Holdfast

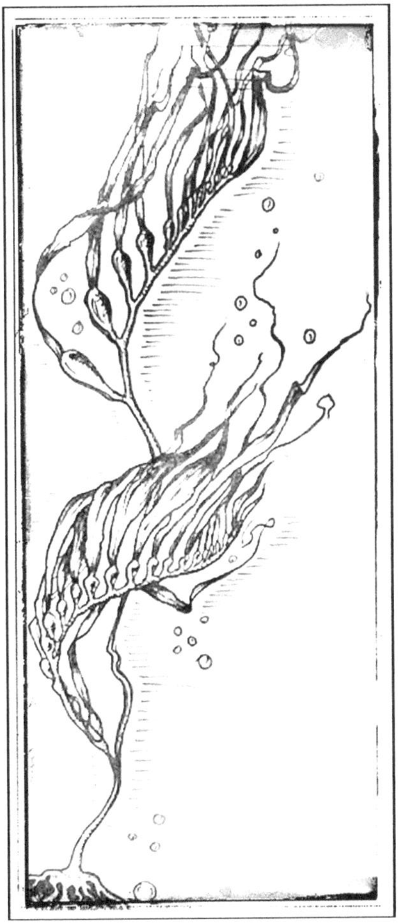

Melinda Field

Published by Wise Women Ink 2024
Printed in the United States

This is a work of Fiction. Names, characters, places, and incidents either are the product of the of the author's imagination or are used fictitiously, and any resemblance to actual persons, living or dead, business establishments, events, or locales is entirely coincidental. The publisher does not have any control over and does not assume responsibility for author or third -party websites or content.

Cover illustration by Howard Pyle 1911, which is copyright free.
Interior and cover design by Lani Cartwright and Jill Voges

ISBN: 978-1-7372821-2-9

First Edition

Wise Women Ink
24142 Shake Ridge Road
Volcano, CA 95689

LATE, BY MYSELF,
IN THE BOAT OF MYSELF,
NO LIGHT AND NO LAND ANYWHERE,
CLOUDCOVER THICK.
I TRY TO STAY
JUST ABOVE THE SURFACE,
YET I'M ALREADY UNDER AND LIVING
WITHIN THE OCEAN.

RUMI

One

The child stood in a dim corner of the room, clutching the hem of her white cotton nightgown, watching her parents dance to the music that poured out of a small stereo. Smoke from a burning stick of incense spiraled in the air making her want to sneeze, so she pinched her nose and blinked fast to try to stop it. Her father put his hands on her mother's hips and sighed deeply. Her mother rested her head on his shoulder and closed her eyes. They kissed long and slow, and the child gagged and looked away. Her father, a big man with a broad mustache, reached back and plucked a white cigarette that was smoldering in an ashtray. She watched from the shadows as he inhaled a long breath. His face looked surprised, his eyes popping out. Lezah hated the smell. He let out air and coughed and held the cigarette to her mother's lips. She watched as he lifted one black lace strap of her mother's slip and pushed it down. Then the other. He kissed her arched neck. They both moaned. Through the front window Lezah could see a big, round moon hanging above the ocean. The far-away sound of the waves told her it was low tide. She turned and quietly crept into the kitchen and out the back door.

The night grass was wet on her bare feet. She bent down and peered at the little drops of water sparkling between the blades. She was hungry. She saw that the light was on at Uncle Brodie's. Maybe he had food. She started along the path to the cabin then stopped, looking up at the triangle window by the roof. She hated triangles—too pointy, not smooth and round like circles, her favorite. She hesitated, remembering the last time. "No," she mumbled, then something in the hydrangea bushes made a loud sound. She looked from her house to the cabin, then hurried to the cabin's wide plank door. Her little fist knocked softly, then pushed at the door, which was ajar. She stood there looking into the half-lit room, feeling, smelling, considering. Uncle Brodie sniffed and moved in his big chair. She tiptoed across the threshold. His eyes were closed, and his mouth hung open like a dead fish. Raspy snores came from his mouth. *Sleep, sleep, sleep,* she thought as she slowly moved towards the kitchen. Her foot nicked a whiskey bottle, and she cringed as it rolled across the floor. He woke up, flailing, blinking, looking around. She froze, hoping he would go back to sleep.

"Lezah? Is that you, little girl?" He leaned forward, saw her standing there. "Come here, baby. What you up to?" She turned and looked at him. "Why ain't you in bed?" She frowned. "Unca said get over here now! Bring

Unca that bottle!" She took it to him, and his big arms scooped her up off the floor and into his lap. He sucked a long, slow gulp. "Want some?" He rocked the chair back and forth. "Big moon, huh?"

His huge hand smoothed her tangled, curly hair. He pulled the dark brown ringlets down straight and watched them pop back up into spirals. "Want to play our game?" he slurred. "What color panties does Lezah have on today?" She sat still, still as she could as his fat, hairy fingers lifted her gown until her belly showed. "Purple!" he laughed, "purple today!" He hiccoughed. She felt the hardness in his lap and wiggled. "Hold still now. Here, let me get our toy out." As he reached for himself, she squirmed and jumped down.

"No!" she yelled. "Hungry, Unca, no dinner!"

"Okay, baby. Some spaghetti on the table. Bring me some too."

Her white gown ballooned out behind her as she scampered through the room and out the open door. Outside, she looked up to the bright lamp of the moon hanging high above the cliffs. Its milky light lit the earthen path, a thin, worn line drawn along the cliff's shoulder. On either side soft grasses swayed in the moisture-laden air, and blooming succulents clinging to the steep walls released their sweetness. The child stopped walking and paused at the edge of the bluff. Below, the ebbing waves broke far out among the exposed, rugged seastacks and caves. She moved back to the path, skipping, feeling the cool sandy dirt on the bottoms of her feet. The path criss-crossed around thorny fields of yellow gorse. The few houses along the Loop Road were dark.

Something moved in the shadows up ahead. She stood and watched small brown rabbits, their bead-like eyes sparked by the moon, sitting up on their haunches nibbling grass. Sensing her, they scattered across the field. "Come back, Lezah no hurt you." But the startled rabbits ran and disappeared into the prickly underbrush.

Another half mile and the trail curved to a jutting point. The path to the beach traversed the starlit cliffs, snaking down and around in a long descent. The last part, almost devoid of footholds, was pocked with small embedded stones. She stubbed her toe but kept going as the steep incline carried her downward. After hopping and loudly counting, "one, two, three, four" down the hard-packed sand stairs, she stood on the beach.

All around were piles of driftwood—some small, some huge—tree trunks, and wave-washed debris. Poised on the damp, silver sand, where pearlescent mussels and smooth ovals of broken agate lay along the foamed lace of the mid-tide line, she looked back along the cliffs to the dull light of her far-away house and the cabin behind it. Still and chilled from the cooling air, she paused. Between the scattered rocks the low tide had exposed small pools studded with lime green anemones and red sea stars. Seaweed clung to the rock tops with hand-like holdfasts of riveted tentacles. Further out, a giant backdrop of basalt several stories high formed an apron for the small stretch of open water. Here, harbor seals, calm and blubberous, let the sheen of their speckled fur drape over rocks as they slept.

The lazy surf swept in, rolled out. The child stood at the water's edge watching, listening, lulled by the soothing pull and the late hour. Stepping in, ankle-deep salt water soaking the hem of her nightgown, she saw the dark shape high up in the rocks, its round head turning, whiskers twitching, large eyes calling. She knelt down, waiting. As the next wave poured in, shot with a soft tremulous light, she lay down on her back, as the foaming swell carried her out into the water.

The A-frame sat back from the road facing the sea. The small dwelling was surrounded by a fence of carefully placed driftwood. The sloping roof was covered in bright green moss that dripped at the eaves after a rain. Rounded bushes of blue, pink, and white hydrangeas grew all around the house, a frilly contrast to the smooth-grained, bleached shingles they rested against. A porthole was embedded in the front door. There were two windows, one on each side of the door. The steps up to the door were stone, built by Opal when she was young. From the beach below, the house seemed suspended, but there was a good piece of land in back and on each side. To the right was a small garden plot, an old garden where perennials had bloomed for fifty years or more. A big twisted cypress towered above the roof.

Inside the front room the gray weathered floor was covered by an oriental rug. Expensive in its day, it had been given to Opal by a "summer bee," her name for the wealthy people who built huge mansions overlooking Banderlay's rock-strewn beaches but usually only stayed a few weeks out of the year. The long, comfortable couch had arrived the same way. Opal knitted there each evening. Her colorful scarves and caps were in demand in the quaint little shops in Old Town where restaurants and bait shops faced the bay. She made her wares from the soft hair of angora rabbits or from local wool from inland farmers. She dyed the yarn herself using plants and vegetables and seaweed. Her Irish grandmother had taught her that knitting was more than making a piece of clothing to warm someone's hand or neck. The art of stitching, the clacking of the needles, the action of hands became a ritual. And depending on what thoughts or pictures were in the knitter's mind, you could either stitch the world together or rip it apart.

The small living room reflected Opal's life—clean and functional yet a bit cluttered. She'd grown up in a filthy hovel of a house in Portland. Coming to Banderlay as a neglected teen had changed her life. She'd worked hard making cheese, processing cranberries, and even working at the lumber mill in her twenties. She'd bought the tiny house for a song. Now the property alone would sell for a million or more. She had always managed, and when she met Roe they had turned the shack-like structure into a home. His knowledge and hard work ethic had transformed it with insulation, a new wood floor, and replastered walls. For months he'd tinkered, fitting river stones to build a hearth where the little woodstove sat in the corner of the galley kitchen. "Tight as a drum," he declared on cold, wind-bitten nights. It was always his job to keep the fire burning. He gathered driftwood, pine cones, and scrap lumber, which were kept dry in a big shed in the back.

Although opposites, Opal and Roe were a good match. Now in their seventies, they were both grateful for the long years of easy love. His books on all subjects lined the handmade shelves: angling, archery, astrology, automotive, all in alphabetical order. He was her left-brain man, orderly, methodical, calculating. So different from her crazy, creative, impulsive, ritualistic self. Her books were not alphabetical. Ranging from poetry to classics to healing ways to Zen and Celtic spirituality, they were in piles on tables and the floor. She was a happenstance housekeeper, while his shed was neat as a pin, and you could always find one between the Os and the Qs. They had no children, but their cats made up for it. Over their time together they had rescued and placed hundreds of strays.

Lezah had come to them when she was five. Those were hard but wonderful times, trying to care for such a wounded, angry, wild, little bird-child. They could never keep her full of anything—food, knowledge, affection, attention, or worldly experiences. Of course they had known her since she was a baby. Her young hippie parents lived just up the Loop Road, next to her Uncle Brodie, a drunken, handsome, charming con man. Opal and Roe never liked him, had always had a feeling about him.

After Lezah was born the parties at the house increased, and the child grew up neglected and dirty, often seen crying in public. When she was five, her parents, both strung out, moved to Portland leaving Lezah in Brodie's custody. He carried her around on his shoulders like a prize, but the pretty little girl rarely smiled. Opal went out of her way to befriend the uncle, taking him fresh garden vegetables and clean yard-sale clothes for the unkempt child. He let her stay with them sometimes. If Opal, who had connections everywhere, heard that Brodie was on a binge, which sometimes lasted for weeks, she would just show up and take Lezah home. They kept her clean and fed, took her to school on time, and thoroughly enjoyed the solemn little soul's company. Lezah loved the beach and swam daily with the seals in the ocean. "More fish than human," Roe would say.

As Lezah matured, Opal tried to talk to her about puberty and cycles. Lezah wouldn't look her in the eye, merely said, "Yeah, I know all about it." There was such sad resignation in her voice. Opal knew in her gut that the girl was being abused. She had gone to the Child Protective Services office, but the worker said that Brodie had legal custody and nothing could be done unless there was proof.

"Are you kidding me?" she responded. "Take her to the doctor, you'll see!" But that could not happen without Brodie's consent. She asked Lezah over and over if her uncle was hurting her, but the child always said, "No, I'm fine."

As her breasts developed, she started wearing Brodie's big T-shirts. Opal took her to Penney's in Lincoln City and bought her clothes and some bras. A quick, shy hug from the girl let her know she appreciated it. On the way home she asked Lezah if she had gotten her period yet. "Yup," she replied, looking out the window.

Another month passed, and the girl was found drunk in Brodie's car parked in front of Dish's Bar and Grill. Brodie said she had gotten into the flask in his glove compartment. Then one day he brought her to Opal's house and, hemming and hawing, said she was having "female trouble" and had been hanging around the Aubrey boy. Could Opal help her out? He called Lezah a slut, then left, slamming the heavy wooden door. Lezah stood there staring at the floor, tears in her brown eyes and a look of shame on her face. Roe suddenly recalled a "project" and went out to his shop.

"Come here, darlin.'" The girl stood frozen, immobile, as Opal put her arms around her. "How long?" The two words broke her, and she started to cry as Opal held her.

Lezah rubbed at the heavy eye makeup she had taken to wearing, her fists wet and black with it. "Two, I skipped two."

"Okay," said Opal, "are you sick?"

"Every morning, sometimes all day. I can't keep any food down."

"Okay, we will figure this out. Have you told Bobby Aubrey yet?"

"No," the girl said quietly, "not him." She brushed her hair away from her worried face.

"It's Brodie, isn't it?" The child froze again. "You can tell me Lezah, I already know. Come on, I'll run you a nice hot bath. Roe found legs for that old clawfoot tub we got at Betty's yard sale." It took everything in Opal not to scream in that moment, to stay calm, guide the girl towards the bathroom. *Just don't open your mouth,* she told herself. "Here, darlin,' are some towels and a new herbal soap I made last week, lavender mint." She took an old terrycloth robe from the shelf. "Put this on afterwards. Take your time—a nice long soak. And when you come out, I'll make us some tea and sandwiches." She closed the bathroom door, went into the kitchen and, with her big strong arms, twisted a dishtowel imagining it was Brodie's neck. Twisted it so hard and tight her wrists hurt for days.

After Lezah came out of the bath Opal settled her with tea and sandwiches. "I'm going to run down to the Shop-N-Mart and get a pregnancy test so we are sure. Be right back."

Lezah lay down on the couch and pulled the soft afghan up around her chin. *A baby, no way! I hate him so much,* she thought, dozing off.

On her way home Opal wondered what to do. *No way Brodie would ever admit it was his. And who would give a twelve-year-old an abortion in this very conservative Christian town? CPS would probably place Lezah into foster care and force her to have the child. Time was of the essence though.* Back at the house she guided the sleepy girl into the bathroom, showed her what to do. The test was positive.

"How will we get it out?" Lezah asked.

Opal sighed. "There are ways, but you could give the baby to someone who would want and love it."

Emphatically the girl answered, "No, no, it should not be in this world."

"We will figure it out, honey. You might have to have an operation."

"Is it a baby already?"

"Yes and no. It won't live if it is born now. Let me study up on it. But we have to do something soon."

"I'm scared. Will it hurt?"

"Yes," Opal sighed again. She hugged the girl. "It will be okay, honey. Now see if you can go back to sleep. Tomorrow is another day."

Once the girl was asleep in the loft Opal read through several herbal books looking for a remedy. *Ruda* seemed to be the most commonly used abortifacient, but where could she get it? She called her friend Esperanza or Espy, whom she had met at a garden show in Myrtle Bay years ago. Espy's family came from Mexico, and she had been trained as a green witch early on. They'd become fast friends, exchanging stories and herbal knowledge.

The phone rang five times before she heard Espy's "Si?" laughter, and then, "Espy's casa of chaos, how can I help you?" Espy greeted her warmly saying how much she missed her. After chatting for a few minutes, she asked, "How old is the girl?"

"Twelve."

"Oh, pobrecita! How many weeks?"

"About eight."

"Okay, si, that should be okay. Are you near a hospital?"

"Yes." Opal heard a baby crying.

"I can get some, know a woman who grows it. It's called Herba de Ruda, botanically, *Ruda graviola.* It is made into a tea to be drunk four times a day. The expulsion should happen within usually a week. Your first time, Opalina?"

"Yes."

"Well, it is pretty safe. There can be heavy bleeding, and you must be sure the placenta comes out whole."

"Can I come for it tomorrow?"

"Yes, sure, I'll be cooking for a quinceañera, so expect a hundred people in my kitchen," she laughed. "And Opal, who is the father?"

Opal sighed, hesitated. "Her old drunk uncle."

"Hijo de la chingada! We have something for him too, a big dose of rat poison. Come by around three tomorrow, all the babies might be sleeping then, maybe we could have a cup of coffee together?"

"Thanks, Espy." Putting the phone down she walked out to Roe's shop, thinking about Lezah. After she told him what needed to be done he said, "Alright, Opal," his jaws tightening. "I'll go to the river for a while. I need to concentrate." He turned away from her. "Gotta glue this window frame here," he said in a shaky voice.

Back at the house she stoked the fire, drank a cup of chamomile tea, then stood in front of her simple altar. An array of flowers and herbs from her last working, a healing for a friend's grandson, was strewn across the surface of the rosewood chest. She brushed them aside and arranged three statues. A white porcelain Mary, her hands folded. A Quan Yin next to Mary. The Chinese goddess's cupped hands held a sphere that represented the world. Finally a carved wooden goddess, her arms raised above her head next to Quan Yin. Crossing the room, Opal retrieved a nest from the coffee table, emptying the stone eggs into her knitting basket. She took a framed picture of a mermaid that Lezah had drawn at age six off the wall and placed it near the goddesses.

She lit a white candle and a spray of dried sage and roses that she set in an abalone shell, then brought the smoke up and around her body. "Dear mothers, I ask for acceptance of what is, for protection of Lezah who must bear the pain of womanhood in a child's body. I pray for the clean hollowing of her womb, for minimal bleeding, and for a full, quick recovery. Please, mothers, send me the wisdom, patience, and strength of all the women through all the ages to be what I need to be."

The next morning Opal drove Lezah to Brodie's house to gather clothes and let her uncle know that she'd be staying with Opal and Roe for a week or so. Opal stayed in the car, unable to control her rage and face him.

In the evening Lezah took the herb with an almost too calm resignation. For three days she lay on the couch, a hot pad on her cramping belly. She bled profusely, which drove her from the couch to the small bathroom down the hall every hour or so. Opal piled books and magazines from the library on a table nearby. The child seemed too distracted from pain to read or draw with the colored pencils in the box on top of the art tablet. Sometimes Lezah moaned, rocking and crying, her arms around her knees. On the fourth day, with her frail body straddling the toilet, she clung to Opal, screaming, as she passed it.

Opal helped her clean up and settled her on the couch. "It's over, sweetheart, now you will just bleed like a period. But you must rest for a few days."

Lezah's face was so pale, dark rings under her eyes. "I

need to see Pinni," she pleaded, "she might have had her pup."

"Alright, in a few days if you feel better. I will walk with you to the beach. You need to eat now. What sounds good?"

"Everything," Lezah replied, smiling.

"Opal's fish and chips?"

"Yes, please."

Several days later, they both had a good night's sleep and woke to a clear sky and a low tide.

"Please, Opal, I'm better. Can we go?"

Opal told the child to slow down as they walked down the damp, moss-covered path. Once on the sand, Lezah started running. Opal caught her hand and shook her head gently. "No," she mouthed.

When they reached the water Lezah called out, "Pinni? Pinni? I wish I could swim out." Opal saw a group of seals clustered on a ledge above the water. After a moment one of the seals joggled itself to the edge and dove in. "It's Pinni!" The seal swam in close. "Oh Pinni, a black one, how cute, such long whiskers. The better to feel with."

The harbor seal nudged the pup closer to Lezah who stood up to her knees in the gentle, sloshing waves. She scooped the tiny pup into her hands, stroked it, and floated it back to its mother. "There you go."

"It's a beauty, sleek and healthy," Opal said approvingly.

It was a relief to see the girl so delighted, but on the way back to the house Opal couldn't help but think about what would happen next. She and Roe had discussed over and over how the girl could stay with them permanently. Opal was willing to call CPS and the police, but Brodie had legal custody, and she was afraid he would somehow talk his way out of it and punish Lezah for wanting to live with them. These thoughts nagged at her as she cooked dinner.

The next morning Brodie showed up rumpled and bleary-eyed and ordered Lezah gruffly, "Get your things and hurry up and get in the car." After they closed the door Opal ran to the window, noting the girl's slumped posture as they headed to the car.

"Roe! Oh, we can't do anything! God damn him to hell!"

He held her as she cried and said, his voice torn and sad, "There there, darlin,' I know, I know."

Later that morning Opal and Roe sat in the living room across from each other, the tea tray on a table between them. Opal's hand trembled as she poured black tea into a cup, adding a swish of milk.

"Thank you." He held the thin, delicate cup that had

belonged to Opal's grandmother in his big, calloused hand. "Tell me, love, why are your hands shaking?"

Opal poured her tea, trying to hold the cup still as she added lemon and sugar. "I am so worried, haven't slept much. He took her back before she healed from the . . ."—she paused, searching for the right word—"expulsion. Such a horrible, traumatic experience for the poor child to go through. I'm just so concerned, and I feel somehow I have failed her. When I saw him at the store yesterday he was hostile. He said, 'She is fine, same little bitch. Don't hover. She doesn't need you.' Roe, I can't protect her!"

Roe set his cup on the tray, stood up, and sat down next to her on the couch. He held her, then took her face into his hands. He kissed her forehead. "I wish I could erase those worry lines. You have done everything possible for Lezah since she was a baby. We both have, and she has that foundation from our love and caring. I know what you are thinking—that it will happen again. All we can do is hope and pray. Brodie is going to screw up eventually, is what I think. The whole town knows who and what he is." He got up and rubbed his lower back. "Gonna go work in the shop, still fixing that window. Chin up. Maybe a walk on the beach this afternoon?"

"Okay." Opal gathered the tea things, walked to the small kitchen, and put the tray down. Back in the living room she moved to her altar. After a moment she lit a white candle. "Mother Mary, I ask for protection of the innocent."

Lezah woke up to Brodie's yell from the dingy kitchen, "Get the fuck up, Lezah!" She rubbed her eyes, pushed her hair away from her face. When she stumbled to her feet she felt a gush. *Oh no!* She rushed to the bathroom and changed her pad, noting that there was only one left. She must tell Opal because this bleeding was going to last at least a month, and Brodie had refused to buy any more. Outside the bathroom window the air was an opaque gray. She shivered. The thought of school cheered her up as she dressed quickly and walked to the kitchen.

"Get the bucket and bait. We're going to the dock. Don't forget the trap."

"But the fog is thicker than snot. We won't be able to even see down the hill. Besides I want to go to school, I've missed so much lately."

"Forget school, it's a waste of your time, and I said we are goin' crabbin.' Make some sandwiches, now, get!" He sat at the table filling his canteen with whiskey, his hands trembling, his long dirty nails black and ragged. "Don't forget the gloves and camp chairs. Put 'em in the car and hurry the fuck up!"

She rushed, trying to spread the peanut butter and jelly quickly. *I hate, hate, hate him!* she thought. He was meanest in the mornings until he got enough booze in him. *Oh, I miss Opal and Roe.* Hopefully later she could go by and tell Opal that she needed more pads and get a hug. Tossing the food into a paper bag she grabbed the buckets from the porch.

He came up the steps. "Where were you?"

When she said, "Hurrying as fast as I could." He slapped her across the face. "Not fast enough!"

"Ouch!" Her hair was wet, wildly tangled in the drizzle. She felt tiny drops of moisture sucked up into her nose as she inhaled and threw the buckets in the back seat with the paper bag.

"Where are the chairs? Jesus, Lezah you're slacking," he yelled from the driver's seat.

After putting the chairs in the trunk she got in, pulling her thin sweatshirt around her body. They could hardly see a thing, though he got them down the hill and into Old Town and steered the car into the parking lot near Dish's Bar and Grill. Visibility was only a foot or so. "Ah, it's gonna be good. Crabs love the fog and cold."

"I'm freezing," Lezah said, her teeth chattering.

"Oh, for Christ's sake! My old coat is in the trunk."

She took the chairs and buckets out while he grabbed the trap. His coat was crumpled in a corner. Reluctantly she shook it out, but it reeked of booze, vomit, and some other horrid odor she could not place. *I'd rather freeze to death,* she thought, throwing it back in. They walked slowly across the lot to the boat dock, at times just feeling their way. The iced air hurt her chest and cut into her slender bones. She heard the slap, slap, slap of the water below, the clanking sound of metal on metal. Little waves bounced the steel panels fastened together beneath her feet. As she walked behind Brodie the slippery floor rose and fell with the water's rhythm.

God I hate this! Sitting all day, having to listen to him. Sometimes the harbor seals were there, their heads bobbing near the pilings. She would lean over the chained railing to see which ones were there and what they were fishing for, and if it was one of her own, she'd get down on her hands and knees, duck her head under the chain, and talk to them. She liked it when other people were there. *But who,* she thought, *in their right mind would come out this early in this frozen soup?* The lighthouse at the end of the jetty bleated out its pathetic call. *Just float,* she told herself as she sat in the canvas chair. *Pretend you are a mermaid wearing a sparkling yellow top. It's summertime and you're swimming with the seals and…*

"Lezah, get over here!"

"What?"

"Come put the chicken guts in the trap." She hated handling the rotten meat, but obeyed him, scooping it out of the bucket and throwing it into the trap. "Now put it in the water," he slurred as she bent down and pulled the trap across the slick metal floor to the edge. Lifting the bottom chain up, she pushed the trap underneath it and watched as it hit the dark water. As she stood and turned, he grabbed her, pinning her arms behind her back.

"Are you ready yet?" He held her, her back pressed against his chest. She smelled his sick breath and fought, kicking, trying to get away, but he was too strong. "C'mon, give your old uncle some," he coaxed as he reached under her sweatshirt. She felt the torn finger of his glove graze her breast. A rush of adrenaline surged through her and she spun away from him and screamed, "Leave me alone!"

"Gonna be like that, little bitch? I'll just force you then." He lunged for her as she stepped aside, ready to run, but he slipped, his big body splatting down hard. His head hit the cold steel floor with an audible crack. He twisted, turning face up. Blood from a gash on his forehead soaked his stocking cap, spilled into his eyes.

Oh no, thought Lezah, stunned.

"Help me! Help me, girl! I'm dizzy, I can't see, help me up!" Fog blew in cold all around them. "Lezaaah...," his voice weaker, "for God's sake, girl, help me!" And then he went limp. Blood gushed from his head, smearing the cold metal floor and pooling near her feet.

Heart pounding, panic-stricken, she looked around—Jonny's Fish Shack dark; the candy store too; no one near the few moored boats; just the cold wind clanging the chains. Moving over to him she bent down, saw his face covered in blood, and with a strength she'd never known she rolled him, her thin arms pushing his body to the very edge. One more effort, and he slid into the water floating face down away from the dock.

Lezah turned and ran up the ramp, out through the parking lot. *Oh my God! What just happened?* She turned right past the jetty and lighthouse onto the beach, barely able to see, her eyes red from tears and the slanting, stinging rain. *Where? What? Where should I go? Opal's? No, she will hate me!* Panic pushed her. The faster she ran, the more the sanitary pad filled with her own blood. *Where? Where should I go? The seals? Should I swim out to them? No! Foggy, high tide, dangerous!* She was out of breath, sweating and chilled underneath her thin hoody. Turning up the muddy path she climbed up the cliff, barely feeling her feet, her ragged tennis shoes soaked. She slipped a few times. *Oh my God! What will happen to me now?*

Reaching the ramshackle house she slammed through the front door, switched on the light in the living room, saw his blood on her hands. *Oh no!* She peeled off her clothes then stood naked, wondering what to do with them. *The shed out back.* She threw on her robe, bundled the clothes and shoes into her quivering arms, and ran outside the few steps to the shed. The big door whined on its hinges. She hated this place. This was where he would take her if she resisted, where no one could hear her screams. Pushing through the stinking, overflowing garbage she made her way to the very back, where the only light diffused through a broken window. She threw the clothes down and moved a metal barrel to cover them.

Back to the house, blood dripping down her legs, she got in the grimy shower. No time to wash her hair. Once out she stuffed a washcloth in her underwear, put on a pair of jeans, a T-shirt, and her pea coat—a gift from Roe and Opal. *Opal! Oh, Opal! Will I ever see you again? What will happen to me now?* Once dressed, breathing so hard she thought she would faint, she tried running a comb through her wet, tangled curls.

Out the front door—the sun was breaking through. *Oh.* Back in, she grabbed her backpack, stood a moment in the hallway, saw his ugly face in her mind, his hands reaching under her sweatshirt. *Breathe, breathe.* Gulping air, holding back tears, she walked slowly, slowly towards school.

After school Lezah walked back to the house. Sheriff Curly Whelan's squad car was there and Opal's old Honda. *Here it is,* she thought, *the end of my life.*

"Hello, Lezah, we need to talk."

"Okay." She looked at Opal, whose face was expressionless, set the backpack down on the floor.

"Where have you been today?"

"Um, at school."

"All day? I can contact the school, and they would vouch for you?"

"Yes, sir, school all day."

"Sit down, please."

"Okay." She sat on the old kitchen chair.

"Your Uncle Brodie's body was found washed up on the rocks at the jetty."

She acted surprised, confused. "Tell me again, please, I don't understand."

"He's dead, had a big gash on his head. Did you see him today?"

"Yes, this morning."

"Anything unusual happen?"

"No. He told me to go to the dock after school, said it would be good crabbing."

Curly shifted his weight from one foot to the other. "Was your uncle inebriated?"

"I'm sorry," Lezah said, "I don't know what that means?"

"Was he drunk?"

"Oh! Always, yes. I heard him up all night."

She looked over at Opal while he wrote on his clipboard. *Does she know? Can she tell by my face?*

"Well, that would explain the two chairs," he said to Opal, who nodded.

"What will happen now…to me?" Tears ran down her cheeks. A vision of herself in a cold, dark hole made her widen her brown eyes.

"Opal, can she stay with you while we find her parents? Brodie had legal custody, right?"

Opal nodded. "Of course! Lezah, go pack your things."

As the girl scurried away, Curly held out the clipboard. "Will you sign this, Opal?"

"What happens now, Curly? You know, with the body?"

He sighed, "Routine, no autopsy. He probably hit his head, bled out, fell in."

Mary Mother of God, thank you, thought Opal. *Should I tell him?* she wondered. *No, best not to.*

Lezah came in carrying her clothes in a garbage bag. Curly went over to her. "I'm sorry, honey, it will be alright. Now go with Opal."

Lezah started to walk to the door but dropped the bag and went back to the bedroom. When she came out, she picked up the bag. In her right hand she held the mermaid doll that Opal had made for her when she was little. The tail was sewn with metallic green yarn, she wore a yellow top, and long, brown, curly wool hair fell over the doll's upper body. Her arms reached up above and her embroidered face was smiling.

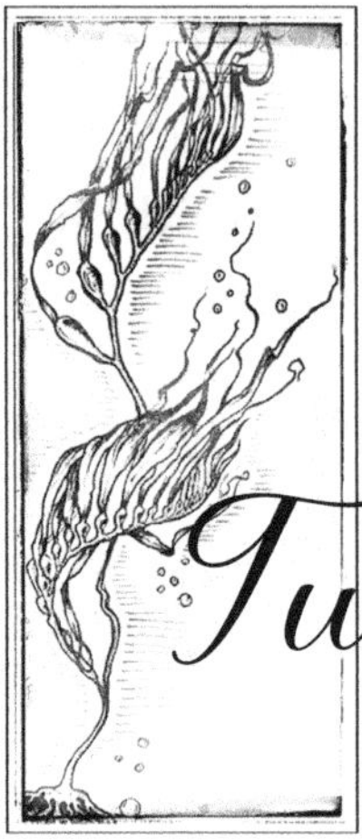

Two

Lezah hop-skipped along the path that led down to the beach. Her bare, painted toes were adorned with rings, and each ring dug into the sand as the trail steepened. Her long, layered skirt dotted with sequins and little hand-sewn mirrors flashed in the sunlight. She wore a purple chiffon chemise under a lace-edged peasant blouse and over it all a light green pea coat. Her impossibly curly hair fell to her waist, and the ringlets bounced with each step. Halfway down she could see the rocks of the haulout, where the seals rested, exposed by the low tide. The huge backdrop of Seal Rock rose up behind, where tufted puffins and long-necked cormorants flocked on the grass-covered top. She shifted the backpack and, putting her fingers to her mouth, blew out a long, shrill whistle. Then, head down, her feet danced faster in their descent, causing her to almost trip from the gathered, downward momentum.

On one of the first sunny days in over a month her heart was glad for the brilliant light that filled the tide pools below. Reaching the bottom she picked her way over, around, and through the littered driftwood clogging the base of the cliff. Alone on the wide beach, she dropped her backpack and began to remove her clothes. She stripped and let herself stand momentarily naked facing the water, sighing as she felt the sun on her skin. Several harbor seals barked in the water, their rounded heads and comical faces bobbing in the waves. She pulled her wetsuit up from her ankles in one motion and wriggled into it easily. It was a constant comfort against the cold, Southern Oregon sea. Only at the height of summer could she brave the water without it. After zipping it under her chin and putting the flippers on she was ready. Taking a few awkward steps, she knelt and floated out into the water. She had always been more at home in the ocean than on land.

They came immediately, rolling off the rocks or nuzzling her from underneath, circling around her, their big eyes and smiling, whiskered faces making her laugh. "Hello, hello." She reached out and petted the head of a female whose pup floated at her side. "Target, look how fat you are!" she called to a big, light-spotted one. "Where is Pinni?" Her finned feet paddled in place as she scanned the rocks. There were a few lounging, their brown, gray, and cream-colored bodies draped over the sun-warmed rocks. Set back from them on a higher ledge she saw Pinni, her familiar since childhood, an old female she called "the Guardian." All of the ten or so others were either the progeny or harem mates of Pinni. Lezah floated on her back as waves splashing through a giant blowhole sent ripples that propelled her towards the old seal's haulout. The matriarch was almost blind, but she raised her head as Lezah called out. Once on the narrow pebbled beach she peeled the flippers off and climbed up to the perch.

Winter had left Pinni thinner. The creature nodded her head up and down as Lezah sat down beside her. "How are you, ole sweetheart?" She stroked the soft, furred skin, then put her arm around the animal's wide rippled neck. They sat like this for a long time, watching the antics of the others as they swam and dove in the water. After almost an hour Lezah scrambled down, replaced the fins, and floated across to the shore. She spotted a couple walking towards her, so instead of changing she left her clothes in the backpack and started to walk. Sometimes when she wore her mermaid tail people waded out into the water to gawk at the strange creature. "Just crazy old Lezah Boudrow," the locals said.

Her bare feet hit a patch of clam holes. She set the flippers down and lifted a little shovel out of the pack as she stomped the sand where water squirted out of several holes. *A good take for a meal,* she thought, *maybe enough for Opal.* She palmed the ridged shells and placed them into a cloth stuff bag. The thought of lemon butter surrounding each slimy morsel made her mouth water.

As she walked towards the cliff path she noticed two

boys bending over the sand. They each held a stick and were taking turns poking at something. She sprinted up to them, curious and concerned. An injured seagull flopped helplessly in the sand. "Hey! What the hell do you think you're doing?"

The boys backed away. "We didn't do it," one of them said, his curly red hair falling in his face. "We found it this way, honest."

Lezah could see that the gull had a broken wing. "How would you like to be poked if you were this hurt? You have no regard for life do you? Get out of here, you cruel little bastards." She jumped towards them. "I said, Get!" Dropping their sticks, the boys took off down the beach. One glanced back with a look of terror on his face.

She dropped her backpack and sat down. She scooped the big white bird into her lap. Too weak to resist, it looked up at her. "It's okay," she crooned. *No way it will recover,* she thought. After her hands smoothed the feathers on its head and chest, the pain in its eyes became resignation. She sang to it as she sang to everything, her flowers and herbs, paintings, the cats, even her old car—a non-song, made up of sounds and hums and lilting cadences that were melodic without words. The gull seemed hypnotized. "There, there." Slowly she reached into the Velcro pocket of her wetsuit. The knife flipped open with a little whir, and she slit the bird's throat just where, moments before, she had stroked it. Its life force ebbed away as blood poured onto the sand. "There, there," she said, settling its body, arranging the lifeless form head down, its wings tucked underneath. She drew a peace sign and circle around it with the tip of the knife, then cleaned the knife with her fingers. "Leave you for the eagles or ravens…you'll go on." Standing, she brushed sand from her seat and knees. She put the knife in its sheath, closed the pocket, and walked to the path that led up to the Loop Road.

Jackson pulled his car into the parking lot of the Cormorant Motel. The older Chevy Nova was littered with papers, shoes, and gum wrappers. A stale powdered sugar donut sat daintily on the back seat. The outside of the car was pocked with rust spots from sitting out in the constant Portland rain. It had belonged to Mary Kay's brother, who had abandoned it in their driveway when he moved to Thailand. Since Mary Kay had kept the small house and Subaru, Jackson inherited the old, green clunker. It had actually served him well over the past five years, not that he'd put many miles on it. He'd become fairly reclusive after the divorce, only driving it to the airport where he had worked as a pilot for a small private airline. The end of that job was the reason why he was here.

Driving up from Granite Pass had left him sore and stiff. He got out of the car, took off the red stocking cap he often wore, and ran his fingers over his short, blond hair. He looked down to the ocean and the towering, scattered seastacks, their shapes carved by eons of wind and waves. A diffuse orange setting sun lit the flat, grass-covered tops of some of the huge islands of rocks. Others, castle-shaped, pointed towards the pale sky. Hungry and in need of a beer, he walked to the motel office to register.

The lobby was quiet, the only sound the soft musical pings of the elevators as they rose and fell. The woman behind the desk seemed half asleep. He filled out the registration form and gave her his credit card, hoping it wouldn't be declined. Key in hand, he started to walk out to the car for his backpack and briefcase, but the flashing, blue neon "Bar" sign beckoned. The room was empty except for the bartender, a long-haired guy with thick glasses. Jackson settled his tall, lean body on a red leather stool and ordered a beer. He sipped at the foam, then took a long swig. Hands folded and head bent, he recalled the scene with Mary Kay yesterday. They had never been in love, but they had remained friends after the separation, trying to make the best of the unplanned pregnancy that had resulted from their awkward few dates. Reaching into his pocket he pulled out his hat and placed it on the bar. As speedy, nervous energy coursed through him, he repeatedly folded it into halves, then quarters. He recalled how hard Mary Kay had cried, frustrated about their now six-year-old son, Owen, who had been diagnosed with cystic fibrosis as an infant: the seemingly endless round-the-clock care that he required, how she often woke in the night to the alarm going off, the worthless caregiver asleep on the couch. Mary Kay had never gotten used to Owen struggling just to breathe, his eyes rolling back in his head, constant body-shaking spasms, his helpless look of fear.

Owen's sweet face flashed in his mind, the blue eyes and head of blond curls. Jackson saw him every few weeks, but visits and activities were limited by the boy's disabilities. Now that he and several other pilots had been laid off, he didn't know how he would pay the medical bills, the caregivers, and other expenses. His life had suddenly become all about money or the lack of it. He really could not afford a weekend away, but by coming to Banderlay he'd hoped to de-stress and find the time and focus to fill out the extensive application for a private company looking to hire pilots. He asked the bartender, who was absorbed in his phone, if there was a restaurant in the motel. "No," he answered, not even looking up. "Go down the hill to Old Town, just a few miles through the beach loop. It's on the bay, Dish's Bar and Grill, tell Lezah Jamie sent you."

Lezah's home and shop fronted Beach Drive, facing the sea. The quirky 1910 cottage had a pointed roofline, small leaded-glass windows, and storm-weathered white shingles. Near the door a sign framed in driftwood read: *The Mermaid - Curios and Original Art - Shopkeeper Lezah Boudrow.*

The large front yard held a jumble of treasures: fishing

nets, old anchors, salt-bleached ropes, and antique bottles whose blue, green, or root beer colors were backlit by late afternoon sun. A dozen wooden boxes held sea shells, starfish, and exotic offerings from other places, as the cold Oregon coast was sparsely littered. A battered wooden dinghy was cleverly turned upside down to display odd containers, wooden bowls, metal pots, and hubcaps planted with rosettes of succulents that still held pools of the morning's rain. These were the same succulents that grew on the flat tops of the seastacks on the long beach below.

Lezah moved to the door as the cat spiraled around her ankles. Inside, the shop featured handcrafted driftwood furniture layered with bright pillows and handmade rugs and bowls. Her large paintings covered the walls. Before going up to shower she checked her messages. One from Carey asking if she could come in to the bar early, one from an antique store in Astoria asking if she had any fishing floats for a customer. Lezah peeled off the wetsuit and pulled on the skirt and blouse from her backpack. She walked to a turquoise door in the rear of the shop, opened it, and climbed the stairs to her apartment.

The large room, which covered the entire top of the shop, was filled with light from the windows that faced the sea. There was a living area, a curtained-off sleeping area, and a well-equipped galley kitchen. Pots and pans hung from old boat hooks mounted on a six-foot length of driftwood scavenged from the beach.

Lezah stashed the bag of clams in the fridge and put

water on for tea—energy for the long night ahead. She searched for an outfit in the ornate armoire that served as a closet. She chose a long-sleeved, coral top and a gauzy print skirt. When the kettle whistled she tossed the clothes on a couch and poured water over loose oolong tea.

On her way to the bathroom she paused in an alcove by a window. A small table held art supplies, paint, and brushes. A large piece of raw canvas lay folded over her easel.

Her finished paintings were hung downstairs in the shop. They were all similar: large, watery, colorful, intricately collaged with dried seaweed, always with a mermaid as the central image. She believed that all art was wholly created in some parallel universe, and it was up to the artist to envision it into existence. She was ready to start another painting, but so far an image had eluded her. *I need inspiration,* she thought. *Maybe there will be someone at the bar tonight.*

She showered, dressed, stood in front of the mirror. At thirty-six she still had the body of a girl, small, lean, muscled. Lately though she'd noticed little lines around her eyes. She put on makeup, tried to tame her wild curls, knowing that in the humidity of the café they would frizz even more. "Oh well." She grabbed her purse, her long white shawl, and the cup of tea and hurried downstairs. The rusted Buick coughed and lurched before starting. She sipped the lukewarm tea as she drove along the beach loop, past motels and elaborate homes for a few miles and then downhill to Old Town, where shops and restaurants circled the harbor.

Dish's Bar and Grill was one of the oldest family-owned establishments, having withstood the frequent business turnover that small tourist towns experienced every few years. More and more the bored and wealthy bypassed Banderlay for fancier Silver Beach twenty miles up the coast highway. She parked and called to a few seals bobbing in between the pilings of the pier.

The jukebox was loud, playing "Georgia on My Mind" as she crossed the sawdust floor, feeling bits of wood catch between her sandaled toes. It was a typical Friday night crowd—fishermen and their wives out on the town, the over-twenty bunch that hadn't gone away to college, and the usual overdressed tourists looking disappointedly at the simple menu. Cary Dish, bald, sweating, and breathing hard, delivered a tray of drinks to one of the tables. Before Lezah could stash her purse and shawl behind the bar he nodded towards a man in a red stocking cap sitting there and said, "Lezah, haven't gotten to him yet!"

"Okay." She moved behind the long, polished bar and asked, "Hey sailor, what can I get you?"

He muttered with downcast eyes, "Coors Light."

Cute, she thought, *shy, not from around here.* She took the can and a chilled glass and set them down on a paper coaster. "Where are you from?"

"Portland." He slid the dollar bills toward her. "Keep the change."

She said, "Thanks!" and turned away, moving to bus a table. She wheeled the cart over and began to clear the dirty dishes. Ketchup and fries were smeared across the table.

The dinner crowd trickled in until 8:30. Lezah kept the man in the red cap in beer, compliments of the house or, rather, her tips. She moved around the big room clearing, wiping tables, and putting chairs back in their places. Around 9:30 she was free to stay behind the bar chatting with the locals, listening to their talk of NOAA and Fish and Wildlife's new rules. They talked about the shortage of salmon and the f-d-up restrictions being put on farmers, ranchers, and fishermen.

She moved on, hoping to talk to the shy man as she wiped down the bar. His eyes were on her, and she could feel their deep probing as she worked. She felt the mixed pleasure the sight of her always had on men. Any man, no matter what age, seemed entranced. Beauty was a curse, she thought, and the sensuality and constant sexuality that ran through her was something she had no control over. It just sparked like some kind of inner circuitry. She did practice discernment, though, and could usually feel whether someone was okay or not. Her empathic nature clued her in. She was only interested in casual sex, never wanting or needing a relationship to define her. The guy at the bar smiled at her, and she knew immediately that there was an innate goodness about him. She would make him stay after her shift was over.

"Hey sailor, what's your name?"

He looked up at her, his clean-shaven angular face held insanely blue eyes. "Uh, Jackson Craig."

"What kind of a name is that?" she smiled, "a last name first?"

He looked away. "After my uncle Thomas Jackson. He was a famous architect in Portland in the '20s."

Lezah dried a glass. "What do you do, Jackson?"

He smiled, "Ah, pilot."

Clancy Cavanaugh waved to her. "Hey, Lezah! What does a guy have to do to get a drink around here? I'm too old and ugly to go home wit' ya. Bourbon, up this time. Hey, fella, watch out for her, she is a man eater!" He laughed heartily.

Lezah let a little smile grace her lips. *He might be right,* she thought. There was that black widow part of her that used sex for inspiration and then never saw the man again. She bent down to reach for a tumbler, knowing he was watching.

She gave the old fisherman his drink and asked, "So Jackson, another beer?"

"No thanks. I'm getting kinda loopy, haven't eaten since... I don't know...lunch. The cook is probably gone, huh?"

She licked her lips, "Yeah, but there's a plate of fried oysters in the warming oven." *And are you ever going to need nourishment,* she thought, looking at his broad shoulders. She turned, her long hair bouncing in dark ringlets as she walked to the kitchen.

He shifted his weight on the barstool. *Is she coming onto me*? he wondered. *Oh brother, you are drunker than you thought.*

The oysters were warm, and she brought tartar sauce and a little cup of vinegar and a napkin. "Enjoy, I've got to finish up."

He watched her walk away and start sweeping. He picked up an oyster. Hot, crisp, salty on the outside, tender-chewy inside—probably the best thing he'd ever tasted.

Several men got up at once. "Old man bedtime, Lezah, see ya."

"Bye guys, later." She put the bottles in order, emptied ice buckets, wiped down the bar for the last time. Except for Carey out of sight, banging pots and pans in the kitchen, it was just the two of them now.

"God, those were good. I'm ready for my bill, looks like closing time."

"Yeah, well I'll lock up. Care to join me for an aperitif?"

"I'm sorry, what?"

"A liqueur, a late-night drink."

"Uh, okay." *Is this really happening*? he thought. "Sure."

"Good. By the way, I'm Lezah." He extended his hand and she took it, feeling nothing negative. "I'll be right back." In the bathroom she peed and thought about the big canvas at home. *Gonna see who you are soon, hopefully. How will I take him*? she wondered as she put on lipstick.

He was yawning when she returned. "Oh, you're tired, maybe another time?"

"No, no, I'll get a second wind."

And a third and a fourth, she thought. She pulled the bottle of absinthe from its secret cubby. She'd made it herself and was pretty sure Carey had no idea it was there. She rarely drank, but when she did she wanted to "fly with the green fairy." The pale green liquid made from *Artemisia absinthium,* and anise was very bitter if drunk straight. Thus the European ritual of pouring it over a sugar cube and adding water as necessary until it turned an opaque white. It created a state of euphoria that was calming and psychoactive. It was known to enhance sex, transforming it into a hallucinogenic experience. Setting the bottle on the bar, she put a small perforated spoon next to it.

"Just a sec." She returned with a pitcher of water. "The water must be ice cold." He watched with curious eyes as she placed the spoon across the top of the glass then set the sugar cube on it. "There," she said, loving the ritual of it all. "Now the liquor." Carefully, slowly, she poured the chartreuse liquid. "Now the water. See how the cube expands and melts and then dissolves?"

He felt aroused watching it. "What's it called again?"

"Absinthe. In Europe they call it 'the green fairy.'"

"Are you gonna poison me?" he asked, half serious.

"Not the way you think," she replied, her full lips smiling. "Try it, you'll like it."

"You go first."

She downed a few ounces and started one for him. "It'll make you feel good, awake, sensuous, and when we've had a few we'll go to my place. Do you like art?"

"Yeah, sure," he said, then sipped. "Like licorice, huh? Yes, I like art but not abstract."

Gathering her purse, shawl, and keys, she went and stood by the door.

He rose from the bar stool, tall and lanky and a little wobbly. "Wait! I didn't pay."

"Oh, it's okay, Jackson, it's on me tonight," thinking, *and in me, over me, around me, through me.* Outside an oblong moon hovered above the hill. "Where are you staying?"

"Oh, that big motel on the loop. I think it's called the Pelican or …"

"Cormorant," she corrected.

"Yeah, that's it. So you want me to drive? Because I'm not sure …"

"No, no, we can take my car. I'll bring you back later." She walked slowly to the beat-up Buick station wagon, feeling the moon's pull. "Here she is, rusty but running."

They drove down the empty street, the surface of the harbor a silver, crinkled patina. The lighthouse at the point bleated out its wail rhythmically.

"You live far?" he asked quietly, wondering what he'd gotten himself into. It'd been a long time since he'd been with a woman.

"No, almost there." They passed his motel. A few blocks later she parked in front of her shop. The yard was eerily lit as moonlight glanced off the bottle collection. The cobalt ones especially seemed to glow.

He followed her through the driftwood gate, saw a sign near the door that said *The Mermaid*. "You live in a shop?" He was feeling very strange. His legs didn't feel attached to him at all. "What if …"

But her buttery voice came from behind him, and her soft laugh was like a rich warble. "No, above it, I live above my shop."

"Oh, I see." But he couldn't really, it was so dark. A shadow moved towards him as they walked to the front door. A big cat rushed him and clawed at his pant leg. "Crap!" He felt its claws sinking into his skin.

"No, Mesmer, no, stop!" Lezah bent down and stroked the animal's body. "No scratching, he's my guest. Go back to your barrel!"

The cat froze, and Jackson swore it glared at him before disappearing behind a huge coil of rope. He heard the waves crashing below. *Shit!* he felt so weird.

She'd gone to the front door and unlocked it. "Come in," she gestured, her small hand outstretched as she flipped the light on inside. Light pooled onto the weather-beaten boards of the porch.

Jackson entered, noticing baskets of shells, ornate driftwood furniture, and shelf after shelf filled with a myriad of objects. But it was the paintings that stopped him. Huge canvases with pictures of women in different poses, life-size, the images so real, touchable, all of them human from the waist up. But then he saw that they all had ornate fish tails—mermaids! The colors were bright or pale or both combined. Some were under water, some lounging on submerged rocks. Their faces proud, angry, or dead calm, their eyes all staring straight at him or through him. He knew Lezah was watching him. "Wow! These are, um, did you paint these?"

She laid her shawl and purse on the back of a coral brocade chair, her silence thick in the strange room. Then she turned and faced him. "Do you want them to be my art? Or someone else's?" She waited.

He stammered, "I don't know the answer to what

you mean, but they are amazing, so large and real." He stopped, confused, lost for words, that floating feeling in his body again.

She began to laugh at his inability to speak, to put his feelings into words. She loved to watch people's reactions to her paintings. But his was so innocent, unabashedly confused, even afraid.

"Of course they are mine."

He relaxed visibly. "You must have loved *The Little Mermaid* movie. My sister made me watch it hundreds of times."

"Well no, I read the original by Hans Christian Andersen when I was ten. I hated that story where a beautiful wild creature who longs for love and a soul is willing to give up her voice, and singing, have her tail mutilated to become feet that will hurt her every step of the way to become acceptable to a prince. Little mermaid is a classical symbolic and sexualized archetype of female sacrifice and the Disney version is just dumb."

Jackson, speechless, just nodded.

"Come," she said kindly, "let's go upstairs, and I'll show you my home. We can have another drink and chat."

He followed her through another doorway and up a short flight of stairs. Mermaid paintings covered the white wall all the way up. *God help me,* he thought as he watched the graceful way she moved, as if her feet were not on solid ground. The mermaids on the walls watched him, their eyes amused. *Run*! he told himself, *now*! But she had opened the door to her apartment and gestured for him to come in.

She felt his uneasiness. She needed to touch him again, preferably his hands; that was usually how she got her strongest intuition. Yes, as an empath she could read footprints on the beach and fingerprints on glasses, but not always. The gift—or curse—was, unfortunately or fortunately, inconsistent.

She took his hand, long warm fingers, slightly damp, tentative. Underneath, a shyness that was innate, not just with her. She sat down on the long low sofa. "I'll get us some more absinthe."

"Oh, I don't know," he said, trying to get his long legs into a comfortable position. "That stuff is different, made me feel strange."

"Just one more. This is my special blend, homemade."

He took the glass from her anyway and watched as she balanced a sugar cube on the little spoon. After making one for herself she settled into an armchair facing him. "So tell me, Jackson, what brings you to Banderlay?"

He sipped the cloudy liquid. "I just decided to stop here for the night. I was visiting my son in Granite Pass, heading home to Portland tomorrow."

"Oh, you have a child?"

"Yes, Owen is six. He lives with his mother. I try to

see him as much as possible." The pungent licorice had numbed his tongue. After an uneasy silence, Lezah, compelled by the fire in her body, stood up and sat down next to him. *God*! he thought as her thigh touched his, *she's burning. Her body heat is intense.*

"Okay, Jackson, so you are a pilot, and I am an artist/shop owner/waitress. What else do we need to know about each other?"

"Oh, well, I don't know. Lisa is it?"

She spelled it, "L-e-z-a-h, Lezah Boudrow, but yes it rhymes with Lisa." She took his hand and put it on her breast, looked into his eyes and whispered, "Let's take another sip and get to know each other." She felt his hand trembling.

"Oh, no more of that stuff, thanks."

"Do you smoke?"

"No, I don't."

"I mean herb, marijuana. I keep a little plant. It's pretty good."

What the hell, he thought. He did indulge sometimes to relax and keep the loneliness at bay. "Alright."

"Oh good." She leaned forward, opened an ornate little box on the coffee table, took out a joint, lit it and puffed gently, then handed it to him.

He inhaled too much and coughed. "Whoa!"

She took his hand again and guided it underneath her silky skirt. His eyes widened as he realized she was naked below, no underwear. She lay down next to him, pulling him to her so that their lips met. When she began to stroke him, he moaned. Hurriedly she undid his pants. Images washed over her. His face as a little boy, not so different from the grown one, sweet and shy, possessing a deep quietness. As she pleasured him, she felt that he was far away, his body somehow floating above.

She sat up suddenly, startling him. She stood as he watched with fear and curiosity, his eyes never leaving her, his senses alive as a cool wind tinged with the scent of seaweed blew in from a half-open window. He watched as she slowly peeled the skirt downward inch by inch until it pooled around her bare feet. Dark, thick curls swirled between her thighs. She held him with her eyes as she pulled the blouse up over her head revealing small, round, upturned breasts. She placed both hands over them, then let one hand trace the muscled contour of her belly, sliding slowly down to her bejeweled navel and beyond, her hand exploring as she sighed and moved her hips from side to side.

"Oh God!" was all he could say.

"You mean, oh Goddess, right?" She smiled at him, turned a few circles around the room then stopped in front of the big canvas draped over the easel. "Let's go for a swim!"

"What?" he responded, "now?"

"Yes! If not now, when? Come on, I'll show you my beach." Swiftly she pulled on her skirt and blouse. "It's a beautiful night." She took the loose canvas off the easel, laid it on the floor and folded it corner to corner then rolled it. Taking a backpack hanging on a coat rack she inserted the canvas. Oh, this made her heart jump even more than the handsome, bewildered man who stood before her. "Come on, Jackson!"

"Really? Won't it be cold?"

"Not with the heat we will make on the beach together." She reached for a second backpack and slung it over her shoulder.

"Want me to carry one? What are in these?"

She stood on tiptoe and kissed him on the mouth. *Reinforcement,* she thought, taking his hand and leading him towards the door. She laughed as they negotiated the stairs. It struck him suddenly that she might be crazy, really crazy! As he followed her through the dimly lit shop and out the door, his caution fought with his desire for her.

They crossed the road and soon were on a path above the sea. The moonlit water below broke far out in choppy little waves. *At least it's low tide,* he thought. Still, not being a good swimmer, he doubted he would go in. In the half light, the tall seastacks looked rigid and misshapen, like curvy skyscrapers or huge humped animals.

Lezah had run ahead on the narrow path. He saw her

slip off the skirt and blouse. Breathing hard to catch up, he watched her naked body trip lightly down a series of plateau-like steps. His soft, bare feet prickled with thorns and sharp pieces of shells and rocks. "Wait up!" he called, but she only waved the skirt above her head and continued on. He saw that there was a small stretch of ocean below backed by a massive wall of stone. He felt dizzy and stood beside her on the cool, wet sand panting a little.

"You alright?" she whispered and touched him. "Yes, you are," she said and walked on. The crests of the translucent waves were lit eerily from within, and he swore he saw something large and dark moving inside one. She stopped at the edge of the water and put her backpack down. Her skin glowed in the moonlight, and her nipples stood erect in the salted wind that washed over them. Slinging the backpack onto the sand, he waited for her to do or say something. He looked across the expanse of water to the submerged boulders and ledges. Caves were carved into the great wall of rock.

Lezah turned and looked deeply into his eyes, her expression far away. She bent down and unzipped the backpack. Grabbing the raw canvas, she spread it out on the sand. She knelt by the other pack, opened it and clasped something, he could not tell what, that sparked and flashed. That disembodied feeling washed over him again as he watched her spread the object over the canvas. He thought he must be hallucinating, because it looked like a fish tail, scales and all.

Lezah sat down beside it and inserted her legs into the waistband then, wriggling and pulling, she eased the iridescent silky material up over her lower body. Her feet peeked out of the flared tail. For a few seconds she lay there on her back, the mermaid tail spread out on the sand.

"What in the world?" he asked softly. He saw that her legs were encased in pant-like sections as she sat up and stood. Able to walk, if awkwardly, she moved into the shallows, knelt and floated out. Mist swirled all around him. He breathed in the moist droplets, watching as she swam, the tail undulating behind. "Holy shit!" Then as fear enveloped him he saw movement on the ledges, rounded shapes like heads with glowing eyes. He heard a splash and watched as flippers cut through the water.

Whatever it was, she called to it, and it swam towards her as they circled one another. Her long hair floated out behind her in inked spirals on the water's surface. He was breathless, awestruck, and he wanted her more than he had ever wanted anything. For a long while he watched her playing with the seal, her laughter echoing. The tide had steadily risen, pooling around the submerged rocks, roiling onto the shore with more force.

"Lezah!" he called out. She waved and dived, then surfaced and swam towards him. He moved closer, his feet in the water. She turned onto her back, the slick, round globes of her breasts pointing skyward, her arms reaching over her head, stroking through the rippled shallows.

Wading out, he scooped her up into his arms. She closed her eyes as he carried her ashore. Once on the sand he leaned down and kissed her wet, salty mouth.

"Put me on the canvas," she whispered.

A few more steps and he bent down and gently set her down on the canvas whose stark, white shape glowed. She shivered, lying there, her hair, caught up with bits of seaweed, splayed out around her upturned face.

"Here," he said, "take my shirt." Pulling it up over his head, he covered her upper body. She pushed it away. "No, I'm not cold. Come, lie by me." Side by side, her wet breasts pressed into him. "Your pants." Hurriedly, he stripped them down and off, threw them aside.

"Here." She took his hand and guided it to the perfectly placed opening in the tail. The first time she saw stars exploding in a purple sky. The next time she heard far-away singing as the pleasure of him deep inside and the fog brushing her burning skin made her shudder. Her toes curled into the sand as she cried out, and the visions deepened. Sweet arrows of fire flew through unfamiliar air. Golden turtles swam in a turquoise sea, calling her name, "Lezah…Lezah." Dolphins flew up, out of the water, spinning webs of foam. She called out again in feral pleasure, then sank beneath the images, falling down and down through unending depths, past a forest of seaweed swaying above the anchored holdfasts.

They were inseparable for the next few days, could

not stop touching each other. They made love again and again. Lezah did not open her shop, called in sick to work. He was life breath to her; she feared she could not live without this sacred touching. The goodness she felt from him was like the purest water. There were few words between them, few questions. Feasting on one another, they barely ate or slept. Their bodies united in a space of something larger, expansive, profound.

She knew that on some level he was frightened of her capacity for pleasure. Attempting to absorb his innocence into her very cells, the sounds she made were unearthly at times. She had never felt like this before. Fine-tuned and stroked so tenderly, each light touch of his beautiful hands tracing her scapula and neck, the delicate, round bones of her vertebrae. The kisses all down her front from forehead to cheek to throat to breasts and belly. And oh, she had never ever felt what his mouth did to her, his lips determined and firm, both a question and a quest.

Out of breath, gulping air, and then, in the afterglow, he spooned her, his hands on her breasts, his heart beating fast against her back, the deep thrum of it matching the rhythm of her rushing blood as visions burst from her, electrically charged, full of color and sound. She'd had these before with men she'd picked up and knew that orgasms brought them on. But with Jackson these were different. She traveled to fantastic portals, mostly underwater, where the mermaids she painted came forth in vivid images and spoke to her—often in unintelligible tongues, nevertheless showing her their essence, their authenticity, the very story and message she was to impart in her paintings.

Lezah and Jackson parted on the fourth day, clinging to each other, tears in their eyes, speaking of the next time, the next time. When? How? Where?

Jackson drove back to Portland, his mind spinning. What was that? He'd never had sex like that. Never experienced that kind of lust and pull. The green drink, absinthe, took him places. It had been scary at first, a separation of mind and body, but the more he drank it the more he liked it.

"Lezah, Lezah," he said her name out loud. Who was she? Her brown-green eyes like polished stone. Her body small, muscular, powerful, sinewy. She was human yet animal too, and something else he could not pinpoint. Was she crazy, from another dimension? Beautiful yet angry and, yes, dangerous? Was there really a mermaid tail? That first night he saw it, made love to her while she wore it on top of the canvas. And the seals—how they called to her like she was one of them. Her strong arms swimming towards them. How they came down from their perches dropping silently into the water. Circled around her, the moon glancing off their dark fur. An artist. He'd never known an artist before. He really didn't know anything about her, but he wanted to.

Reality hit as his cell phone rang. It was Mark, probably wanting to know if he'd submitted the application. He let it go, put the phone back on the seat. He thought of Owen, his little hands grasping his. *Get real, Jackson! You need that job! Buck up, get your head out of the clouds. You need that job desperately.* Once home he vowed to focus and get the application in ASAP.

Three

She walked along the path to the beach, the backpack bouncing softly against her shoulders as she started the descent. Her mind would not relent. Why hadn't he called? It had been two weeks since their time together. Was it real? Did it happen? Was he just another user? Sleepless and upset, she retreated to the ocean, knowing she would find solace—if not peace—being near the water. Once on the beach she took off her sandals and let the backpack fall from her shoulders. She sat quietly, absorbing the many sensations around her. The feeling of her bare toes and feet digging into the sand, its weight and warmth. The insulation, like a gritty blanket, comforted her restlessness. Leaning back, taking in deep breaths of the fishy, oxygen-laden air, a mixture of stink and cool sweetness, she plunged her hands into the sand, then brought them up, spiraling the tiny nibs between her thumbs and forefingers, able to distinguish the individual grains.

She remembered the first time Roe had shown her sand magnified a hundred to three hundred times. Her amazed joy at the sight of the tiny bits of intact shells, rocks, and coral. There were pieces of sea urchin spines, quartz crystals, mica from mountain lakes, even lava from fire fountains. Roe told her each grain of sand spoke of a moment captured in time, because somewhere on its path from creation to erosion it recycled back to the earth. He said each grain was beautiful and unique, like people. So walking on sand was like stepping on a million years of biological and geological history. She thought of the first four lines of the long William Blake poem, *Auguries of Innocence*:

To see a World in a Grain of Sand
And a Heaven in a Wild Flower
Hold Infinity in the palm of your hand
And Eternity in an hour

A colony of seagulls flew over the sunlit seastacks, squawking and diving, interrupting her reverie. Now midday, the summer sky was a vivid blue, like the color of his eyes. Those eyes sometimes shy, other times intense, filled with tears as he spoke of his suffering child. Those eyes that lay lash-edged on the cliffs of his cheek bones as he slept. Again, she felt the anxiety that ached throughout her entire body, the empty pit in her gut, the literal weight on her tight chest.

Searching for release and distraction, she focused on the waves. As she had seen from her window this morning the waves were perfect for body surfing, good-sized but not too large. She counted—yes, about ten to twenty seconds between each one. Waves were her first playmates. Her tiny girl self had run into them, the white, tickling foam all around her naked body, then had run away screeching in delight as they chased her. She had spent hours in the water. At night falling asleep in her crib her body had still rocked with the ocean's ebb.

After she'd come to live with Roe and Opal she had become obsessed with body surfing. She had learned everything she could about waves. How they were driven by two forces: the generating push upward of water and the gravitational force pulling back. All waves move out from where they are created in a spiraling motion. Then the surface waters, blown by powerful winds, travel thousands of miles across the sea until they break on shorelines.

Fascinated by the fact that wind generates waves and by the distance they travel, Lezah wondered where today's waves had come from. She unzipped the backpack, took out her wetsuit and flippers. She pulled the long T-shirt that Jackson had given her over her head then held it close to her face, breathing deeply. Sighing, she folded it and laid it in the sand. Scrunching the rubbery wetsuit down, she put her feet in and pulled it up to her thighs, then stood up and wiggled and pulled it up to her chest. After putting both arms in the sleeves, she eased it up from her ankles again, smoothing it over her body like a second skin. Content that it was secure and comfortable, she sat down and pulled on the rubber fins. She duck-walked closer to the shore and paused to study the waves. They didn't seem to be bottoming out or breaking too close to shore. The crests of the waves were about six feet high, the troughs about the same, not choppy or rough. She waited until they retreated then waded in and dove into the shallows.

Swimming out to wait for the next set, then paddling in place, she looked behind and saw another group gathering and building. She held her body forward stiffly, one arm in front, one behind. Kicking out fast and turning towards shore, she swam as the swell came from behind. Caught in the upsurge, she was blasted forward with tremendous momentum, immense energy, rushing toward the shoreline with insane speed. Again and again she surfed, losing track of time or place, simply part of the living velocity of water and force.

Then unexpectedly as she paddled in the foaming slosh she looked back and saw a giant crest moving faster than any of the others. Leaping forward she swam, kicking as fast as she could. Glancing back she realized she could not outswim it, that the monster would consume her body. Just as this thought flashed through her mind she knew she was in danger of being pummeled and barreled. She slowed, then tried to become limp, hoping to float above the wave instead of being swallowed by it. But no, it overtook her, and she was tumbled over and over as the wave threw her towards shore. Spinning inside it, her body turning crazily, she felt sand engulfing her. Fear exploded as she blacked out briefly. Tiny lights sparked around her. She left her spinning body and looked down at it from above, a scream silent in her sand-filled throat.

She felt one of the fins come off. Helpless and afraid the wave would slam her down into the rocky bottom, she stiffened her body, arms at her sides, so she wouldn't land on her head. She raised her knees to stand as the rogue wave broke on the shore. Breathless, spitting sand, she staggered forward onto the beach, her chest heaving, her head pounding. Mother Ocean, her oldest friend, had humbled her, showing her that nature, no matter how familiar one was with it, holds the last card. She bent forward, hands on her knees, tears streaming, her mind crying *Jackson, Jackson, Jackson.*

She watched the water, each wave a reminder of what had just happened. *I have become weak,* she thought, *letting myself be this distracted by a man! You need him,* her heart whispered, *want him. Need? Want? What the hell? Never, ever really needed anyone—except Opal and Roe. Or yes, Robin, the college boyfriend who died in a car accident. Thought I needed him, but life goes on.*

The thought of never seeing Jackson again made her nauseous. She brushed off the sand, stared back at the water. *I need to work, to paint, to find out who the mermaid is on that canvas we made love on.* With this thought she felt a rush. "Stop it," she told her body. The canvas was still in the back of the Buick. *Go to Roe. Build a frame, stretch the canvas, see what the mermaid says.*

Roe brushed varnish onto a kitchen cabinet. "Lightly, lightly, old man," he told himself. He heard a clanking sound as wind slithered down into the little pot belly stove that heated the shop. Laying the brush down he straightened his tall, thin body and went outside to look at the chimney but could not see anything. From down the hill near the stairs he heard Lezah calling.

"Roe? Roe? You here?"

"In the shop." He ducked back in. "Hey, you're dressed for the drizzle."

"I just almost died bodysurfing."

"Sounds like fun. Where?"

"Up the beach from the jetty. Where is our favorite person?"

"I believe she's having lunch with Espy and then going to a spinners' meeting. What's up?"

She gave him a little sideways hug. "Wanted to see you anyway, need to make a big canvas. Got any wood? Gonna be six feet by four feet."

"Check that barrel over there. I think there are some long ones. Want me to make it for you?"

"No, but thanks. I need, I mean I want to make this one myself."

"Another mermaid?"

"Yes. This one is…important."

"Here, let me clear you a space on the table." Carefully he removed the kitchen cabinet door and leaned it against the wall. "There, that should work."

"It's in the car. Be right back."

Roe placed the miter saw on the work table, then found the corner brackets, screws, and the driver that fit.

Lezah pushed through the door. "This is heavy!" She took the canvas out of the pack and unfolded it. Smoothing it with her hands she felt heat rising from it. Gathering it up by its corners she moved it to the shop couch and laid it down. "Okay, frame first." She cut two four-foot and two six-foot pieces. Screwed in the brackets at each corner. "What kinda wood is this?"

"Pine I think."

"Alright, Roe, got sandpaper?"

He handed her a sheet, and she ran her hand lightly across the fine surface. "This is good. I'll put it on the table." Vigorously she chafed the slim boards until they were smooth and free of splinters. When she flipped the frame over, a little pile of blond dust puffed up, then sifted onto the table. Again she worked each piece with the sandpaper.

"It's a big one, huh?" Roe raised his eyebrows.

"Now the test. Take that end, please." They held the frame, wiggled it, tried to make it shimmy, but it held solid. "Strong one—yay! I could use some help with the stretching." She felt an anxious quiver in her belly when she touched the heavy white canvas. Roe reached over and took a corner. The other side unfolded itself as trapped sand slid to the floor. Lezah let out a breath. Here was proof she had lain on these grains with Jackson. "Uh oh, I'll sweep it up, Roe."

"No worries, life is messy. Are you gonna staple it on?"

"Think so, but not sure. Hmm. Hate staples, they are so loud and ugly. You still have those colored tacks?"

"Yup, we bought a thousand didn't we? Well, I'll be back in a few. Guys gotta go, ya know?"

"Okay, I'll choose tack colors and figure which way I'm going to stretch it. Pee ya later."

"Funny ..."

"On second thought I think I will stretch it at home. Walk out with you? Thanks. Tell Opal I love her."

Roe always felt like the air had been let out of him whenever she left. Her energy was so bright, effervescent. God, how he loved that girl. He and Opal had been through so much with Lezah, fear and heartbreak shot through with their greatest joy. He and Opal were just settling into the A-frame, happy as two clams and hoping for a child of their own, when they first met Lezah, a solemn, dirty, and malnourished two-year-old. She became their baby, protecting the innocent child their mutual mission.

Opal had suspected the abuse first while he had doubts. But Brodie had turned out to be the lowest form of slime. Roe still remembered the dark feelings that had haunted him while she lived with Brodie. He saw himself as a bit of a wuss, but he had served a tour in Nam and could do what he had to. In his need to protect the child Roe had nightmares about stopping him in any way possible. Opal didn't want him to engage Brodie for fear that they would lose access to Lezah. Brodie's death was a godsend, and the fact that they were able to adopt her was some kind of miracle.

Lezah was very athletic and played sports all through middle and high school. They loved going to her swim meets, soccer games, and dance performances. She was tiny but a muscular powerhouse with a will to win. Although she'd had a good deal of counseling, Opal worried about her shyness and lack of friends. *Don't know where that shyness went,* he thought. Nowadays she was outspoken and expressive, seriously trying to educate people about the environment, but she came across as prickly, even angry. *Still single at,* he counted, *thirty-six, she seems content. And anyway,* he thought, *where is the guy that could be both kind and strong enough to be with her?* He put the cabinet door back on the table, dipped his brush in the varnish, and started a second coat. *Let her stay that way,* he chuckled to himself, *less worry for me.*

Lezah drove home with the frame resting on the back seat of the Buick. With the backpack slung over her shoulder, she held the frame with one arm as she picked her way through the cluttered front yard of her shop. She unlocked the door, noticing how the late afternoon sun lit up the cobalt blue medicine bottles on a high shelf. She had to do a little dance to get through the turquoise door in back that led to her apartment. Going up the staircase she was careful to not disturb the mermaid paintings hanging on the wall. At the top she maneuvered the frame through the beaded curtain. Inside, she noticed the early morning candle was still burning. *Damn it, always forget.* She leaned the frame against her oversized easel, then tossed her backpack on the loveseat in the alcove.

She washed her hair in the shower, surprised to see how much sand rinsed out. *Can't believe I wore the wetsuit all day.* Tying on an old terrycloth robe, she towel-dried her hair, not bothering to comb through the mass of curls. She heated up a bowl of salmon chowder, carried it to the alcove, and watched the sun's downward journey while she ate. Yawning, she knew she would be asleep before sunset. Her whole body ached as she settled into her bed.

She relived the morning, the rare feeling of being out of control as the ocean tossed her around like a piece of seaweed. Burrowing in, a lightweight quilt around her shoulders, she drifted off. A half hour later she was awakened by the phone. She listened to her message. "Hi, this is Lezah Boudrow, owner of The Mermaid located at 936 Beach Loop Drive in Banderlay, Oregon. Please leave a message." Guessing it was Opal checking in, she sat up.

"Um hello, Lezah? This is Jackson Craig."

She flew out of bed and ran across the room, her heart galloping. But just as she was poised to answer something stopped her. *Wait, breathe, listen to his message first, see what he says.*

"Lezah, it's Jackson, are you there? Lezah, are you there? Listen, I would have called sooner but my little boy, Owen, has been in and out of the hospital for the last few weeks. I am so sorry but ..."

She couldn't stand it. "Hello, Jackson, I'm here."

"Oh thank God. You must have thought I wasn't interested in," she heard him take a breath, "you know, in getting in touch with you."

"Well I did wonder." Her hand shook. "Is your son alright?"

"Yes for now. It's been rough, and Mary Kay, his mother, is working now so it's been up to me to stay with him. He is doing better. Lezah, I want to see you again. Mary Kay's temp job is over next week. Can I come and visit on my way back to Portland next weekend? Would Thursday work?"

"Yes, I want to see you too. I'm sure I can get the

weekend off, even if I have to call in sick."

"Great, I am so relieved. I will check in, see you soon. Take care."

"Oh, you too, Jackson." She hung up. "See you soon," she sang out loud, dancing across the room. "See you soon, Jackson. Yes we will." Her heart felt light. "I will see you soon," she said quietly.

The next day at the café Lezah was forgetful, unable to focus. She hammered the last colored tacks into the back of the frame. The tedious work had taken hours, but the canvas was well secured, tight enough to bounce a quarter into the air. She walked the canvas over to the large easel Roe had made for her. Because she was short but worked with large canvases, he had lowered the mount bar so she could reach the top of the painting. Setting the blank canvas in place, she backed away from it and opened a can of gesso. Mixed with chalk, the thick, white substance would prepare the canvas for the acrylic paints she used. Inserting a stir stick, she swirled the opaque substance clockwise. Then she dipped in a wide paintbrush and painted a broad, wet stripe from the top left to the top right. The gesso dried quickly, so by the time she had reached the bottom she was able to apply a second coat.

The setting sun left a rosy wash on the ocean below. Bringing a delicate handblown glass and the bottle of absinthe to the side table next to the loveseat, she poured a tiny amount into the glass, ignoring the usual ritual. A tingling warmth slid down her throat and into her belly as she settled against the worn velvet. Feeling her limbs relax, she stared at the canvas. The white was not a warm tone but cold and antiseptic. All of her paintings started this way, but by the time they were finished they glowed with prismatic colors, and the watery environs the mermaids inhabited seemed to shimmer and ripple.

Each painting emanated a specific yet mysterious emotional energy. Lezah did not believe they were her creations alone. The essence of the three-dimensional creatures was sparked by her ideas or images and oftentimes a question she wanted answered. Yet they appeared in her dreams and told her what they needed to impart. Each brushstroke was like a tarot card revealing a secret. Her question this time, of course, was about Jackson. She took another sip of absinthe, her heart beating faster at the thought of his name. Looking at the canvas it seemed there was always this moment in the beginning, the yet-unmanifested expanse of pure possibility that overwhelmed her with both fear and joy. Fear that she might fail at capturing or interpreting the image, mood, or meaning, and joy because she was embarking on an unknown journey of discovery.

The white rectangle confronted her. Gathering pencil and paper, she let her imagination create a list of what "white" could mean or inspire.

ice
a birth caul

moonlight on bare skin
a wedding dress
a gull's angled wing
white puffy clouds
snow
shroud of death
a white curtain
a veil worn by Mary and her sister Magdalen
a splash of sperm
a crescent of fingernail
the white inside a rose
the underbelly of a field mouse
a bloodless menstrual pad
cream
ashes
a white lace corset
a perfect oval egg
the high trough of froth inside a wave
white phosphorus used in war
the skeleton of a sand dollar
a sinking moon

Setting the pencil down she took another sip and read over the list. Not knowing what was pertinent or what to choose, she stood and picked up a piece of charcoal. Standing in front of the canvas she closed her eyes, waving the charcoal just above the surface, letting her hand dance over the large space. Raising it from the bottom to the top, then moving her hand down slightly, she opened her eyes and drew a circle in the middle about a quarter of the way down from the top. *Hmmm... is it a head, a sun, a moon?* She glanced out the window—a fat, glowing moon hung in the sky. "Yes," she said out loud, "a moon." *Okay, we will go with that for now,* she thought.

Filling a cup with water she returned to the canvas. She squeezed a glob of yellow and then a smear of white acrylic paint onto her palette and mixed them together to create a buttery cream color. With a medium brush she filled in the large circle, leaving a rind of pure yellow around the outside. Suddenly tired, she washed the brush in the sink and laid it in the dish rack to dry. She turned back to look at the canvas with the yellow circle. *A moon. But is it a morning moon, a daylight moon, or a night moon?*

Later, Lezah stood at the window watching the storm gather over the ocean. Wind rattled the loose latch, so she put the little piece of cardboard on the sill inside the space. Pewter waves rose, swelled, and crashed on the shore below.

She removed the sheet covering the canvas, a pale space, a yellow moon near the top. Thunder made the ceiling lights dim and come back on. Lightening clawed across the day dark sky. She stared at the canvas. In the kitchen she opened a screenless window and reached her arm out. Filling a jar with rainwater, she carried it to a table in the alcove. The ancient box that held her brushes and paints was on the floor. More thunder, lightning, then the wind picked up as violent sheets of rain hit the glass. She put a paint rag under the loose latch knowing it would start to leak. Right then she heard the doorbells jingle downstairs. Damn it. She washed her hands and went down.

When she opened the front door she saw a couple standing beneath a huge umbrella in the cluttered yard. They were both so tall, over six feet. She was struck with how much they resembled one another, fair hair and skin but ruddy in their cheeks. They were big people, not fat but big boned. The man's light blue collared shirt peeked out of a thick cable-knit beige sweater. The kind advertised in high-end catalogs as "Genuine Irish Wool." His big face was hairless. Something about the way he offered his arm to the woman and helped her step over a large coil of rope seemed extremely tender and considerate. They turned then, the woman looking towards the porch, her face different yet so similar in a feminine way, the way Lezah had observed some married couples resemble one another. Her smile showing big, white, horsey teeth.

"Afternoon folks, sorry I'm about to close. Are you here for the weekend?"

"Terrance McClaren here, my wife Maeve. Beautiful this Banderlay."

"Hi, I'm Lezah. Have you been here before? Where are you from?"

"Oh well, no, our first time. We've let the Carpenter's house for a few months. Actually, we just arrived here yesterday. We have been in America now for several weeks visiting relatives. We're from Scotland. Shutting up shop, eh?"

"Sorry I've got to be at my other job soon."

"That's alright with us. Tickety boo, you know we will be back. Right?" His wife nodded and they turned and went out through the gate.

Lezah locked the gate after them and looked at the car for the first time. The man waved before he got in the sleek brand-new navy-blue Cadillac. Hmm, not knowing clearly what she felt she just said, "Strange," aloud and hurried into the shop to shower.

Four

Lezah, half-awake, turned over in bed, her hand brushing Jackson's back. His quiet, steady breathing told her he was asleep. He had arrived late last night, and they had stayed up talking, then made shy, soft love before falling asleep in each other's arms. Jackson stirred, opened his eyes, and reached for her.

"Good morning."

"Yes, it is," she replied. "Are you hungry?"

"Always."

"Well then, I am going to make us a feast for breakfast. Do you drink coffee or tea?"

"Coffee, strong and black. Could I take a shower while you cook?"

"Sure." She brought him her old terry robe. "Everything you will need is in the bathroom cupboard."

She whipped up batter for coffee cake, mixed brown sugar, butter, and oatmeal for the topping and put it in the oven. Unwrapping a package of sausages, she slipped them into a frying pan. The coffee bubbled and dripped into the pot, filling the room with what Lezah thought was the most pungent, rich, and sense-stirring aroma on the planet.

Jackson came into the little kitchen clean-shaven, looking handsome in her robe. "Ah, smells so good! My mouth is watering."

So is mine, she thought, *but for you.*

Lezah opened the oven door and stuck a knife into the cake, the scent of cinnamon wafting into her face. "Almost done. Pour yourself some coffee." Pushing her hair up, she twisted the thick curls into a bun and secured it with one of Opal's knitting needles, then smoothed the flowered caftan she wore. She broke brown eggs into sizzling butter.

"I love breakfast, best meal of the day," he said, sitting down at the table in front of the window. "Foggy this morning, huh?"

"Yes, but it will burn off later." She put the steaming plates down. They ate heartily, filling their coffee cups several times.

"This is so good. Have you always lived here?"

"Yes." Lezah turned in her chair, wondering just how much she should tell him. "I was born in Banderlay. Right here in this building. There was no upstairs then. Roe and

I built this addition after I came back from art school."

"Your folks live here too?"

"Um no, my parents died when I was twelve. Roe and Opal adopted me then."

"What happened to your parents?"

"Car accident."

"So sorry."

"It's okay, long time ago. Shall we go for a walk?"

"After I help you clean up here." He reached across the table, took her hand. "Thanks—that was the best!"

A thin fog drifted around them as they walked along Beach Loop Drive. Lezah was excited to show Jackson the seals. "Wonder where the pod is today?"

"Pod?"

"That's what they call a group of seals. Here is the path that goes down to Seal Rock." They stood at the overlook. Below, the island, which was eight stories high and about a mile long, was partially shrouded. In the middle of the rock face was a huge blowhole that allowed incoming and outgoing waves to pass through. They held hands; no one was out yet except one person walking a dog. The fog was visibly lifting as they passed the quiet houses. "This way, be careful, it's slippery."

Once on the beach they waded through piles of driftwood. Whole trees lay like pickup sticks. The beach at very low tide formed a damp apron of sand. She let go of his hand. "Come on, let's see if they are here."

"Who?"

"My seals." She scrambled like a crab over the rocks, crouched low, almost on all fours, sidestepping the tide pools.

He caught up. "You are fast!"

"Yeah. Do you remember when we were here that last time? At night?"

"Sort of. That was an interesting night. What do you call that drink you gave me?"

"Absinthe."

"I was pretty buzzed."

"Here, come this way. I think they are on those rocks to the right."

He followed her, feeling strange knowing that where he walked would be covered in water at high tide. He saw movement near the spot Lezah was approaching.

She turned and gestured. "Look, see these red sea stars? There used to be so many more. The last few years there have been a lot of changes." She bent and gently poked her finger into the center of a bright chartreuse anemone. The creature's short tentacles twitched as Lezah pulled her hand away.

"Do they sting?"

"Not me. I know when to withdraw. These guys are few and far between too."

"Why do you think?"

"Many reasons. The ocean is warming. Marine animals' food is becoming scarce. The kelp beds are dying." She gestured again, "I see their haulout."

"Their haulout?"

"Where they gather together." She hopped onto a long cluster of boulders. "Here they are!"

"My God, they are huge!"

"Yup. They can weigh up to four hundred pounds."

Jackson kept his distance. Several of the seals were basking in the sun. One looked up, its sleepy face scanning him, its long whiskers twitching.

"Hey guys!" At the sound of Lezah's voice the others raised their heads. Enormous and blubberous, they began to move towards her.

"The way they move over the rocks reminds me of worms."

"Yes, actually the way they move is called galumphing. A perfect example of onomatopoeia. Do you know that word?"

"No, don't think so."

"It's when a word sounds like what it refers to. The seals GALUMPH over the rocks." She laughed. "It's perfect. And so are you, Old Girl. This is Pinni. I was five when she was born." She squatted and petted the head of a spotted one. The seal rolled over, its belly wrinkled in rolls.

"Their flippers are so short, their tails too."

"On land they are slow and clumsy, but in the water they are gloriously agile. They can stay under for twenty-five minutes." A movement in the water caught their attention. A round head surfaced and swiveled like a periscope. "Oh, Annie, you had your pup!" Lezah went nearer the water. "Oh, it's a pretty white one." Jackson watched her cradle the pup then put it into the water. "Okay, back to napping. Shall we go to the cave?" Lezah asked.

"The cave?"

"Yes, one of my favorite places. Where did you grow up?"

"Portland."

"How was your journey to adulthood?" she asked as they continued walking.

"Um, well my dad died when I was five. I was raised by my mom. I have an older sister who lives in Chicago. My mother moved back there to help with Carla's big family—six kids and counting."

"Was it a good childhood?"

"Yes, for the most part. We didn't have much. Money was always a struggle, but there was lots of love and support."

"Oh, I am so glad for you!"

"What a funny thing to say." He turned to her and, seeing those full lips, leaned in and kissed her.

"Yum. After the cave maybe we should go back to the apartment?"

"I think so." He watched Lezah bend down to pick up a sand dollar.

"Look, a whole one! This is rare. I usually only find pieces. Sand dollars are really flat sea urchins. This," she held out her hand, "is a skeleton. When alive they are purplish brown and fuzzy. The flower shape is where their mouth is."

"You know a lot, don't you?"

She laughed. "It's just because this is ALL I know. Move me inland and I can't tell a fern from a tree, not really." She put the treasure in her pocket. "I'll save this one. Sometimes I like to dip them into paint and make prints. The cave is just around the corner."

Jackson looked at the scattered seastacks rising out of the water. "Is it a cave we can go into?"

"You'll see." She ran off ahead laughing. "Over here!"

He caught up, and they stood before a huge A-shaped wall of stone. In the middle of the wall was a slit. "Oh good, there's no moat, so we can leave our shoes on." She took his hand. "Come on in."

Jackson stepped inside. The cavern was large, the ceiling seemingly endless. It took a few minutes before his eyes adjusted to the filtered light. He heard a wave crash somewhere nearby and looked at Lezah, puzzled. She pointed. On either side was a tunnel that led out to the open sea.

"Wow! The cave is filled with water when it's not low tide, huh."

"Yes, and as a kid I would tempt fate and sit here waiting for the water to rise. Come on, you've got to see something."

"I don't know. Is the tide rising soon?"

She laughed. "Not for a while. Follow me. It's slippery, walk on the exposed rocks."

"Whoa." He watched Lezah duck down and move carefully along the narrow passage.

"It's alright, Jackson, trust me. Look at the walls!" He moved forward and saw hundreds of chartreuse anemones clinging to the wet surfaces. "Come on further."

Hesitating, he tried to find his balance. "Are you going all the way?"

"Yes! And so are you!"

Shit, he thought, watching her step easily to the open end and disappear. *Where did she go*? "Lezah?"

"Come on, it's safe."

He moved forward slowly. At the opening he saw her sitting on a rock just to the right. The breaking waves were closer. "Jeez," was all he could say. He sat next to her. After a moment he asked, "How long do we have until, you know, the tide comes in?"

"Plenty of time. Isn't it awesome to be this far out in the ocean?"

"I don't know, I guess. You know I don't swim very well."

"You will be fine. Look out there," she pointed. "Those seastacks are called Cat and Kittens. See the big one looks like a cat, and that line of smaller ones are the kittens."

Jackson nodded, watching a huge wave break twenty feet away. "Alright, I felt that one on my face!" he shouted.

"Okay, let's go back," she called. Sighing with relief, he led the way back through the tunnel. Once inside Lezah hugged him. "You okay? Didn't die of fright?"

"That was incredible, those anemones lit up like that."

"Yes, they are beautiful. But before we go I need a kiss—always wanted to kiss someone in here."

"You mean you haven't, ever?" She shook her head.

"Well then come here." They kissed long and deeply.

"Oh, and one more thing before we go. You've got to hear the acoustics in here." She moved to the middle and began singing. Her voice bounced off the damp walls and rose up to the ceiling, a cadence of uplifted notes, drifted above them. A crashing boom sounded, and they heard and saw a wave break at the end of the tunnel, water starting to pour in.

"You live on the edge, don't you?" he said, smiling.

"I try," she answered. They came out squinting, the early afternoon sun blinding at first. "So what shall we do? Go down to Old Town and get some lunch? Are you hungry?"

"Hungry for you."

"Oh, well that can be arranged." They walked back to Seal Rock and up the path. It was only a few blocks to her shop. They held hands, the heat palm to palm tangible.

A car on the road slowed and pulled over. Cary Dish leaned out. "Aha, Lezah, I caught you, thought you were sick," he said with a twinkle.

"I am sick, Cary, sick of work!"

"Okay, kiddo, you deserve it, have fun." He looked at Jackson. "Take care of her, whoever you are."

"Cary, this is Jackson Craig. Jackson, my boss Cary." Jackson nodded.

"Great to meet you. See you Monday, Lezah." He pulled back onto the road and waved.

"He seems nice."

"Oh, he is the best, like family really." As they picked their way through the cluttered yard of her shop Lezah, overcome by desire, reached out and took Jackson's arm. He pulled her into him and kissed her on the mouth. On their way upstairs they kissed again as Jackson reached under her shirt. Head thrown back she moaned. "Let's go, I can't wait!" she said, hurrying up the stairs.

Jackson saw a mermaid staring at him out of his peripheral vision as he followed. He shook his head. The beaded curtain made a crescendo-like sound as he entered the apartment. Lezah had already stripped her clothes off and virtually pushed him down on the bed, pulling off his pants, lifting the sweatshirt up over his head. "Can't wait, can't wait," she whispered as he kissed her breasts, her belly, her thighs. He took her then as she called, "Yes, yes," searching his face with her wild eyes.

Afterwards, in each other's arms as their breathing slowed, Lezah opened her eyes and saw the yellow moon on the otherwise blank canvas staring back at her.

They sat outside Tommy's Fish Shack devouring crab cakes, fried clams, sharing a beer. Afternoon sun stippled the bay. They laughed about Jackson's fear in the cave, as

Lezah wiped tartar sauce from her mouth. The sky darkened, and a frigid fog swooped in and surrounded them.

"Wow," said Jackson, "chilly all of a sudden."

"That's the coast for you, mercurial and unpredictable. Let's walk a little. I am stuffed. Wanna go to the book store?"

"It's crab season, right? Can we walk down to the dock? Maybe we can get a fresh one for dinner."

"Sure," said Lezah, buttoning her sweater as Jackson paid the bill. They walked around a sitting area where the benches were covered in tiled floral patterns. "Pretty, huh? The high school kids did them as a project."

The metal planks of the floating docks were slick with moisture. The clang of the chains that held the panels together and the undulating movement of the floating pontoons made walking unsteady. Through the fog they could see only one large woman sitting in a folding chair.

"Do you ever crab?"

"No, Roe is a master fisherman. He keeps me supplied."

Freezing fog swirled all around them. As they approached the woman she muttered, "Shit," as she pulled up an empty pot and threw a piece of rotten chicken in the basket. Lezah smelled the chicken and shivered, feeling suddenly nauseous.

"You cold?"

"Uh-huh."

"Shall we go back?"

"Yes, let's."

Jackson laughed, "Alright, but first a kiss." Taking her by surprise he lifted her up off the dock, her body small and light. The fog was so thick now he could barely see her face. The fog horn bleated.

"No! No!" Lezah cried. Jackson startled, set her down and put his arms around her. She pummeled his chest with her small fists. "Nooo." She turned and ran, sobs of terror trailing behind her.

What had happened? Jackson ran after her, found her clutching the edge of a sink where people cleaned their fish. She was breathing hard, seemingly unaware of his presence. "Lezah? Lezah? What's wrong? What happened?" He tried again to hold her, but she pulled away.

Oh God, indeed what had happened? Her jeans were wet; she'd peed her pants. *Get it together,* she told herself. "Give me a minute, Jackson."

"Okay," he said, but he was shaking.

They walked silently up the hill to Beach Loop Drive.

The night before Lezah attempted to explain what had happened at the dock without going into details. "It had to do with a memory from my childhood before Roe and Opal adopted me. I'm trying to make sense of it. Please be patient, I will let you know more when I do." Jackson seemed to understand and did not ask any questions.

The next morning, they had made love, a quiet, gentle connection that made Lezah feel even more vulnerable. After breakfast she filled their cups with the last of the coffee. Jackson watched her lick the honey spoon, her eyes on his. "Yeah, um yes I do this but not in public I promise." She laughed.

"My little boy does it too. 'Waste not want not' my grandmother used to say."

Lezah poured cream into the lukewarm coffee. "Tell me about your child."

He smiled, "Owen is six. People say he looks like me, he's blond, blue eyes. He has his mother's big smile. He was born with cystic fibrosis. Do you know what that is?"

"No, not really."

"The disease compromises the lungs and pancreas. The pancreas can't digest fats and proteins. These kids are usually small for their age. Owen is a tiny guy, looks more like four than six. His lungs get covered with thick mucus which of course causes breathing problems. It's so severe he needs a bronchial airway draining at least twice a day for thirty minutes. If he has a really bad attack, we have to percuss his chest by hand. He is very susceptible to pneumonia. On the average he gets hospitalized three or four times a year. We are in debt, for hundreds and thousands of dollars since I was laid off, I have no benefits and the insurance company just refused to pay for respite care. As you can imagine Mary Kay is very stressed." He sighed.

"Oh Jackson, your sweet little boy! How hard for both of you."

"We separated three years ago. Believe it or not Mary Kay got pregnant during our one-night stand. We stayed together because of the baby. She is a really good person and mother but we are so different. She suffers from depression. Sad story huh?"

"What's he like, little Owen?"

"He is just the greatest. Happy, I guess because it's all he knows. He is super smart, loves books and puzzles. Owen is a dinosaur freak like I was. Well, that's enough about me. Have you ever been married?"

"No, I haven't." Stacking their plates, she moved to the sink. Jackson brought the coffee cups and set them down on the counter. "Can I ask why, is it too awkward?"

"Of course not. Everyone wants to know why an almost forty-year-old woman has never been married. Here is the short answer, I'm too independent. The long answer is that I like my own company. I'm solitary by nature. My shop and work at the café are social enough…and I've yet to meet a man that I could do the 'day-to-day thing' with. My observation, familiarity breeds contempt. I'm joking but not. How about you, do you date a lot?"

"No, I'm a loner too." He looked at his watch. "I should go, it's a long drive."

"Jackson about yesterday, I want you to know what happened had nothing to do with you or us. Shall we get together again?"

"Okay, well thanks for everything." He picked up the backpack by the door.

"Let me walk you out." She stood in the cluttered yard. A brief hug before he got in the car. Waving as he pulled away, she felt something both physical and emotional, a sickening dread that she might never see him again. *Stop thinking,* she told herself. But her relentless mind said, *did you see his face when you asked if you'd be getting together again, the weak way he said, "Okay"?*

Jackson pulled away from Lezah's shop with a knot in his chest, her scent still on his shirt. In the moment he could not name the thoughts and feelings that rushed over him. He had such empathy for the wounded, vulnerable child part of her, seeing her hysterical running for her life like that. What the hell had happened? Had he triggered it? The worst of his fears that she might just be crazy or mentally unstable. But she seemed so strong, so together. He turned onto the highway choosing to take the coastal route. Images of their time together floated up as he drove through the heavy rain. The way she was with the seals, her devotion to them, the time in the cave, the way she humored him about the rising water. Sometime, if there was another time, he would tell her about his drowning incident. Their sexual connection…so deep and wild like nothing he had ever experienced. He knew one thing for sure, he couldn't wait to be with her again. Even though she pretty much told him she didn't see herself in a relationship. His cell rang; he didn't recognize the number.

"Hello."

"A yeah," a deep voice said, "Is this Jackson Craig?"

"Yes, it is."

"Hi, Ski Rakowski here. Your friend Mark said I should call you. You're a pilot, right? Still looking for work?"

"Yes, I am. What kind of job is it?"

"Well, we will discuss that when we meet. I'll be in Portland on Wednesday, can you meet me at noon?"

"Yes, sure."

"Okay do you know where the Bob's Bigboy Burger Restaurant on 6th and Main is?"

"No, but I will find it. Thanks."

"Right, see you there. Bring your resume. Take care."

"Okay, thanks." That's weird meeting at a restaurant. Rain slid down the windshield in steady sheets. God, hope this works out. His cell rang again. Mary Kay.

"Hi there, how are you guys?"

"We're alright and you?"

"Just heading back to Portland. What's up? How is Owen?"

"Doing better, he had a small incident last night. Listen, the pediatrician's office called."

"Oh no, unpaid bills?"

"No, not this time. They have a new drug trial going and they wanted to know if we want Owen to be part of it. Supposedly it alleviates the thickness of the mucus. It's untested at this point, she said it's promising. Checking in to see what you think."

"Hmm…it's untested, first trial. I don't know, he is on so many meds right now. It worries me, what do you think?"

"Yes, I agree. Did you hear back from the insurance company about continuing the respite care?"

"No, not yet. I'll get back to you tomorrow. By the way, I've got a job interview on Wednesday. Keep your fingers crossed."

"Sounds good. Owen wants to talk to you."

"Mary Kay, how are you?"

"Today is good. Slept five hours. Here he is."

"Hi Daddy, where are you? What are you doing?"

"I'm driving to Portland. What are you doing?"

"Playing with my dinos. You know how we read about the Rexes and the Spinosauruses, how they fight. Remember?"

"Yes, I remember."

"Well, Dad I want to have a party for ALL my dinos. Do you think they would get along if it was for a party? Mom is making me little cakes out of playdough."

Jackson smiled, "Yes, I think they'll get along. Whose birthday is it?"

"It's not a birthday party. It's a going-away party for the Pterodactyl. He is flying away to visit his dad in another country."

"I see, well have fun. I will Skype with you at bedtime and you can tell me all about it."

"Okay, Dad. Bye. Love you more than the stars in the sky."

"Me too Buddy, see you tonight."

Five

Lezah paced around the shop not knowing what to do with herself. The beach, I've got to move. But the high tide, it's treacherous, boiling boomers made a walk impossible. Opal, I need Opal. But could she explain what had happened yesterday without telling her about Brodie? Should I tell her? No, she might hate me, withdraw her love. I couldn't stand that. Then again maybe it was time for that old secret to be told. Go!

She grabbed her jacket and put it on as she rushed out the door. She jogged the five blocks to Opal's. Breathing hard she stopped at the set of stairs that led down to the A-frame. Calm down. Breathe, she told herself as she took each stair slowly, deliberately.

Lezah gave the big wooden door her usual one knock then opened it and called, "Hello, anybody home?"

Opal came down the hallway toweling her hair. "Lezah! Hi, I haven't seen you in days. Do you have time for tea?"

"Sure, that would be nice, where's Roe?"

"Fishing."

Lezah followed her into the galley kitchen, watched her fill the kettle, take down cups and spoons, and set them on a red lacquer tray. Over her shoulder Opal said, "So what have you been up to? Painting?"

"No, remember that guy I told you about last month?"

"Uh-huh."

"Well he came for a few days …"

"And?" Opal poured boiling water into the teapot and picked up the tray. "Let's sit in the living room."

Lezah followed her and sat in the small, overstuffed chair that had been "hers" since childhood. "This man is different," she paused, "special."

"Really, how so?"

"He is," she searched for words, "so sweet and kind. I have feelings for him. Feelings I haven't felt before."

"Well, how wonderful, honey. What's his name?"

"Jackson." Her voice trembled, caught. "We had a beautiful time together this weekend but yesterday something happened that will probably turn him away." How can I tell her, she thought, without telling her about Brodie? She teared up, sniffed, rubbed her eyes. Opal took a handkerchief out of her pocket and handed it to her. "Sorry."

"Don't be. Are you going to tell me what happened?"

"Yes, I showed him my world, the seals. Oh, Annie had her pup, a white one. We went to the cave, the tide was coming in, he was scared…he's not a good swimmer but so funny about it. We came back to the shop and then went to Tommy's for lunch. We shared a beer and ate crab cakes and talked and laughed. And then he said could we walk on the dock and I said, sure. The sky clouded over, a thick fog came in. When we got to the dock, no one was there except an old woman I didn't recognize. She was crabbing. She threw a rotten piece of chicken into the crab basket, the smell of it made me feel sick. Jackson asked if I was cold and I said yes. I felt so strange and then he picked me up and leaned in to kiss me. Oh, Opal, I don't know what happened, but I was there on the dock, but it was another time when, when Brodie …" She paused, her breath coming fast. "Oh Opal. I just lost it. I ran up the dock screaming in terror, so out of control. Jackson came after me, but I fought him off and ran to the fish sinks. It was horrible. Jackson was so confused and worried when he spoke to me. That's when I came to my senses and realized that I was with him, not Brodie."

"Lezah, what really happened the day Brodie died?"

"I can't Opal, I can't. It would change us; you would think of me…differently."

"Impossible. I've known ever since the Sheriff questioned you that morning there was more. It's time, no more secrets."

Lezah looked at this woman who was literally her savior, her mother, her best friend. "Okay." A strange calm came over her. "Brodie wouldn't let me go to school that day. I really wanted to; I had missed so much. He was already drunk; said we were going crabbing. It was just getting light out. He yelled at me to make the sandwiches and load the car. The fog was heavy that morning. We set up the chairs and crabbing gear on the dock. No one was there that early. I was so cold; I'd forgotten my jacket. He kept drinking, yelling at me to load the bait into the crab basket. The chicken was rotten, it smelled awful, but I picked it up and threw it in and closed the lid. After I tossed it in the water, I turned around to sit when he grabbed me. I remember kicking him as he lifted me off the ground putting his ugly mouth close to mine, he said, 'Come on Lezah, you better? Gonna give me some?' He reached under my shirt, started touching me. I screamed 'Put me down' and kicked him in the groin. He slipped and fell down hard. Blood poured out of a big gash on his forehead, covering his eyes. He said 'Lezah, Lezah help me. I can't see, I can't get up, girl help me.' I didn't know what to do, I was so scared. And then his eyes closed, and I didn't see any breath, but I didn't know if he was dead or alive." She paused, looked at Opal's face. "That's when I did it," another pause. "I got down on my hands and knees and I rolled him to the edge of the dock and pushed him into the water. I got up and ran home, stashed my bloody clothes in the back shed, washed up and went to school." Silence, for what seemed a very long time. Lezah saw tears in Opal's eyes.

"Honey, I am so sorry." Rising, she paced around the room. "Good riddance, I say. He was a monster and, and you just a child only twelve years old! What you lived through, my heart breaks to think of it. The pregnancy and abortion. You were still on your period and he was going to rape you again and keep doing it. You had no choice, it was survival."

"That's what I've been telling myself all these years. I thought it was over."

"If Jackson is the right one, when you tell him he will understand and see what a kind and wonderful woman you are."

"I didn't want him to know! He will think I'm weird or that I'm damaged, or worse guilty of ..." She couldn't say the word.

"Lies and secrets kill relationships. No matter how careful one is, the truth always comes out."

"What about you, Opal? Did you know? You never brought it up."

"I knew something was amiss even though it was feasible that he was alone. You answered the Sheriff's questions perfectly, but I knew in my gut there was more. Look, Roe is coming home soon. Do you want to stay for lunch?"

"Thanks no, I'm gonna go. I need a nap, hardly slept last night." She stood up. "Please don't tell Roe."

"Alright, come here, my girl." Lezah stood up. She leaned into Opal's embrace; tears of relief streamed down her cheeks.

"Forgive yourself," Opal whispered.

"I'll try."

Once home she felt exhausted, barely able to keep her eyes open. Her body too was heavy, needing to lie down. She slept fitfully, waking up feeling frustrated, uncomfortable, sweat on her forehead. Rising up, stretching she padded barefoot to the canvas in the alcove. The creamy moon hung suspended against the stark white. Yawning, she stared at the canvas, "What do you want to be?" she asked it.

"Show me please." She lit a fresh candle. Nothing came. She sat down in the love seat, looked out of the window. The sea below was so mercurial. Shifting in and out of darkness and illumination. Could she forgive herself? Had she…almost? Her higher self knew that what she'd done was not evil. Below the sky changed to a yellow green, the water bright turquoise. A group of rowdy kids and dancing dogs blazed through the dunes, the children running, screaming into the surf, daring it to catch them.

Brodie's face came across her mind. She shivered, made a cup of tea. The next step was to cover the entire canvas with a background color. Hmm, she thought, wondering what color was forgiveness, not for him, never

ever, but for herself. One of the children below ran with a brightly colored kite. The wind lifted it high above the boy. Brodie had stolen her childhood. Her mother had deserted her, the energy it had taken to endure it...what else had she lost? The security of protection, of being treated like an innocent child, nurtured and loved unconditionally. The sky darkened again, the far-out waves roiling, tossing every which way. The huge pounders serrated at their peaks, their frothy curves like the classic Japanese images. The symmetric rise, break and spill throwing up foam along the sleek sand, the sound below booming like solid thunder.

"You fucking bastard! How dare you do that to a little girl, an innocent baby!" She paced, her body shaking, letting it happen. Across the room sat a big, clear glass vase she was pricing for the shop. Flying to the shelf, she grasped its neck and threw it high in the air, watched it crash onto the hard, planked floor. The shattered glass rearranged itself as it rose up then and tumbled down with a loud tinkling sound.

Methodically, Lezah swept the glass into the dustpan. She glanced at the canvas. What color was innocence, forgiveness, wholeness? Blue, she thought, blue. A clean, pale, soft gentle light blue. She moved to the cupboard and lifted the case down that held her paints and brushes.

Hurrying, trembling, she mixed the baby blue color and with her widest brush painted the background, skirting the moon. Her body tense, her thoughts scrambled,

Jackson's face hovered before her, those eyes, so clear, so changeable, from light blue to deeper blue-green. The way the dark sweep of his lashes framed them. Squeezing out a glob of blue then green paint onto the mixing tray she knew suddenly the area below the moon and sky would be the ocean.

Dipping her favorite bamboo brush into the water, she swished it thoroughly then laid the fat bristles into the two colors. She watched the way they spiraled, still separate but bonding, becoming a new color. Could people do that, blend two entities to create a new, unique whole? She lifted the brush from the tray and stroked it across the width of canvas. She backed up, squinted at it. Was the color right? Almost. Twisting the lid off the cadmium yellow, she squeezed a bit onto the brush. The tiny streak blended in, brought the perfect light needed.

By the time the storm subsided the canvas was covered. A slim sky of pale blue at the top; a butter-yellow moon seemingly sinking into a turquoise sea. *Hmmm, where is the mermaid going to go?* She stood back, brush in hand. *Close,* she thought. She knew there would be many layers of color over the water as the image was completed. *This turquoise, though, will shine through the overlays like his eyes.* Moving away from the easel she sighed, "Stop it. My God …" But, it was deep, a knowing so clear that Jackson was not just a lover but a teacher. Good or bad, she needed him, and she knew it.

Ski Rakowski parked his truck in the almost empty parking lot. A slim moon lit up the only other two cars. He ducked his six foot three inch frame and stepped down. Just off a shift, his niece Brandy had left a message saying his dog Toby had been hit by a car that evening and was in critical condition. *Toby, Toby,* was all he could think of at this moment. He walked to the front of the veterinarian's office and searched for the buzzer they said he would find. He heard it go off as he looked through the glass door, saw someone walking up the dim hallway towards him. *Toby.* He brushed tears away with his huge hands. *Toby, best damn dog on the planet,* his baby, his girl may be dying. A woman in blue scrubs put her hand up in greeting and opened the door.

"Mr. Rakowski? Hi, I'm Dr. Stone. Your dog is in recovery. We finished the surgery a few hours ago. Two broken legs, left rear, front right. She also had a concussion. Does she chase cars?"

"Not that I know of. Why?"

"Well, it was a hit-and-run. Your niece said she heard the tires screech, went outside and found your dog. The car pulled away fast."

Did anyone get the license number? I will kill them, he thought.

"Mr. Rakowski?"

"Please call me Ski, everyone does," he hiccoughed. "Is she going to die? Because she is only four and …"

"We don't know, but her youth is in her favor. As far as a full recovery, it could be a long haul." She removed the surgical mask from her forehead and twisted it. "They were clean breaks, and the concussion was substantial but not severe." She noticed tears sliding down the big man's face. "I'm not supposed to tell you this, but I think she will be fine in a month or two. Let's go take a look."

They walked down a long hallway past a woman mopping the floor. "Right here, Mr., um, Ski." She opened a door and there was Toby laid out on the table, her legs in casts, tubes and IVs everywhere. Ski moved closer. "Just don't touch her, please."

"Toby? Aw, look at ya. Ya gotta get better, ya hear. How long will she stay?"

"A week or two. Your niece said you work out of town a lot. Will she be taking care of her? Or perhaps your wife?"

"Yes, we share a duplex. I'm not married. When I'm gone she watches her. She adores her."

"Okay, well I have to go home and feed my baby. She will be up soon for the midnight feeding. Do you have any other questions?"

"Can I pay extra for extra care, the most expensive food you have?"

"No, everyone pays the same."

The man fingered the keys in his pocket. "Thanks so much. Can I visit her?"

"Of course, she would love that. Should be more alert by tomorrow. If there are any changes we will call you."

"Okay, thanks a million. You don't know what she means to me."

"Oh, I probably do," she smiled. "Let me get my purse, and I'll walk you outside." She went into a room and came out with her purse over her shoulder. "Here, I'll let us out." They left the office. "Try not to worry. Goodnight."

Ski watched her walk to her car and waited until she warmed it up and pulled away. You never knew who was around. He stepped up into his cab, willing his sixty-eight-year-old body to cooperate. *Toby, goddamn it pup, you better be okay. Best damn pup.*

Once on the road he realized he was hungry, not just hungry but ravenous. Bob's Bigboy sounded good. He flipped a bitch mid-highway, making sure the hundred and eighty-degree turn was complete even though there was not a soul to witness the maneuver. A few blocks back he pulled into the parking lot. At the counter he smiled at the sleepy looking kid.

"Hi there, having a hard time staying awake?" He put his big hands on the counter and laughed. "Can I have a Bob's Bigboy, make that two, with extra mayo, pickles, mustard, cheese and onions?"

While he waited at a table near the front he watched the neon signs blink on and off across the street and thought about Mom. He had been an only child, and his dad had run off when he was a baby. She would be gone now—he counted: he was forty-five when she had stroked out in front of the TV, so twenty-three years. Bob's had been their go-to place. They both agreed that the burgers were the best and, after all, they contained nutrients from all four food groups! God, he missed her. The kid slid his tray on the counter and called "Ready."

"Thanks, ya can go back to sleep now." He sat down and dove in, the special sauce dripping down his wrists. He finished the second burger and wiped his hands, took his tray to the bus station.

He drove home, the sky blank of stars, murky. Parked in front of the same duplex he had grown up in. After Mom died he bought the other one, let Brandy stay there rent free because he was gone so much and she just loved Toby. Didn't know what he would do once she graduated from nursing school. He yawned, unlocking the door. Changed into his sweats, flipped the TV on. Some news anchor whining about climate change. *Suckers!* He nodded off, the TV still on, his last thought, *miss my Toby.*

Six

Jackson rolled over, glanced at the clock, picked up his phone, 4:45 Mary Kay, "Hi what's up?"

"I can't do it anymore, Jackson. Been up all night. He's resting now but I'm taking him to the doctor's at ten. I need help, Jackson, please find out about insurance. I'm losing it. I've got to have respite, or I don't know what's gonna happen. This not sleeping is killing me." She took in a breath.

"Okay, I'll call again. If you would only move back here, I could help…I know, your mother and all of Owen's medical stuff is down there but this isn't working. Maybe I can come down next week. I've got that job interview today, not feeling so positive about it though."

"Why?"

"I don't know, the guy called me, wants to meet at some burger place downtown. Not professional, and you know it was Mark that set it up, and we both know about Mark, right?"

"Okay sorry to bother, I just hit rock bottom. Gonna go lie down now while Owen sleeps. I hope it's just a cold. I'll call you this afternoon. Thanks for listening."

"Sure. I'm sorry, take care."

The appointment was at noon so there was time to wash his slacks and button-down shirt. *Okay, coffee,* he thought, *heal me now!*

He punched in the address, but the GPS couldn't find it. The morning had been a shit show, an ink pen in the laundry, no creamer, and a line at the gas station. He was probably going to be late. Bob's Bigboy Burgers where are you? Just then he saw the sign out of his peripheral vision.

He pulled over two lanes in time to make the entrance to the parking lot. The place was packed. He walked to the front door wondering how he would find the guy inside. A huge man approached him. "Hey Bro, can you give me some change, I'm really hungry." Jackson said, "No, sorry" and proceeded to walk away. The man followed, called, "Hey are you Jackson Craig?"

"Uh yeah! How did you know?"

"The picture on your resume," the guy busted up

laughing. "The look on your face when I asked for a handout, priceless. Hey, I'm Ski Rakowski, sorry for the little joke. Thought I'd try to find you out here. It's so crowded. We've got a table, come with me …"

What the hell? thought Jackson as he followed.

The place was packed and loud for a lunch crowd. Waitresses in pink ruffled aprons dashed here and there with pink lipstick smiles. Jackson followed Ski through the length of the restaurant as he examined Ski's huge Hawaiian-type shirt in front of him. The man was light on his feet though, dodged and weaved like a lawyer. Was he a lawyer? He couldn't remember what Mark had said. Was this the manager? The boss? Ski stopped at a booth at the very back of the dining room. They both sat, facing each other.

The handshake hurt. He pulled his hand back, played with the edge of the napkin, waiting.

"You live in Portland?"

"Yes, I do, all my life."

The waitress came over. "Hi Ski," she said rather flirtatiously. She was older, silver hair tied up in a ponytail. Too much eyeliner. She handed them menus.

"Hi Verna, busy today huh?"

"Yes sir. Anything to drink?"

"Extra-large root beer. Jackson?"

"I'll have a Coke please."

"Okay boys. Be back for your order in a minute."

"Ever had a Bob's Bigboy Burger, Jackson?"

"No, my first time here."

"My favorite. Since I was a kid really, used to come with my mom." Ski opened his menu. "I always get the same thing, but I look anyway."

Jackson was hungry, the stressful morning had left no time for breakfast.

"What do you usually get?"

"Me? Oh, I get two of the double deckers and fries."

Verna was suddenly at the table. "Decide yet? Need more time?"

"I'll have my usual," Ski said, "with fries, side a ranch also."

"Okay, and you?" She winked at Jackson.

"I'll have a cheeseburger and fries please."

"Okay boys, be back soon."

"Can't wait, Verna, you're looking good."

"Ah, Ski," she smiled, obviously pleased.

"Alright, well, where were we? Hey, there is a history that goes with Bob's Bigboy. One year, my mama dressed me like Bob for Halloween. Little too short shirt, belly sticking out. I already had the big belly even when I was little. So...okay...back to you, you've lived in Portland all your life?"

"Yes."

"You're a pilot?"

"Yes."

"Saw on your resume, both private and charters, ever do commercial?"

"Yes, I tried it for a few years. Didn't like it. Boring."

"Uh-huh. Been laid off, huh?"

"Yes, our provider went bankrupt."

"When are you available?" Ski sipped his root beer.

"Anytime. Need work now. Can you tell me about this job please, Mark didn't say much."

A group sitting at the next table got up to leave, a little kid holding a cup tripped and spilled his milkshake into Jackson's lap. The kid started crying. Jackson tried to comfort him as Verna rushed over with a towel. "Here ya go," she tossed it to him, *Jesus what else,* thought Jackson.

"I can't tell you about the job yet. This," he waved his hand across the table "is just the preliminary. I can tell you two things: it involves flying airplanes and it pays a lot of money."

"Okay sure, what's next?" Jackson sighed.

"Meet me at an undisclosed location next week, I will email you the details. You got family here?"

"No, well my mom and sister live in Chicago. I have a child, a boy Owen, he's six. I'm not with his mom. Owen has…issues."

"Like?"

"He has a disease called cystic fibrosis; it affects his lungs."

"Here ya go," Verna set down the heavy plates. "Been bowling lately, Ski?"

"Nope." He had rolled the paper sleeve holding the giant burger and was about to take a bite.

"No, we should go again."

"Yeah, we should!"

"Okay later." She rushed off.

"Nice lady," he said, his mouth full. "So, do you see your boy often?"

"As much as I can. He lives in Granite Pass."

"You guys have good insurance, I hope."

The pink special sauce dripped onto his shirt, landing right on the bird of paradise.

Jackson had never seen someone enjoy a hamburger this much. "I don't have any coverage after the first of the month. We're behind in bills and they have cut off our respite care."

Both were quiet while they finished the meal. Ski took the bill, "On me this time." They shook hands in the parking lot. "You'll be hearing from me." Jackson nodded and thought *no I won't, must be some kind of shaky outfit.* Ski unlocked his truck, got in. "You do okay? Good girl for waiting." Ski pulled out of the parking lot. He petted the dog's head. "Got a good one, Toby. Desperation always helps."

Roe stood on the little porch looking over his gear: rod and reel, cast net, knife, folding stool, bait bucket, spare spool of line, pliers, and rain poncho. He sat down on the bench and slipped off his shoes. Pulling on his ancient rubber boots, he checked the slash on the sole to make sure the layers of duct tape still held. Oh, if these boots could talk. He remembered the day on the commercial fishing boat when he had ripped the rubber sole by stepping on a random hook someone had dropped on the deck. Luckily, his foot was not cut. He was amazed that they were still wearable. They must be at least forty years old he thought, as he loaded the gear into his bucket and picked up his rod.

He'd "read" the beach, the sky, the water from the house window during breakfast. It was overcast, misty, the high tide strong at wave break. He set out down the few steps that led to the path to the beach below. The beach path snaked down the hillside. Once on the sand, he walked to the shore and set up his stool, the bucket nearby. He took three live shrimp from the bucket and pushed them onto the hook. Moving closer to the water he saw the sand bar where the fish hid. He cast overhead, aiming for the sand bar. Once cast, he set the pole on its stand and waited.

A circus of tufted puffins flew by, heading for their nests on Seal Rock. He thought of the time out in the boat when one of the men accidentally hooked a puffin, how it had come on deck flapping and squawking. After getting a good look at it he'd thought that describing a group of puffins as a "circus" of puffins was correct; they *did* look like clowns. He sighed. Twenty years as a commercial fisherman. How had he done it for that long?

After Vietnam he was lost, drinking heavily, not able to expunge the demons. He'd hitchhiked from LA to the Oregon Coast. Banderlay was in the midst of a fishing boom and needed workers. Being inexperienced hadn't mattered; he learned on the go, whether salmon, halibut, or whatever was running. It was the hardest work he'd ever done but physically satisfying, easing the pent-up anger and resentment he had towards the war and what he'd done there.

Banderlay was a beautiful distraction. On days off he still drank heavily, a tribute to what a thirtyish body could handle. Commercial fishing was dangerous and had a ten times greater death rate than other American occupations, but for him those years, until he quit at fifty, were a doable battle each time out. Sure there were times when nothing happened, but he'd even loved those days as he studied everything—the sea, its myriad patterns, colors, winds, weather, and creatures. He'd told Lezah about the strange and otherworldly things he'd seen and heard while the boat was so far out that the water was Prussian blue in color.

Towards the end, as he rapidly approached elderhood, it all bothered him. Being wet and cold and miserable, or sweating your guts out. No clean underwear; salt-stiff hair; itchy scalp; strong odors, both human and fish. Meeting Opal in his early forties had changed his life, and she had graciously done his stinking laundry for years.

Something jumped in the surf distracting him. Only a seal, probably one of Lezah's. Oh well, the expected competition. Mist moved to drizzle, so he put his hood up. *That woman,* he thought, *how did I get so damn lucky*? After almost thirty years together they were still as close as two peas in a pod. He'd first seen her when he dropped the daily load off at the fish processing plant in Old Town. Her big smile and blue eyes emboldened him, and he had asked her to coffee. Afterward, she'd taken him up to Beach Loop and showed him the dilapidated A-frame she had just purchased. They'd been together ever since that day. No one had loved him like Opal, openly, without judgment or fear. And she tolerated his need for order, whether it was books or the shelves in his workshop.

Yes, they had suffered over that dirty, underfed, and

abused little girl, but even that had turned out alright. Lezah was the light of his life, no buts about it, and she loved him back. He had supported her fascination with mermaids since she had told him once, when she was small, "I'm your little mermaid, and you are *sooo* much nicer than Ariel-on-TV's mean father."

As she grew up and started painting she begged him to tell her stories about being a fisherman, especially the unexplainable things he saw and heard out on the water. Like the day he heard the mythical sirens. They were anchored in a calm sea while work was being done on the temperamental engine. He was the only one on deck when he heard the most incredible singing coming from all around the boat, voices melodic and harmonic, not of this world. Or the day the whales, traveling back from Mexico with their newborns, circled the boat closely as if showing off their young ones. Lezah loved the story of the dolphins jumping for pure joy, leaping so close they looked him right in the eye.

He felt his line jerk and walked towards the water as, more than likely, an ocean perch on the other end tried to unhook itself. He reeled it in slowly and steadily, watched it bounce over the high surf. But when it came into view it was not a fish but a big octopus. Oh, he loved these guys. Cephalopods fascinated him. This one was a mottled rusty orange, its eight arms dotted with suckers their whole length. It was frantically waving its arms around its mouth. Roe walked into the surf up to his waist—so much for not wearing his waders. He lifted the line gently, talking quietly to the creature. "If you hold still, I can get the hook out." As if it heard him the arms relaxed and splayed out, floating on the surface. He only had a minute before the next wave broke. "Okay, here." He reached the end of the line and felt where the hook was embedded. The body was squishy in his hands. The hook came out easily. Roe saw the octopus change color as he ran back to the beach. The wave rushed in, partially submerged the octopus, then pulled back. The gorgeous thing rode the wave back out, its big head swiveling. "See ya," Roe called. *God, they are alien,* he thought. He knew their DNA matched no other on earth, and they had three hearts.

Soaked to the gills, he sat down on the beach and emptied his boots. *Can't wait to tell Lezah,* he thought with a smile. As he packed up his gear he heard Opal ringing the signal bell from the house. *Lunch is ready,* he thought. As he walked home Lezah's sad, serious face came to mind. The girl was obsessed with the changing environment. He'd noticed over the last twenty years how the seasonal patterns and fish migrations had changed due to global warming. The decline was dangerous; she was right. *Mercury runs amuck, so many fish not edible. Shitting in our nest, we are.* The bell rang again. *Alright, old woman, I'm coming. Hope she wasn't planning on fish and chips.*

Roe put the fishing gear away in his workshop behind the house. He washed his hands using the bar of Opal's handmade soap that was sitting near the makeshift faucet. He went to the house and pushed in the heavy door. "Anybody home?"

"In the kitchen."

"Well, hi there, "Inthekitchen." He came up behind and kissed her cheek. "Hope you weren't planning on fish and chips for lunch? 'Cause no bites at all, except I caught a big octopus. Took out the hook, sent him back. Smells good. What are you making?"

"Salmon chowder. Do you want bread and/or coleslaw?"

"Both. I'm wet, cold, and hungry. Gonna change."

"Alright, be hot when you come back."

"Whoa." He stopped in the living room after changing, spotting Opal's little altar. Flames sputtered up from three lit candles, and burning incense spiraled wisps of black into the heavily scented air.

"Okay, Opal, who died?" he called.

"No one, silly. Come and eat. Lezah came by."

"Is the arsenal on your altar for her?"

"No, not really. Sit please."

"Mmm, what's the different flavor?" asked Roe, dipping sourdough bread into the chowder.

"The tarragon is up. Thought I'd try it since the dill isn't ready."

"It's good. What's up with the rest of your day?"

"I need a nap, I think. Broken sleep last night."

"Yeah." He reached over and took her hand. "Can I join you?" He stroked her cheek. "What about—what did we decide to call afternoon delight, an 'elder nooner'?" He laughed, wiped his mouth with a cloth napkin.

"It's not noon. It's 2:15. Sure, do the dishes and I will meet you in there."

"Aha, bribery. Okay, will do. Bet you are asleep before I get there."

"We will see," she said, yawning.

"I'll jump in the shower real quick."

"Okay, yes," she whispered, heading towards the bed. She stripped off her sweats, leaving her bra and panties intact, and lay down on the bed.

Roe came in with a towel around his waist. He could hear her sleep breathing, along with that little half snore. *That's alright,* he thought, *just want to lie next to her.* He slid in on his side, rolled close to her. *Ah, her skin.* She moved against him as he stroked her back. She rolled to face him, and they kissed warmly, softly holding each other. He slipped his hand into her bra, sweetly stroking her. Aroused now, Opal held onto him as he did what he knew how to do to pleasure her. Although he couldn't make love as in his younger days, she knew how to pleasure him too.

Afterwards, in each other's arms, Roe asked, "How is our Lezah?"

"She's in love, Roe, I really think she is."

"Who is it?"

"A man from Portland. Never seen her like this. So, so over the moon but doubting herself."

"About what?"

"Her worth, whether she deserves happiness." She would not tell him about Brodie, not now anyway.

"What the heck? She's so deserving, what we've always wanted for her. Is that why the altar is lit up like Christmas?"

"Partly, well yes." She yawned. "I need a nap."

Roe put his hand on her hip. "Always loved your hips."

"They're getting wider," she said sleepily.

"You'll always be my hippie chick, Opal."

Rain fell on the little house. In the door yard, pale blue hydrangeas nodded beneath the heavy droplets. Roe and Opal spooned, then slept in the familiar shelter of each other's bodies.

Lezah moved around the café, wiping down tables, straightening salt and pepper shakers, pushing in chairs as the dinner crowd would be in soon. She plucked a newspaper from the bar but on the way to the trash can, the headline caught her eye. *"Dead whale's stomach filled with 76 pounds of plastic."*

"A young male sperm whale, 15 feet long and weighing over 1,000 pounds, likely died of starvation and/or dehydration as a result of the plastic filling its belly. After it beached and died, a marine mammal expert said after the necropsy, 76 pounds of plastic were found in its otherwise empty stomach. We found plastic bags, tangles of nylon rope, and hundreds and hundreds of plastic drinking straws."

Lezah picked up the paper, rolled it, hitting each table with it on her way to the kitchen.

"Carey? Carey, look at this!"

He came out of the kitchen, wiping his hands on his apron. "What's wrong, Lezah?"

She waved the paper near his face, "Look at this!"

"Jesus Lezah, I don't have my glasses on, what the hell is it?"

"Plastic, that's what it is. Whales dying from their bellies full of plastic. Plastic killing seabirds and the ocean." She gripped the rolled paper and hit her thigh with it, her voice rising, "and we, we Carey are guilty of contributing to this murder!"

"What the fuck, Lezah, quiet it down, what if someone comes in. Another one of your causes, huh. Girl, chill. It's the world...you can't change it by yourself, it's just life."

"Fuck you, Carey! I can change your life today. Either you," she narrowed her eyes, "get rid of plastic straws and start recycling or I quit," she hissed.

Carey sighed, "Look, girl, I spent a fortune on the paper to-go boxes you made me get. They leak and don't stack as well as the Styrofoam. Now you want me to get rid of straws? People need them, they like them."

"I don't care. They don't need them. It's a habit, that's all. People are perfectly capable of drinking right from the glass!"

"Lezah, look at you. You are so upset all the time about this stuff. You do your part but you can't control the world. I'm worried about you."

Lezah pushed a curl behind her ear. "I'm serious Carey, stop using straws or I give my notice as of now."

Carey sighed again. He'd known her since she was a little girl. She was the hardest worker he'd ever had. People came in because of her. People loved her...Christ, the place would not be the same without her. He looked at her serious face; she meant it. He knew he couldn't do it without her.

"Goddammit, Lezah! No straws but that's it, no more of these eco demands. Gotta go fry up the fish and chips." He headed for the kitchen, shaking his head. He heard her say, "Thanks Carey, every little bit does help," as he pushed open the double doors.

She found the scissors in a drawer behind the bar. She cut the article out carefully, found a glue stick, pasted it to the back of a menu. In Carey's untidy little office, she found a blank piece of xerox paper and a marker. She printed, *"We are no longer providing straws to our customers."* She tacked the sign up next to the daily menu. "Okay," she said to herself. She grabbed a rag from the pile, ran it under hot water, and began wiping the bar top clean.

She went into the kitchen, grabbed a paper plate, lifted the fry basket up and took a small piece of fish and a few fries. Carey was busy shredding cabbage for coleslaw.

Squirting ketchup over it all she looked up at him. "Still love me?" she asked, licking her fingers.

"Yeah, yeah. But I gotta make a living, Lezah. Hard enough to do with the seasonal ups and downs. You know I depend on the locals, just don't want to piss them off."

There was a long silence while she finished the food, then putting the plate in the sink she turned. "Well maybe if people complain I could talk with them, educate them."

"No! That's where I draw the line! Just what I need is you yammering away while folks are trying to enjoy themselves. Understand? No talking with people about any enviro stuff. Get it?"

Lezah sighed, "Got it." Walking back to the bar, she looked at the clock, hmm 5:10, soon the dinner crowd would be in. Better pee, she thought, heading to the bathroom. While there she replaced toilet paper, cleaned the sink, picked up a dirty diaper from the floor. "God people are pigs," she said out loud. Washing her hands, she heard the bells on the front door jingle. A quick glance in the mirror, her curly wreath of hair more wild than usual.

Coming out she saw a man at the bar, his back to her. Something familiar about him. He was doing something with his hands, holding something red.

Oh my God. She stood there across the room from him, out of sight. Frozen, her breath caught in her chest, as her brain sent panicked opposing messages. Run! Could she get to the kitchen unseen and sneak out the back door? No, no, wait, what? He turned his head, picked up a menu. His hands, the long slim fingers. As she stood there feeling both terrified and ecstatic, guarding hope for what might be, she took a breath and walked slowly across the room.

Where is everyone? he thought. *This was a mistake, she wasn't there, he'd drink a beer and go.* "Jackson?" He turned, watched her move behind the bar. "Hey, you're here."

"Yes, on my way back from Granite Pass. Hoped to see you." She noticed he nervously folded and unfolded the hat. "Wasn't sure if …"

"Yes, I wanted to see you too. Do you want something to drink?"

"Coors, please."

Lezah took a chilled glass from the fridge, filled it at the tap, set it down before him.

"Thanks." His eyes held hers. "I miss you, Lezah, but not sure how you feel about us, the possibility of us?"

"Can you stay over, Jackson so we can really talk about it?"

"Okay."

"Are you hungry?"

"No, I stopped on the way."

"I'm going to call in another girl, I'll have to work a few more hours. Do you feel comfortable waiting at my place?"

"Sure."

"The key is in a dish of shells by the front door. Go upstairs, make yourself at home. Gotta go let Carey know."

Jackson watched her rush away to the kitchen. A big party came in, Lezah greeted them, sat them down, gave out menus and took drink orders. Back behind the bar she put glasses on a tray. "It's all set, Jackson, I should be home by eight.

"Okay sounds good. See you there." By the time she took the food order in to Carey, he was gone.

The porch light was on, thank goodness because he remembered how Lezah's cat had clawed his leg that first visit. He found the key, opened the door, the shop being larger than he remembered. He could make out tables holding bowels of shells and crystals in the dimly lit room. Walking to the back of the long room he left the keys by the cash register and opened the turquoise door. He found the light switch at the bottom of the short set of stairs. As he slowly climbed up, he stopped to look closely at the four mermaid paintings. The first, eyes closed, naked from the waist up as all of them were, floated on her back, her long red hair drifting behind her, her tail just below the surface.

The second, a beautiful dark one, was curled on a rock, her eyes defiant, her persona almost frightening yet powerful. "Geeze" he said aloud, as he stepped up to take in the next one, which showed a mother mermaid nursing a newborn in a sheltered grotto.

The last, totally immersed, the mermaid's arms outstretched as she swam through a forest of seaweeds. The kelp and seaweeds, their colors so bright, so real, almost three dimensional. His last thought before he ducked through the beaded curtain was: Although he knew nothing about art, her paintings were amazing. He was surprised to find a candle burning in the alcove next to the coral loveseat. Across from which sat the giant easel with a paint-spattered sheet draped over it.

He went to the kitchen, could smell the herbs in little clay pots all along the windowsill. He turned on the hot water, palmed a bar of soap then began washing his hands, then his face, leaning over the wide porcelain sink. "*Was this a mistake?*" he wondered, drying his hands. "*Maybe should have just gotten a room?*" He yawned. Saw a black shawl hanging on the shoulder of the loveseat. He went there, exhausted from the long night before with Mary Kay and sat down. Taking the shawl into his hands he brought to his face. Softer than it looked, some kind of knitted material. Her scent was there, and he breathed it in.

Lezah had the new girl follow her for the next hour. "Don't worry if you get behind, most people come here to hang out and visit. The dishwasher will help you bus tables. Carey presents as a grump, but he is really a sweetheart. It's gonna die down around eight thirty 'cause there is music at the pub tonight."

"You're doing great." Lezah ripped a page out of her order book, wrote on it. "Here is my cell number in case you need me. Keep all the tips for tonight. I really appreciate you coming in on short notice. Carey will lock up. Questions, concerns, comments?"

A halfmoon lit the seastacks along the loop. Lezah sighed. Jackson. He was there, here, at home. Mesmer's eyes lit up from her headlights as she parked in front of the shop. There were butterflies in her belly as she went upstairs to the apartment. She found Jackson sitting upright sound asleep in the alcove, her shawl held close to his chest. He stirred, opening one eye. "Hey, oh wow, I crashed. Hi." He stretched his arms out in front of him. Not knowing how to reach out to him, she stood before him. Then blurted, "Jackson, it meant so much to me that you came here, to see me. I've missed you also and wasn't sure how you felt after the last time. I'm starving, was going to heat up some soup, join me? And we can chat and catch up, okay?"

"Yes." He stood up, reached for her, took her in his arms, "Yes," he whispered as he bent and kissed the top of her head. "Yes."

Seven

Jamie looked at his watch, Lezah would be coming by soon. He sat in front of the computer making notes to share with her. Closest friends since high school, she was absolutely one of his favorite people. His partner, Zachary, loved her too and the three of them had such amazing conversations not to mention some crazy adventures over the years. She would often come into the Cormorant Motel where he bartended after her shift at the café. After the 2008 crash his job as a marine biologist with the Department of US Fish and Wildlife had been cut back to four days a week, so bartending filled in the holes and paid the rent. Zachary's shop in Old Town was popular and did well in the spring and summer but quiet winters were a challenge.

Jamie was watching a video showing the white lines being laid down by several planes. He checked the screen, trying to figure out who had created the video. He found a woman's name and looked up her profile: from Portland, Oregon, a solar energy systems engineer. *These Are Not Contrails* was the title of the two-minute film. "Contrails? What were contrails?" He googled it…

"**Contrails.** *Short for 'condensation trails' or vapor trails, are line-shaped clouds produced by aircraft engine exhaust or changes in air pressure, typically in aircraft cruising at altitudes several miles above the earth's surface. Contrails are composed primarily of water in the form of ice crystals. They last approximately forty seconds."*

Jamie took off his glasses, "Hmm, if all planes emit these why have they only been visible lately?" An activist group in School's Bay had a website about the strange clouds that were sprayed by seemingly unmarked planes. Viewing them had informed him and Lezah that these chemical trails (as the website referred to them) stayed in the sky sometimes all day. Several planes would lay them down in the morning over a clear blue sky. The trails would bond and mingle causing the blue expanse to become a haze of gray or white that blocked the sun. If normal-looking storm clouds were present the planes flew through them, their lines of white visible, and the next thing they saw were those clouds thinning and then completely disappearing.

He heard the front door open. Lezah called, "Hey, anybody home?"

"I'm in the office," he responded.

"Hi there friend, whatcha doin,' researching again?"

Jamie stood up. "Look at this." He pointed to a website.

"The School's Bay library is having an informational meeting, next month on the 9th. We should go. It says geoengineering will be discussed."

"What time? I'm working."

"Let's see." He leaned into the screen. "Eight pm."

"Okay, good, I'm off at six."

"So other people are seeing the trails, lots of deniers though, many just don't believe it's happening, say it's just normal emissions, contrails they call them."

"It's not about belief Jamie, it's about observation. We see it almost daily now."

"Okay I know." He put the computer screen down.

They heard the front door and Zach's voice, "Honey, I'm home. What are you two nerds up to?"

Lezah hugged him. "How was your day?"

Zach sighed, "Well if you factor in that the upholstery delivery was three days late…yup, when I opened it you guessed it, wrong material! The folks waiting for their new couch are pissed at me and let's see, the bank called, I'm overdrawn because I was gonna deposit the money for the couch tomorrow. Other than that, it was a bitchin' good day. Who wants wine? I'm pouring." They followed him to the kitchen.

Jamie turned the halibut over in the skillet. He took baked potatoes out of the oven, then shook up the salad dressing of olive oil, garlic, and rice vinegar. He put butter, salt, and pepper on the table.

Zach handed each a glass of cold white wine. "Kitchen or dining room?"

"Kitchen," said Zach, carrying plates and silverware to the yellow '50s dinette set. "Find anything out about those sky stripes you two are obsessed with?"

"Obsessed is the wrong word. More like curious and researching," said Lezah

"Okay. I get it." Zach lifted a plate, "Lezah? Fish?"

"Yes, please. This your secret sauce, Jamie? Mmm," she licked her finger. Zach pretended to slap her hand.

"Where's your manners?"

Lezah smiled, "Bottom of the ocean."

Jamie buttered his potato. "I learned some things today. Contrails vs. chemtrails, but we are going to learn more next month because the School's Bay library is having a presentation led by a Portland activist group. Lezah's going. Wanna go?"

"Umm, no thanks. I'll leave the investigating up to you two. My question is why? Why are these weird stripes in the sky? Who is doing it?"

Jamie put his fork down. "Unmarked military planes

and I've read maybe even commercial flights. It's not just here…all over the world and yes who, what and why?"

Oh, he felt bad, really bad. Ski Rakowski held his head in his big fat hands and moaned. Damn headaches. He took three more Vicodin, tried to lie down on the couch but couldn't be still. Pacing the small apartment back and forth he felt the iron-like grip on his forehead easing up. *Need soda,* he swigged a Dr. Pepper halfway done, poured the rest in the sink. He tightened the belt on his robe, felt that warm rush making his legs feel loose, the muscles in his back let go. "Okay, okay," he said out loud.

Toby lifted her head, yawned then curled back up in her bed in the corner. With the high, his thoughts pinging from one to the other, came the initial release of all tension, thoughts of work, as his deep loneliness lifted up and off him. He stumbled as he put the can in the trash. "Whoa!" He steadied himself, swayed, walked across the living room. The bunker, he'd go there. Where was the goddamn key? Back in the kitchen he took the lid off the cookie jar, and reached in. Fuck, why did he lock it anyway? No one ever came here except his niece.

Flipping the light switch, he turned on the CD player as the Star-Spangled Banner played quietly. Cold, he shivered and moved to turn on the heater. American flags covered all four walls. He sat himself clumsily in the recliner, his weight tipping the chair back slightly, and sighed. To his right was a life-size blow-up doll of Popeye. "Hey guy, how's it hangin?" There were photos of Vietnam buddies, their eyes bright, filled with youthful hope and excitement. There were aerial shots of the jungle, roads and villages and picture after picture of storm clouds. A poster high on the wall read, "Make mud not war!"

Feeling good but woozy he struggled to get the eight-millimeter reel on the projector. He stood up too fast and lurched towards the light switch. Back in the chair the click, click of the film lulled him. "Ah look at that plane, woohoo coming in for the...there it is coming down over the jungle...perfect!" He watched the images over and over until he could barely keep his eyes open.

Lezah glimpsed the cerulean blue ocean beyond the humps of grass-covered dunes. She wore a small fanny pack and gestured to Jamie who walked behind her. "Yes, it's a good question, fair I'd say. Let me think about it. How are you and Zach? Did he get caught up in the shop?"

"Yeah, he settled down. My workaholic, type-A, sweet man. He's looking forward to spring, designing a new set of pillows."

They stopped where the narrow path ended, removed their shoes, tied the laces together, and took off running.

Lezah yelped, "Beat ya there, James," as she sprinted away from him.

"Game on," he called. He watched her small body rushing away, then saw her stop and face him. She started doing jumping jacks! Her antics made him laugh out loud. Goofball! But he loved her, had ever since junior high. They had run track all though high school. "Okay, come on, midlife body." He could tell that his muscles had warmed up. He picked up the pace, feeling the sand, cool and firm, under his feet.

Lezah had told him about this new guy. *Curious to hear about him. Was she serious? Was she in love? Lezah? Be a first, except for the guy from college.* Now she was running back towards him, swinging her shoes in circles above her head. *Her dedication to her art, the seals, the café—these filled her life.* Two miles down, a half to go. Then they would turn around and run back. They did these five-milers a few times a week.

"God, you are slow!" She whizzed past him. "Half mile ahead."

"Just cruising 'cause, you know, I'll win in the end."

"Ha!" She knew he might just beat her, and he knew she really did not care.

All the way back to the dunes she thought about Jackson and what Jamie had asked: what about him was different? She stood facing the horizon, her breath slowly coming back. The sky so blue, the water bluer. *Cerulean. What's the root of the word? Oh yes, from the Latin, dark blue. Right.*

Jamie ran towards her, stopped. "Get that smirky smile off your face," he said, wiping his forehead with his bandana. He took his glasses out of his fanny pack and put them on.

"Water?" She passed him the tiny thermos.

"Thanks. Felt good, huh? You?"

"Yep, we should do it more. Sit a minute?" she asked. She drew spirals in the sand in front of her. "Alright, I thought about why I'm so attracted to this man. Well, the sex was otherworldly." She paused, "It's his scent."

"You mean his cologne?"

"No, no. His scent, clean, sweet, earthy, almost like almonds or …"

"Oh wow, wait?" He was thoughtful, his eyes on hers. "You like his body odor?"

She shook her head yes.

"Aha, a good sign, truly necessary. Animals know it. Gotta love the way your sweetie smells."

"Stop it. This is serious! For me, scent is so intense, the energy a person puts off has an odor. Did you know that?"

Jamie nodded, a comical then a serious look on his face. "Yes, I agree. Okay, number one, he smells yummy. Good. Number two, what else?"

"His energy is slow and easy. Never seems annoyed

or rushed. All the cells in my body feel effervescent when I'm near him. Not just sexual, there *is* that kind of spark. This is another fire that ignites the life force." She trickled sand through her fingers. "Like our blood flowed in the same direction, an ancient pact, who knows?"

"Okay, number three, he lights you up. What else?"

She was thoughtful, "Something must have happened while we slept. You know I always sleep alone, never ever let a onesie stay over or come upstairs. Jamie, when I woke up next to him, I've never felt like that before." She looked out to sea. Gulls circled the Buddha rock like a living crown.

"Hmm, well interesting, never seen you like this."

"And you know what? The most amazing thing—Mesmer loves him!"

Jamie snorted, "Sorry, did I hear that right? Mesmer loves him? How do you know this?"

"She jumped into his lap, curled up, and started purring."

"Well, I'd keep an eye on my balls if she was in my lap! And there is no way that Mesmer is capable of love. No way a demon succubus from the far-right side of red-hot hell can feel. She's planning something, possibly murder. So let's see: (1) sex is through the roof; (2) he smells yummy; (3) he has good energy; (4) you slept through the night with him; (5) Mesmer loves him. Your guy better start asking the Egyptian cat goddess Bast for protection."

"Oh, Jamie."

"Hey, I still have that scar on my ankle! So, sounds like a good start. I'm happy for you."

"Well, it's complicated. He has a sick child. He lives in Portland. I don't know ..."

"Oh my! You've got it bad, girl. Let's walk to my place and have coffee."

"Well, it can't hurt. My new painting is being elusive as hell."

"Aha, an elusive man, an elusive painting. I see heavy mists on the horizon, blue, green, a splash of copper after rain."

"Oh, you shut up." She smiled. "How's work?"

"Interesting. Scary, what we are seeing, the extinctions, consequences of ocean warming. In just two centuries, humans have shat in their nest. Given up their freedom for comfort. The Cormorant is slow, but I'm making rent. Can't complain, and Zach and I are good."

On the way back to Beach Loop they stopped at an overlook, a large new sign before them.

For sale 75 acres
Pristine cliff-to-sea property. Seal Rock views.
Call Jolly Biggs 541–658–6691

"Ugh," said Lezah, spitting on the sign.

"Whoa, girl, that's gross!"

"Oh, and the development of essential habitat that should be protected, isn't?"

"Touché," Jamie said. "Touché."

The wild Oregon-California coastline slipped by with one spectacular ocean view after another.

"Ever been to the redwoods?" asked Lezah.

"Yes, I think so. I was little. Vague memories. You? Do you go often?"

"To this one place. Roe and I used to go to this certain beach. From near there you can hike up into a spiraling canopy of redwood trees. But first we will go to the mouth."

"The mouth?"

"Yes, Requa means mouth of the river in the native language. It's where the fresh water from the estuary flows into the salt water."

The ocean was one enormous blue mirror as she drove through the small coastal towns. They laughed telling each other stories about high school as they listened to oldies on the radio. They played the "what if" game. "What if you could live anywhere?"

"I'd stay in Banderlay."

Jackson thought a moment. "I'm not sure, it would

have to be somewhere close to Owen." They stopped in Silver Beach at an overlook and ate the egg salad sandwiches that Lezah packed.

"Another hour, we're almost to Crescent City."

"Okay, can't complain, awesome scenery, beautiful chauffeur." He reached over and took her hand. After a comfortable silence, she asked, "So how is Owen? You said there were issues with…his mother. Feel like talking about it?"

"Sure, it's the same set of problems that come up over and over again. Mary Kay is tied down because of Owen's illness. Our insurance, I think I mentioned, doesn't cover respite care, and with me being out of work, I can't pay for it out of pocket. When I go down there, I can stay with her and Owen. Free her to spend a night away but she doesn't. Lately she seems more depressed than usual.

"Oh, that's a hard one, for all of you, I'm so sorry." She turned down a road with pastures on either side. "Oh, look! An elk herd."

"Wow, so many!"

"I know, let's park here. We'll check out the beach first then walk over to Burnt Ridge where the trail starts. So, bring your jacket, yeah? I'll take the day pack, some water and snacks." She reached into the back seat. "Want to carry the binoculars?"

"Sure." He put the strap around his neck, watching her lock the car.

"This way." She led him through a grassy area where crude wooden structures, a sweat lodge, a dancing pit, and a few other small buildings sat. "This area is still used for ceremonies." They straddled a narrow path through a section of shrubs and elderberries, over root-risen ground and boulders as they came out onto the beach. They could see way out where the mouth of the river had blown through a sand bar, the cross currents creating huge powerful waves.

Near the calmer shore, sea lions cruised the waters, barking loudly.

"Funny bunnies, huh?" called Lezah.

They paused, looking out as an osprey flew down from the forest behind them and dove, rising from the water, a whipping thing in its beak.

"Is that a snake?"

"No, it's an eel. The natives still catch and eat them. So, this is the mouth of the mighty Klamath River. Pretty cool, huh? Incredible energy where the ..."

"Yes, so wild. You can just feel it."

Which made Lezah smile. "So, we're going to leave the car here and walk to the Burnt Ridge trail and hike up through the redwoods." They walked about a quarter mile to a large pond. As the creatures sensed their presence, the sound of duck squawks and wings ruffling water reached them as the mallards and mergansers flew low over yellow lily pads to the other shore.

Skirting the lower edge of the pond, they followed the damp overgrown path, which rose up slowly, switchback after switchback, through the groves of three-hundred-foot redwoods.

"Do you know how old these trees are?"

Lezah turned to him. "They're ancient, some over a thousand years old." She reached up to a lower branch. "See how small the needles are? I love how it smells," Lezah called as she breathed in the moist minty resin. Light splintered through the serrated spears of ferns. "You doing okay?"

"Yes, I'm good."

After climbing a mile up, they stopped for water, passing the bottle back and forth. "Did you know these giants have really short root systems? You'd think they would be deep considering their height, but they only go down six to twelve feet. It's the intricate, intertwined roots that anchor them."

Upward, they passed huge burnt-out circular husks and fallen trunks, bridging the duff-packed trail. "Look!" called Lezah. She was bent over a delicate mushroom, its purple pleated skirt brushing the ground.

"Oh, that's a neat one," said Jackson. "Know what kind it is?"

"No but since there seem to be many here, I'll take this one home and make a spore print to identify it."

"A spore print?"

"Yes, you leave it on a piece of white paper overnight and it drops its spores in a certain pattern, which can then be identified."

As they climbed, streams and seeps trickled down through the canyon. Lezah stopped. "It's humbling, don't you think? Energy here is so old and protective in a primitive way. I feel so small here. Comprende?"

"I'm sorry, what?"

"I asked if you understand how I feel here?"

"Yes, I do," he said, looking at his hands, then lifting his eyes to hers, "I do, it's indescribable."

Lezah pushed her hair back. "Kind of indescribable, like this hair of mine. Good grief, it's like a damp, unruly nest." She smoothed it back with both hands, twisted it and tied the long tail into a knot. "There, maybe that will contain you for a while."

Birdsong sounded from below.

"That's the first bird I've heard," said Jackson.

"Uh-huh. There isn't a lot of wildlife, not much food here. I mean there are coyotes and rarely mountain lions. The salmon spawn in the streams nearby. An endangered seabird, the marbled murrelet, nests here or in nearby old-growth Douglas fir stands. There are owls, ravens, osprey, and bald eagles."

"How do you know what you know? Did you study biology?"

"Really, I learned it all from Roe. He has family here. We came often to fish and visit. As you can see from these huge, burned stumps there was fire here. Some burned but most lived. Redwoods have really tough, thick bark and it's moist between the layers so they can survive."

They reached a wooden foot bridge, crossed, and climbed uphill once more. Nearing the top, the overstory still towering above, Lezah called to Jackson, "Come up here." She stood at an open overlook where they could see all the way down to the rock coves below and hear the faint barking of the sea lions.

"Wow, cool."

"Shall we sit and have a snack before we go back down?"

"Sure, sounds good."

They found a log and settled next to one another. Lezah took the day pack off and set it down. She pulled a cloth napkin out and laid it on the ground. With her knife she cut an apple into eighths and sliced the pepper jack into strips. Each ate silently, absorbing the hushful quiet, the little prismoid drops of fog refracting in the intermittent sunlight.

"I'm a go pee," Lezah said getting up and moving into a brushy area.

When she came back, Jackson was lying on his back holding the binoculars looking up at the nearest tree.

"Their cones are small."

"Yes." Lezah turned. "Let me show you." She reached up, grasping a low branch but couldn't quite reach the cone.

"What are you doing? Need help?"

"Oh, that's right, you're tall, that cone right there, to the left of that branch?"

"Uh-huh," he took the binoculars off, stood up.

"Could you get it for me? I want to show you something."

"Cost you a kiss?"

"Oh well never mind I don't need another redwoods cone anyway." She started to walk away. He stood there not knowing what to do when she turned suddenly and ran straight into his arms, her mouth searching for his, their bodies pressed against one another. He started with the zipper on her coat as his cool hands searched under her sweater.

He backed up, his lips still on Lezah's, managing to unzip his jacket and pants and let them fall to the ground. With his hands on her shoulders he helped her lie down, kissing her warm lips, her eyes. Her cheeks flushed, her breathing quickened as she rolled from side to side saying his name. He took her shoes off, hurrying with the laces, tossing them aside. He rolled her pants down to her ankles as she kicked them off calling, "Jackson, Jackson." She pulled the sweater over her head where he saw her breasts so white compared to her tan belly, he bent and kissed them both gently and hard.

"Oh, Jackson. Bring me, bring me." Guiding him in, she was lost. Her body imploded in pleasure again and again. She flew, rising up through the fragrant spires, wraiths of fog drifting with her. Above the windblown crowns of the trees she found herself out over the endless blue water. Below, the mouth of the river crashed into the sea. Down and down she floated to a rocky cove and there half in half out of the water the vision, a mermaid her arms up in the air as if she were reaching for something. The face was hidden and partly covered by her long hair. Suddenly transported back, she heard Jackson's voice.

"Lezah, you alright?" Her eyes rolled back; her body shook.

She blinked a few times. "Yes." Sitting up slowly she put the sweater and jacket back on, retrieved her pants, pulling them up. "Just coming back to earth." Shivering as cool tufts of wind rose up through the canyon. She tied her shoes, speaking softly. "We should head back down."

"Alright." He stood up, found his pants, slipped his shoes on. Reaching for her, his hands under her arms, he helped her stand. She still seemed dazed, unsteady on her feet. He fastened the fanny pack around her waist.

"Thank you, Sir."

They stood at the overlook for a moment. The sun low on the horizon, the ocean laminated in silver. An eagle flew overhead weaving its way through the canopy, its loud, long call echoing above.

"Come on, we'll be racing daylight if we don't leave now. Much as I love the gloaming, not fun to hike in the dark."

"The gloaming? Don't know that word."

"Old English word for twilight or to grow dark."

As always, the path down seemed shorter than the up-hill climb. After half an hour they stopped as Lezah took a chocolate bar out of the pack.

"Here, eat."

Jackson, taking the piece of chocolate said, "Lezah, what happened after we made love? You seemed so far away."

"I was in my painting."

"I'm sorry, what?"

"Sometimes when I have sex I kind of leave my body… and have these visions about my art. This time I saw a mermaid in a cove with her arms reaching up to…I know not what."

He was silent a moment. "That's um…you are…lost for words," he paused.

“Weird huh, don’t think we are going to make it back to Banderlay before dark. Maybe the inn will be open.”

“The inn?”

“Yes, its nearby, just across the river.”

“Okay sounds good. Hey, look, the first stars.”

Lezah took in a long breath. “The trees’ scent is so unique, you know. Maybe it’s because they breathe in starlight that took eons to reach earth.”

Back at the car it was almost dark. Silent except for the soft swish of low tide waves in the estuary. The inn was open, and they ate a dinner of vegetable soup, salad, and fresh sourdough biscuits with herb butter. Their room was small and cozy, furnished with vintage furniture. They showered together and fell into the feather bed. Jackson was asleep immediately. Lezah’s last thought as she spooned him, “Safe, safe, safe.”

Eight

The freak storm had poured rain between Banderlay and the School's Bay public library where the meeting was being held. Jamie slowed down as they entered the parking lot in the wake of cars ahead skirting the puddles.

"Look at all these cars, Jamie."

"Hmm, wonder if there is something else going on besides the geoengineering meeting?"

They found a place to park, jumped out into the deluge, umbrellas up, and walked to the large building. A sign inside the glass door said GEOWATCH MEETING ROOM 920. Shaking the dripping umbrellas in the foyer, they headed down the hallway to a large room filled with many people. They sat near the back, Lezah looked around the room, maybe seventy-five to a hundred people. Singles, elders, families, kids. She spotted the Scottish couple near the front; they were both turned in their seats facing the door intently watching people enter the room.

“Hmm?” She tapped Jamie’s arm. “See the older couple in the second to front row” she whispered. He nodded. “That’s the couple I told you about, they’re from Europe.” The crowd chatted quietly, Jamie wrote the time and date in his notebook.

A young woman walked to the podium and stood in front of the crowd.

“Hello my name is Maraya Perez, I am the admin for the group geowatch.com and I am the liaison for GeoWatch Activists Now. Thank you for attending this evening in spite of the rainy weather, thank you for your time and interest. Our group is made up of scientists, physicians, meteorologists, pilots, and people like you. Something is happening in our skies. Not just here but around the world. We see unmarked planes and commercial flights spraying something into the air creating these long white clouds. We are here this evening to try and understand what this operation is about, why it’s being deployed and by whom. There will be several speakers. On the table in the back of the room you will find packets with each of the speakers’ resumes and groups they are affiliated with. I ask that we hold questions and comments until everyone is finished. Our first speaker is Jane McIntosh.”

A short-haired woman in her fifties left the front row and stood before the podium. Maraya handed her the microphone.

“Hello, my name is Jane McIntosh and I have been a solar energy systems engineer for over twenty-five years.

My job is to test or evaluate photovoltaic cells and review specifications to achieve solar design objectives for commercial and industrial systems. About three years ago I noticed a significant decrease in solar output for the companies I work with. I was confused, we were only getting 60 percent and then I noticed the trails in the sky day in and day out. It took many months of observation before I realized that the trails were dimming the sun. After speaking with colleagues who agreed that something wasn't right, we were introduced to Bryant Holmes who has been on his own journey of discovery. Both Bryant and I live in Portland and have observed similar scenarios."

A tall man with glasses came forward and took the microphone.

"Hi, I'm Bryant Holmes. I'm retired now, but I was a commercial pilot for over thirty years. Let me first just say there is nothing good about this program. It is neither legal nor moral. This attempt to control nature has predictable, dangerous consequences. As Jane stated, I have been aware of geoengineering for many years and I have done extensive research and interviews. Before I begin, I want to say how important it is to use the correct scientific term and that term is not "chemtrails," it is Solar Radiation Management or SRM. What is it? Why are they doing it? Who are they? This is not a conspiracy theory, and the main denial of the existence of this program is that the chemical sprays we see in the sky are just condensation trails, or contrails from domestic airlines. Nope, it is impossible for a contrail to last longer than forty seconds. As we have observed, the chemical sprays stay in the sky for hours, bonding with others and eventually covering the clear blue sky in a thin layer of white, blocking the sun. Why? The unofficial word is that the ozone layer is more damaged than the public knows. Solar Radiation Management is to protect the inhabitants of earth. Really? Who is behind this secret program? It is our own Military Industrial Complex. Both unmarked military planes and commercial airplanes are used. And how do they do it? By spraying certain chemical and nanoparticles that reflect the sun's light away from earth. But there is more to this. It is also to weaponize the ionosphere for star-wars-like engagements. It's called Weather Warfare. President Johnson once said, "Those who control the weather, control the world." SRM is combined with the use of giant ionospheric heaters known as HAARP or High-frequency Active Auroral Research Programs, which by microwaving the chemicals and nanoparticles can create weather. And by the way, you can research and find where these installations are located around the globe. These operations create cloud cover in the stratosphere, 33,000 to 42,000 miles above the earth, greatly affecting weather patterns, blocking the jet stream from reaching coastal areas or causing extreme storms or drought. Crazy weather huh? Is it just climate change? We don't think so.

"Weather warfare was first attempted during the Vietnam War. Between 1967 and 1972, 5,000 northern Vietnamese troops maintained 12,000 miles of secret roads known as the Ho Chi Minh Trail to protect their essential supply routes. The US decided that the best way to block the roads and deny them access was to start OPERATION POPEYE. From bases in Thailand and Guam, our pilots flew cloud-seeding flights daily spraying silver-iodide over the Ho Chi Minh Trail, causing years of extended monsoon seasons and flooding that caused landslides, washing out river crossings and basically creating havoc for the enemy. The saying, 'Make Mud, Not War,' originated with Operation Popeye.

"The differences between Operation Popeye and the issues today are many. The chemicals being sprayed today are aluminum, barium, and strontium. Lab tests around the country are revealing high levels of these chemicals in people's bloodstreams. Well, it's got to go somewhere. Right? Has this protocol ever been tested on flora, fauna, humans, the environment? Nope. After being ramped up in the nineties all across the world, there has been an incredible push to normalize what's happening in our skies. How has this operation remained secret? No one is looking up because so many folks are looking down at their phones, right? But seriously the logistics are undercover and completely compartmentalized. For example, pilots are told weather modification is helping to save lives, and weather warfare is in the interest of national security so that enemies cannot enter our airspace with their new tech weapons.

"Most pilots are single, childless, many elder, many

ex-military, or commercial or private airline pilots. These pilots make five hundred thousand per year. They are told not to speak to one another, they are rotated every few months, then they are transferred to another base. They rotate between day and night flights working five days on, seven off. Along with flying certain routes, the pilots make course corrections, perform takeoffs, and landings. Satellites control the aerosol dispersals. When it looks as though latrines are being emptied, chemicals are loaded on.

"Planet-wide geoengineering is the main cause of global warming. It is why the oceans are warming. It's political: if we control the weather in a country we can starve its people, or create floods and storms. Please commit to educating yourself. And now Bill Short will speak to you."

"Hi, yes my name is Bill Short and I am an atmospheric meteorologist. We study principles of science to observe and forecast the earth's complex atmospheric phenomena and discover how it will affect the earth and its inhabitants. In other words, I track and predict the weather using complex computer graphic equipment to make weather maps. I've been aware of geoengineering for quite some time, and I believe that what was said here is right. This secret Military Industrial Complex program is causing global warming by manipulating the weather, and ionizing the skies for weather warfare. It's these operations around the planet that have dimmed the sun, holding and retaining a canopy of hot air, nanoparticles, and chemicals that create the man-made cloud cover. It is my opinion that the extreme wildfires of today are directly related to geoengineering. These droughts happen because the jet stream is blocking moisture along coastlines, and remember the particles and chemicals are also accelerants. In closing, please stay informed and help people understand that this travesty affects the health of the entire planet's ecosystems. Now I'd like to introduce Dr. Lambda V. Sahay, neurologist, and Dr. Irma Vidmeyer, pediatrician. Both have established practices in Portland."

"Yes, I am Dr. Sahay. Over the past few years, colleagues and myself have seen a ten-fold increase in neurological diseases. It seems as though this rise has been observed coinciding with the rise of Solar Radiation Management. Yes, there are many other environmental variables that can be contributing. My major concern is what are these nanoparticles doing to our bodies' various systems. I'm one of the physicians that have been studying the chemicals in blood samples and the levels are extremely high. So yes, please let's inform people and stop this untested, toxic operation." Maraya took the mic and handed it to the next speaker.

"Hello, I'm Irma Vidmeyer, pediatric physician practicing in Portland. My concerns are similar to Dr. Sahay's. There has been a tremendous increase in childhood allergy, asthma, autism, eczema, and skin rashes. I can't help but wonder what these substances do when they are breathed in, incorporated into our food and water, and absorbed by young, growing minds and bodies. I and other pediatricians have formed a group to exchange and compare, and to start looking at the chemicals in children's blood. Thank you for your interest," she nodded at Maraya and sat down.

"Well, this concludes our program for this evening. Please take the free materials in the back of the room, sign our mailing list, and share this information with friends and families, and politicians. The speakers will be available to answer questions in the back of the room. Many thanks to supervisors Smith, Watkins, and Kathy Adams for attending tonight. If you are interested in having an informational meeting in your community let us know. We will come. Goodnight and drive carefully."

People moved, put on coats, had to wait in line to reach the exit. The mood seemed quiet but intense, a sense of disbelief. Lezah walked as quickly as possible, weaving through the slow-moving crowd. Jamie followed knowing her need to get out quickly.

They were silent walking back to the car. The rain had stopped but the sky was still threatening. Lezah in shock, sat mutely, shaking her head as Jamie drove onto the highway. "Weather manipulation, engineered droughts, global warming...human-caused? Oh my God, Jamie, is this really happening?"

"Afraid so," he sighed. "The speakers seemed top notch authentic and educated. I picked up their resume packets while you were in the restroom. I'll have their contacts now and can query them to learn more."

"Jamie, what can we do? I need to learn more too so I can speak about this, this, fucking travesty. It's so unreal, a sci-fi movie or dystopian novel, but it's happening right over our homes." She rushed on, "What can we do to stop it?" She sat up straighter. "We need flyers and let's go to the next meeting and do you think Zach would let us use the shop as an info center?" Her hands were trembling in her lap.

"Yeah, we need to be on top of this for sure. I'm gonna research all weekend." He parked in front of the shop and leaned over. "You gonna be alright, want me to come in for a while, huh Lezah girl?"

"No thanks," she sniffed, rubbed her eyes. "I'm okay, I mean I'm not, but you go home, I just need some time, that was so much to take in."

"It sure was. Talk tomorrow."

Clouds parted as she unlocked the door to the shop. A walk, she thought; I'm too wired to settle in. She threw her purse on the desk inside, locked the door and took off running to the path above the dunes that would lead to the bluff. Tucking her arms into her sides, she ran through a tunnel of tall gorse, the thorny branches and plush yellow flowers glowed. There were rustlings, faint stirrings, bursts of startled bird sounds inside. The moon so bright she could see small brown rabbits browsing, then their panicked scatter when they heard her feet pounding the sand. Once through the dunes, she burst onto the beach, gulping salt air, picking up speed, her thoughts wild, rambling. "How can they do this? Why would they do this to their own people?" She passed Maiden Rock, the round stone face looking up at the sky, next the upright seastack she called the Buddha. The faster she ran the harder her breath came the more her mind let go its fearful rant. The tide wasn't low enough to enter the cave, the little mote in front blocking entry. A squadron of pelicans flew along the shoreline.

Another mile ahead, she could almost make out the island. Out of her peripheral vision, a moving shadow crossed in front of her, a crab galloped away. She felt "held in" and that if her body stopped moving, her thoughts would drown her. After another two miles she was aware that she must slow down, even stop for a moment as an unfamiliar feeling of exhaustion overcame her. A few miles more, she slow jogged the rest of the way. She checked near the island but there were no seals in sight. "On the back side," she thought.

Climbing the steep path to the top of the bluff, her clothes sweat-soaked, her hair a tangled mess. She made it, her chest heaving then slowing down, she looked out as moonlight silvered the open sea. Seastacks rose up from rows of perfectly symmetric waves and near the island, the humped shadows of the seals hauled out on the rocks below. On either side of the endless beaches, their driftwood-strewn sands, winding both north and south. She felt salt-dusted air, long draughts of it coming from above bathing her, cooling her. The view filling her with a momentary peace. She heard it before she saw it, the low buzz of a distant plane. Turning to the sound, the plane began emitting a white plume as it rose up, finally aligning and blazing a swath of gauze across the moon. No longer able to hold the weight of sorrow, she fell to her knees and wept into the sea grass.

Lezah had worked long hours carrying the large canvases downstairs and arranging them with others around the shop. After the geoengineering meeting, she had searched for a way she could help and raise awareness.

Her ten newest paintings all had an environmental message; for example, the one with the mother and child had a large red starfish clinging to the rock the mother mermaid was perched on. The title card next to the painting read: Mother and Child. Area of Interest: Multiple species of sea stars have experienced mass die-offs along the West Coast.

On others, she had collaged dried seaweeds and kelp, noting the decline of the kelp beds and coral.

The bell on the shop door jingled, startling her since the shop was closed, now someone knocking. Jeesh, then she noticed that the open sign had not been turned around. Shit. She was sweaty, paint-stained, her hair, twisted into a giant bun, had escaped, tendrils wisping around her face. "Alright, I'm coming."

"Hi, sorry but we are closed today." She flipped the

sign, looked up: it was the Scottish couple who had come once before and had been at the meeting.

"Oh dear, our timing, it must have been off. We are so curious to see your art. We came before, do you remember us?" He handed her a card. "We are co-owners of a gallery in Portland, Oregon. We've heard from the locals that your mermaids are spectacular."

Lezah looked at the card. Seemed legit. "Well thanks for your interest. I just finished hanging the show but I'm afraid there are ladders about and my floor is littered with cut papers and masking tape. Not to mention, myself—I'm rather a mess too, but um alright, give me five minutes to clear a path and you can come in."

"Sure, sure we will look at your lovely trinkets out here."

"Hmm." She closed the door, moved the ladders out of the way, picked up the debris and put the bundle of it in the trash behind the counter. She glanced around. "Alright." She looked closely at the card to see if she knew the gallery. It said the Park Gallery, fine art across from the Portland Botanical Gardens. *What?* She did know the gallery, had gone there for shows while she was in art school. Old, established and one of the city's finest.

"Alright folks," she called, opening the door. "Welcome, come in."

"What a lovely shop," said the wife.

"Enjoy." She moved behind the counter and pretended

to look at her computer. It is impressive, she thought, having a moment of surety instead of insecurity. The thirteen paintings glowed against the freshly painted white walls. The couple stood together in front of each one, pointing, murmuring quietly to each other. The man read each card out loud, letting Lezah know that her writing was both clean and informative. After almost an hour they stood in the back and talked quietly for a few minutes, both nodding, then came up to the counter.

"Miss? Lezah, is it? These are so very wonderful, unique, timely and I must say your mermaids are all so… distinctly individual. The colors so prismatic and your handling of their watery domains feels as though one is there. Where did you study?"

"Portland Art Institute."

"Ah, a fine school." His blue eyes widened.

"Well, I'll be forthcoming, we would like to offer you a show at the Park Gallery. Are you interested?"

Her ears heard it; her mind questioned it, but her body trembled inwardly with the possibility of it. "Sorry did you say show?"

"Yes, yes allow me to explain. The gallery is committed to environmental awareness through art. We have been gathering international artists for a six-month exhibition featuring art and ecology. Your works would fit in quite nicely."

Lezah let out a breath, the one she had held while he spoke. "Yes, I'm interested."

"Fantastic! Do you have slides?"

"I will by tomorrow."

"Excellent. I will send them to my partner who I'm sure will send you a contract with all of the details and percentages of consignment sales etc."

Lezah swallowed, moved from behind the counter. "When does the show begin?"

"Next month, yours is the last collection to be chosen."

"Well, thank you so much. Paperwork will be mailed to me, you said. I will have my lawyer look at it and get back to you."

"Wonderful, and just so you know the gallery will take care of everything. We will pack up and transport all thirteen canvases to the city, hang your show with your final approval and oh yes, all will be covered under the gallery's insurance and liability."

"Nice, um, may I ask you a question, what did you think of the geoengineering meeting in School's Bay?"

"Oh, were you there? Well yes, we thought it was so well done. We have this issue in Scotland as well and are interested in forming an activist group in the town where we live. And you? Were you as impressed with the speakers and their expertise as we were?"

"Yes, I want to organize a group here."

"Well, ta-ta, we must be on our way. We will be in touch."

The silent wife gave a little wave as Lezah was struck again with how much they resembled one another.

Did that really just happen?! She danced around the big room, then stopped, dizzy mermaids spinning around her. That night she went to sleep, her thoughts were not so positive, wondering if this really was legitimate, a scam somehow or could she trust that that they wouldn't be stolen while being transported to Portland? But the next morning FedEx delivered the contract to the shop. She contacted Zach, who was a paralegal before becoming a shopkeeper. They had gone over the packet thoroughly and he felt sure it was on the up and up. When she sold a painting, the gallery would take 40 percent, which was fair and competitive.

The next day there was a call from the gallery saying people would arrive the following week. All happening so quickly, she felt overwhelmed. They wanted her to come to Portland to tour the gallery, discuss the pricing of her work and to pose for photos and interviews along with the other American artists. *Oh. My. God. Is this happening? Really?* Carey gave her the week off to go with just a "congrats" and a shrug as he liked the new waitress.

On the day the truck arrived she watched as a crew of young men took each canvas and most efficiently wrapped each one in bubble wrap then brown paper. They were carried out and packed away in the large van. There was a small panic as she stood on the shop's porch watching them pull away with the most important work of her life.

Upstairs getting ready for the dinner shift she stopped in front of the easel. Pulling the sheet off, she stared at the image. "It's just you now," she told it, "and I have no idea who you are or why you are there or whatever you are so passionately reaching for."

Nine

Lezah, in front of the mirror changing clothes, changing her hair, trying to contain the changing circumstances of her life. She had finally decided on a gauze skirt, long-sleeved leotard top, boots and, as if she had a choice, her hair down and wild. On the two-hour drive she thought about the gallery opening, wondering how it would be to meet Jackson there after a month apart. The gallery had rented suites for the artists attending at the fancy Woodlark Arms Hotel across from the gallery with a view of the park. Her thoughts so random, all over the place, she passed the exit. Pulling into the parking lot of the gallery, she turned the engine off, sitting for a long minute listening to her banging heart, nauseous from a lack of breakfast. *Deep breaths, girl, deep breaths.* All so surreal, she locked the car and stood reading the large sign, Art and Ecology International. The bright banner listing the names. Hers, the last one. A man came out of the glass double doors hurriedly then stopped to speak to her.

"Oh hello, can I help you? The gallery is closed until this evening."

"I'm, I'm Lezah Boudrow, one of the artists in the show."

His brown eyes widened, "Oh, hello, I'm sorry—I've only seen your picture and…welcome, Lezah, I'm Hank Berella the gallery manager."

She smiled shyly, "Hi, nice to meet you."

The rest was a whirlwind blur of meeting so many people from the gallery, the artists, the folks who attended wishing to chat with the artists before they purchased their work. Jackson was late, apologetic and so handsome, actually hot, she felt a rush of blood to her cheeks as he crossed the huge lobby. She had held onto his arm and whispered jokingly but not "Don't leave me."

"Alright," he whispered back.

At the end of the evening, they were approached by Hank, who held his hand out to Jackson, "Hey, nice to meet you, I'm Hank! Lezah, letting you know one of your paintings sold, the mother and child. Congratulations."

"Oh my, thank you."

Lezah was exhausted when they checked into the suite around midnight.

"That was—wow, are you famous? What an event. You do this kind of thing often?"

"God no, this is my first show ever outside of Banderlay. I'm pinching myself. All happened so fast." She yawned, turned down the bedding, slipped her skirt and shirt off, and slid into the long opulent king-sized bed. "Sorry Jackson, so so tired." She patted the other side. Her eyes drooping. "It's comfy…see you in the morning," and she was out. Jackson stood there looking at this most extraordinary woman asleep in the fairy-tale bed in the fairy-tale room, feeling his heart so open it hurt.

After the loving in the morning, they'd ordered a huge breakfast from room service compliments of Hank Berella. "Let's go to the Japanese gardens. Want to? I haven't been in years."

"Okay, me neither."

The morning lay hot and humid as they drove through the city. The gardens, exquisitely laid out into areas of interest, the Mediterranean gardens, the flowering cherry trees, a cultural village, and the koi ponds. It was there that they settled until late afternoon, where the calm splash of waterfalls, the arched bridges, the gigantic bright orange and black silken creatures swirled through the lotus-filled water.

They were served tea sitting across from one another at the red lacquer table where they talked for hours, sharing personal stories about their families. Lezah always shared from the time she was with Opal and Roe. Lezah felt something under the table near her foot, thinking it was Jackson's she responded with her toes brushing him. A sudden sharp jab landed on her ankle, and she pulled away, the small chair scraping the pearled gravel. "Ow, Ow. What are you doing?"

"What, what is it? I'm not." They both stood up, bent over to look under the table and burst out laughing. There in the middle of the space where their feet were perched was a turtle, its jaws opening and closing, munching on a piece of rice cake. Lezah, who had just taken a sip of tea, waved her arms, laughing out loud and snorted as tea came out of her nose, which made them both bend over holding their sides. They were the last to leave, embracing in the parking lot clinging to this newfound feeling, talking about the next time they could be together.

"Okay gotta go. Love you, Lezah."

"You too." She waved, waited until he pulled out of sight before getting in to her car. She felt so happy, weightless as if she could just float away.

It was weeks after the geoengineering meeting but Lezah could not let go of her constant obsessive thoughts. Today she brought flyers to give out and had stood a few doors down from the café after her shift. Mostly people ignored her, said "No," or walked away. One teen yelled,

"Conspiracy Theory Much!" as he whizzed by on his bike. And just now, the new girl came out of the café.

"Carey told me to tell you if you don't leave now you're fired!"

"Well, thanks for relaying the message, Sheila." She said *shit* under her breath as she walked to her car.

Driving home she felt suddenly exhausted. Angry at the attitudes of the people she was trying to inform and their nasty remarks. Jamie had warned her that Zach was skeptical, worrying they were becoming "conspiracy theorists." Jamie said that people couldn't go there, that they couldn't believe their own government would do this to them. The words for this denial were cognitive dissonance. She yawned as she parked in front of the shop. Mesmer met her in the yard, meowing and circling her ankles. "I know, I forgot, come on." She let him into the shop and fed him.

Walking up the stairs to the apartment she missed her mermaid paintings that now hung in the gallery in Portland. Parting the beaded curtain, she saw the painting on the easel. It was so long ago that she and Jackson had made love on that canvas. Still no clues as to who and what the picture meant, she grabbed the sheet and threw it over the damned elusive thing. Yawning again, she changed. Wearing only a T-shirt and underwear, she lay down and immediately fell asleep. Her phone chimed. Not quite awake, she listened.

"Hey Lezah, it's me Jackson. Um, checking in. I'll be coming your way next week. Will you be around Monday? Hope so. Let me know."

Oh good, she thought, and fell back to sleep.

Lezah yawned, rolled over onto her belly, her first thought, the need to paint, not an urge or desire but the need. She hadn't held a brush in days. Jackson had left at dawn with a hurried goodbye as there had been some crisis with his son.

Again, their time together had been…words cannot, she thought. They had stayed up late, cooked together, listened to music, danced. The new girl at work gladly covered Lezah's hours so she could take off work. They had explored Banderlay, the beaches, lakes, lighthouses, and museums. Jackson was so interested in the myths and history of her home place. Roe's friend Joseph had taken them out in his boat. Roe talked story the whole time, making Jackson laugh at his wild tales about being a commercial fisherman. Looking over at the framed picture from that day, she thought, it's real. It happened. It was the best time.

She threw on her robe and opened the curtain, *What in the actual fuck?*

A blue sky but four thick white lines formed a tic-tac-toe box. Inside each section was an X or an O. She grabbed the phone.

“’Lo? Morning, Lezah.”

She heard him yawn. “Jamie, look out your window!”

“Uh oh, okay. Whoa. Look at that!”

“What are they doing?”

“Looks like they’re having fun. Okay, not awake, after coffee I’m gonna call my friend at the county. What’s your day like?”

“Work the shop today, café tonight.”

“I’ll get back to you, hey how was your visit?”

“Sublime.”

“Good, okay later.”

By the time she washed the dishes, the lines in the sky had lessened, leaving an unnatural-looking haze. What chemicals were they using to make the trails? Was it falling into the ocean? Would it affect the seals? Not knowing what to do with herself, she moved to the big canvas in the corner. Pulling the paint-splattered sheet off, she stood in front of the painting for a long time. The six-foot by four-foot canvas held a pale blue sky, a pearlescent full moon sinking into a turquoise sea that covered the rest of the canvas. She squinted, then closed her eyes, remembering her vision from the redwoods. Squeezing some silver, mixing it with water and a smidge of aquamarine, she put a small brushstroke in the middle of the painting. This would work to sketch the body. “Hello? Where are you? Who are you?” she said, the brush held in midair.

Recalling how in the vision, the mermaid's body was arched, her arms reaching upward, Lezah drew with the tip of the paintbrush a head thrown back, with long wet hair. Her face turned away, the features not visible yet.

Beneath the water, she painted a ruffled tail. Glancing at the clock she set the brush in the water jar. Enough for now…with the kettle back on she made toast, buttered it, took a bite, set it down, not hungry. Her ringtone chimed.

"Hello."

"Hi, Lezah, Jackson here." He rushed on, "I just wanted to check in, not the way I wanted to spend our last morning together…you there?"

"Yes, I'm here. Everything alright with your son?"

"Well, it's not about Owen this time. It's Mary Kay, she is having some kind of breakdown…not sure. She's in the hospital. Her neighbor took her. Guess they had a rough night. Owen's asleep. How are you? Lezah…I miss you already …"

"Me too, Jackson. I'm good. Just getting ready for the day and …"

"Oh, gotta go, another call. I'll get back to you—"

"Yes, bye."

His cell rang. "Hey there, is this Jackson Craig?"

"Um, yes?"

"Well, this is Ski, Ski Rakowski, remember me?"

Jackson looked at his watch, shit he needed to start Owen's treatment. "Yes, yes, yes, I do ..."

"Well, hi we had a preliminary meeting about a job opening?"

"Yes, yes I do remember."

"Well, I'd like to meet with you again and talk more about the job but there is a problem. I'm going to be in McMinnville tomorrow where the base is...I'd like to show you the ropes. I know it's short notice. Are you still interested in the job?"

"Um yes. I am, certainly. Tomorrow, what time?"

"Oh, let's say two o'clock. Would that work?"

"Yes, I think so."

"Do you know where the base is?"

"Yes, approximately, I'll GPS it."

"Okay, it's all secret service stuff to get in—go to the gate and park. I'll leave a clearance for you at the front desk."

"Okay, see you there at two. Thank you. Good bye." How the hell this is going to work out is beyond me.

Oh, Jackson, she thought. *How did this happen?* In a daze, she wandered to the bathroom. Looking into the mirror she sighed, *Medusa hair today huh? Crap*. She looked closer at her face. Something was different, unfamiliar. What? A softness, a lack of tension?

"It's because you are loved," said a voice in her head. *Yes,* she thought, nodding. Floating back to the kitchen she poured the boiling water into her favorite mug and settled into the loveseat. She held the cup with both hands as the thought surfaced again, "You are loved."

"Yes," she closed her eyes, took a sip.

"That is," said the voice, "UNTIL HE KNOWS!!!"

Her hands began to shake. The scalding water spilled onto her thumb, then slid down the inside of her blue-veined wrist. Brushing it away with her other hand she stood up, the cup falling to the floor. Emotions racing through her, tears, outrage, and finally, a sadness so dark and deep she staggered to the bed and as the truth ravaged her, she howled into the pillow where traces of his scent still lingered.

Downstairs, Opal knocked on the door. The sign said open, but the door was locked. She heard strange sounds coming from the upstairs window.

"Lezah? Lezah it's me." Waiting, concerned, she heard Lezah open the inner door.

"Coming." Soon, she unlocked the first door. Opal took in her wild matted hair, her red swollen eyes.

"What, what happened, is it the man?"

"Let's go up, oh wait! Need to change the sign, be right there." Opal waited.

"I'm not okay, not gonna lie."

"Did something happen in the redwoods?"

Over her shoulder, as they climbed the stairs Lezah said, "Oh yes something happened." They settled at the kitchen table. "Something so unexpected so amazing, Opal." She pushed the mane back behind her ears looking at her hands, then into Opal's eyes. "We are kindred. He and I, we love each other."

"But that's just wonderful, I'm …"

"No, it is not wonderful because once he knows what happened back then…at the dock, it will be over and I won't blame him. How could he ever trust me again? No," she shook her head slowly back and forth, "no. Oh Opal, I'm just going to break it off now instead of waiting, that would be torture just waiting for it to end."

"Lezah, wait, slow down, perhaps he will understand once he knows about Brodie."

"He will see me differently, damaged, dirty, some brutalized sex toy."

"Oh Lezah, not if he's the man you say he is." Lezah's cell rang.

She looked at it. "Oh no, it's him, I can't talk to him right now…maybe not at all."

On speaker, they heard him say, "Hey Lezah it's Jackson," his breathing audible. "I'm almost to Granite Pass. Not sure yet what's going on."

Something in his voice, his words so measured like he has trying to maintain some kind of control.

"Hi, Jackson."

"Oh Lezah, hi, glad you're there. So, Mary Kay won't be discharged until the end of the week. I'll explain it later. Anyway, I have a, problem. I've got a job interview tomorrow in Portland and no one to watch Owen. I hate to ask you, he's in a really good place health wise right now, but this interview is important. It would be for four or five hours."

Lezah had a look of terror on her face. "Well, uh, okay Jackson let me think." She shook her head no at Opal. Opal mouthed say "yes I will help."

"Well, okay Jackson, what time will you bring him?"

"I'll leave early, be there around ten. The interview is at two. I should be back by five or six. Does that work?"

"Yes, okay Jackson see you then."

"Oh, and Lezah, I will bring his meds and his percussive vest. It's easy, heck he can show you how to use it. Thank you so much. Bye."

Lezah turned to Opal. "Why did I do that. I shouldn't see him, I should have said no!"

"Lezah don't 'should' on yourself. It may not work out, but you can help him out for a few hours, right?"

Lezah nodded, "Yeah, I guess."

"But I don't know a thing about kids, what if he gets sick?"

"I have some experience from my caregiving days. We can figure this out."

Lezah flopped down on the loveseat. "God I'm so emotional. What's wrong with me? This man has changed my life...I feel so upended."

"Okay, so let's start with food. Did you know kids love Mac and Cheese?"

"No."

"I didn't think so. He is ill, how so?"

"Cystic fibrosis—thick mucus in his lungs causes infections, pneumonia, asthma."

"Okay, but can he go to the beach?"

"He has a snazzy wheelchair, Jackson told me."

"Good because you know a wheelchair can make it on the dock ..." The look on Lezah's face silenced her. "Or we can go to the state park beach. Whatever."

Jackson parked in front of the house. He hurried to

the front door but with his hand on the doorknob, he paused and took a breath, wanting to be calm for Owen's sake. He knocked, not wanting to surprise or startle anyone. "Hey, is anybody home?" Not even all the way inside Owen was right there putting his arms around Jackson's knees. "Daddy, Daddy, you're here."

"Yes, I am. How are you? Who's here with you?"

"It's Mrs. Jacaranda, she's watching me while mommy gets better." An elderly dark-haired woman approached them.

"Hi, I'm Jackson, Owen's dad. Thank you so much for staying with ..."

"Sorry." She grabbed her purse from the hook. "Sorry, but I'm late for work. Nice to meet you but...could we have a private conversation?"

"Sure, Owen, did you brush today? No? Better go do it okay?" The child skipped away towards the bathroom.

The woman sighed, "Um Mr. um, Jackson, how well do you know your wife?"

Jackson looked down. "As you know I live in Portland, why? What should I know about Mary Kay?"

"She's been seeing this guy; he drives a beat-up mustang. My daughter who lives with me says he's a drug dealer. Mostly meth and such. He is here most nights, and people come to the door and ..."

"What? Are you saying? Mary Kay???"

"I'm so sorry, we live just across the street and can see everything. Why I'm here right now? They had a fight. He threw her out on the porch, she was screaming. I found this in the bathroom." She had wrapped the syringe in a paper towel, held it out to him.

Owen came back in. "Daddy I did it until the light came on." Jackson lifted him up and kissed the boy's head.

"Here is the hospital number and her room number. I have to go; my number is on there too. So sorry, what will you do? He's ready for his treatment in ten minutes." Her eyes met his. "So sorry, such a sweet boy." As she walked across the lawn, Jackson called "thanks so much," then hugged his son, hoping to keep his panic at bay. "C'mon Owen, let's go choose a book to read while you have your treatment. Okay? Then afterward I need to make some phone calls."

"This where mommy is?" Owen took hold of Jackson's hand. "I know this place!"

"Yes, you do. Mommy is upstairs resting. We are gonna visit her in a few minutes."

The receptionist looked at a chart.

"Oh yes, number 531—bed B. Elevator to your right."

Owen skipped ahead of Jackson, down the corridor. Thank God he is healthy right now, he thought. He glanced at the number on the room. "Owen, over here."

"This mommy's room?"

"Is that my Owen?" came a weak voice from behind the curtain.

"Mommy!" He ran to the bed.

"Hi, love."

"Owen, be gentle," said Jackson. "She has a needle in her hand that is giving her medicine from that bag hanging there."

"Oh yeah, are you better mommy?"

"Yes, I think so."

Deep dark circles under her eyes shocked Jackson.

"Umm, Mrs. Jacaranda told me some things…I need to know what really happened." His long arms hung at his sides.

"Hey is this a party?" a young nurse looked into the room. "Oh, is this your son? Hi, I'm Wendy." Over the intercom, they heard, "Visiting hours will be over in fifteen minutes." She bent down to Owen. "How would you like to come with me for a minute? I happen to know where the key to the ice cream freezer is. Mom and Dad, can he go have ice cream with Nurse Wendy?"

"Please?" said Owen dancing towards the door.

"Okay, see you in a little while." She took Owen's hand in hers and left.

"Jackson, I'm so sorry." She started to cry.

"Alright Mary Kay, what is going on?"

"Okay, I met Mike at that little park by the post office. He was there with his niece. He seemed very nice, and we would run into each other there and talk while the kids played. One day I asked them over for dinner. Only Mike came. He was a great guy, considerate, played with Owen. We started seeing each other, you know? After Owen went to bed he'd come over. Once after Owen and I had been up all night he offered me an oxycontin to help me sleep. At that point I didn't know he was using and oh God Jackson after so many years with broken sleep it was a miracle and if I didn't wake up to care for Owen, Mike would wake me and tell me, 'The boy needs you.'" She paused, looking at him.

Jackson in shock, disbelief, felt sick. "How, how could I have missed this?"

"Owen was always well cared for, I promise. After I became addicted, I realized Mike was dealing drugs out of the house. I told him to leave but he threatened to cut me off. Oh, Jackson, I'm so ashamed. I've tried to be the best mother, but, but I can't anymore, not for a while. I have an opportunity to go to a rehab for three months in LA, all paid for. You know I'm not a drinker or a druggy, don't you Jackson???"

He nodded yes, tears in his eyes.

"Can you take care of Owen? I'm so sorry, I'm weak I

need a break. I will come back strong and healthy and be there for him again…I promise."

"Okay, alright," he took her hand. "Don't worry I will figure it out…I may have a job."

They heard Owen, "Look! Mommy, Daddy," as he burst into the room. "Look what I got!" He held a dinosaur helium balloon.

"We kinda had to break into the gift shop for that, huh Owen?"

"Visiting hours are now over," came over the speaker.

"Well you all heard it, I'm kicking you out," said Nurse Wendy. She bowed to Owen, "Nice meeting you, sir. I'll be back."

"Bye."

Jackson said, "I'll call you tomorrow. Be better, Mary Kay."

"Bye mommy, kiss."

"Bye baby."

The nurse came back in. "Okay time for your eight o'clock meds. Wow, now what a nice lil boy and his father? How did he take it?"

"He is sad for me, he said don't worry it's his turn, he's the best …"

"Really?" She made a face. "A good man, OMG kidding me???" She laughed, walking to the door.

Mary Kay sat up in the bed. "Hey, thank you for this morning. For listening to me. For you know, seeing who I really am…instead of what this looks like right now."

"No problem." She picked up the empty water pitcher. "You know I'll tell you something, I was where you are, and I beat it. Find a good Narcotics Anonymous program. It works well. I can tell you are going to be fine. Try to get some good sleep, even though you know, we will wake you up at least four times during the night." She laughed. "Take care, Mary Kay, good luck."

After dropping Owen off in Banderlay, Jackson drove to the EcoAir base. He parked where the guard pointed. He walked through three check points, finally arriving at Ski's office. His secretary let him in.

"Oh Heya! Jackson? Right? Come on in, sit down."

Jackson took a seat in the chair the big man pointed to. "How was your drive? Sorry about the timing. Can I get you anything? Coffee? Soda?"

"No thanks, the drive was fine. I came from Granite Pass. That's where my son lives." He glanced at the clock, wondering how long this would take.

"Okay, how is your boy? Did you tell me he is sick? Something?"

"Yes, thanks for asking. He has a disease called cystic

fibrosis, but he's doing well right now."

"See him a lot?" Ski asked.

"When I can. More often since I've been laid off."

"Divorced?"

"We never married. We haven't been together since Owen was a toddler, he's six now."

"Got a picture?"

Caught off guard, Jackson smiled and said, "Sure do." Ski watched him pull the photo from his wallet, "Oh he's a cutie, looks like you huh?"

"That's what people say."

Ski reached across the desk. "Here you go. Let's talk about the job! I see from your resume that you are qualified. Commercial pilot, National Guard, Air Force, some private companies. The flying part of this job is easy. You'll be cruising over certain pre-selected locations, in certain formations while the chemical dispersions are computer controlled."

Jackson, confused, looked up. "I, um maybe I misunderstood. Are you talking about agricultural spraying?"

"Nope." He got up, his stature overwhelming in the small office. *Nope,* here goes he thought. Explaining it was always a challenge.

"This is a secret military program to shield the planet from the sun because the ozone layer is damaged beyond what people know about."

Jackson stiffened, sat up listening as Ski went on. "See, your plane will be equipped with nozzles. These chemicals when sprayed combine to create a 'mist' effect that dims the sun, thus protecting the planet and people from the damaged ozone layer. This protocol has been around for a while but was ramped up in the nineties. Mostly the military fly unmarked planes but our company supplies planes too. This is very hush-hush. Do you understand? Top secret. Get out now if you can't keep a secret, it's serious. Ya know what I mean? People have disappeared."

A thousand red flags waved in Jackson's brain. Ski was staring at him, waiting for an answer. "Oh well let me think about it."

"Its five hundred grand a year, full benefits, five days on, seven off. Interested?"

"Well yes, but I need to know more ..."

"That is impossible. Here is the deal, Jackson. It's a worldwide secret operation. All the other stuff EcoAir does is just a front. Rule #1. No contact with other pilots or personnel. That means your friend Mark too. You live in Portland, right? Can you start next week?"

Jackson broke out in a sweat sitting up straighter in the chair. It seemed impossible with Owen to be considered now, but the bills were stacking up and oh God, what should...

Ski leaned in, looked him in the eyes. "I thought you

needed this job to help your kid? Okay, it's alright, I've got other applicants."

"No, no, I'll take it, thank you. Can you give me two weeks before I start, Owens's mother is um, unable to care for him now. I need to make arrangements ..."

"Sure, sure, that will work. Congrats!" He got up and grabbed Jackson's hand and squeezed it hard. "Stop at my secretary's desk and get the paperwork, fill it out and sign. There is no time frame. It's month to month. Glad to have you on board. See you in a few weeks."

"Oh, and Jackson remember, you tell NO ONE about this operation, understand?"

"Yes, okay." Ski walked out with him.

"Ginny, give Jackson here the paperwork. He starts in two weeks. Okay pal, see ya later."

Jackson left the office, made his way to the car. He sat there for a while going over the interview, wondering how he was going to take care of Owen. It was a bonus that he would have time to spend with his son but on work days, what would he do?

He drove slowly through the Portland evening traffic but made good time once he cut over to the coastal route. He felt a major sense of relief having talked to his mother on the way. After hearing about his issues, she said she would come to Portland while Mary Kay was away and gladly take care of Owen.

An hour out from Banderlay, a pre-sunset wash of tangerine flared across the sky. He wondered how this new situation might affect his and Lezah's relationship. Was it a relationship? Well, there had been no words to that effect, but he sure hoped so. He thought about all he must do, pick up Owen, drive to Granite Pass, pack up the boy's things, empty the fridge, shut the house down and then return to Portland in a few days to get his place rearranged so he and Owen could share his room and his mom would have the spare room. Then the job would start. The job. Ski was weird but nice enough. At the end of the interview, he offered Jackson an advance, enough to keep the bill collectors at bay. That offer had solidified his decision to take the job. The secret stuff was concerning but he had no choice.

Liquid gold speckled the darkening water as he parked in front of The Mermaid. He got out and paused at the silhouette of his son sitting in the dingy in the cluttered yard, facing the sea, the cat Mesmer perched on the prow gazing in the same direction. Barely visible in the shadows on the porch he saw Lezah. The light was so unique the boy and cat haloed by it, he thought, was it possible? That he could have this someday. Just then, Owen turned and saw him, running through the gate to jump into his arms, "Dada, Dada," he called.

"Hey Owen, how are you?"

"I'm good and I had fun and I like the ocean and Opal made Mac and Cheese and Dad can we come back sometime?"

They walked to the porch. "Well that depends on Lezah, if she invites us again, right?"

Lezah, her smile directed at Owen. "I think you better come back soon so you can see the seals...and sure I guess your dad can come too."

Lezah patted the boy's hair. "Hey its late—why don't you two stay the night. I have a casserole in the oven."

"Dad, can we?"

"How are you feeling, Owen? How was your percussion today?"

"Good, oh super good. I showed Lezah how to work the vest. They, her mother is Opal, took me to the beach. Next time I maybe can walk to the seals instead of staying in my chair? Huh Dad can we sleep over?"

Jackson smiled, hugged the boy. "Okay, yes but we have to leave early."

"Well come on guys, let's go upstairs and have some dinner."

"Yay," yelled Owen, "I'm a hungry, hungry hippo."

While they ate Jackson told Lezah about the job; a private company based in McMinnville. He was grateful to be close to home so he could help his mother with the boy.

After they settled Owen down for the night, they came down the stairs. Jackson held her afterwards, kissing her forehead thanking her for all she had done for his son. So gentle, so tender his soft words against her cheek. The comfort of him so close, then a rush of fear as she held back tears. This man and now this boy, how had this happened, was it possible under the circumstances? She did not know in that moment and did not care.

There were still stars above the water when Jackson fastened the half-asleep child into his car seat. With arms tightly wrapped around one another he and Lezah whispered their goodbyes. "See you soon," he called as he ducked into the driver's seat, a smile on his face. Lezah stood in the street in her white nightgown waving until they were out of sight.

Ten

Lezah brushed her hair for the third time, the curls bounced backed with each stroke. She was nervous with Jackson arriving any minute. Glancing out the window, the sunset was resplendent, metallic red and gold at the edges of clouds. The special dinner was prepped and sat waiting on the counter. The crab was steamed, the butter melting. She'd made a small salad—arugula, tomatoes, and red onions. There were new potatoes from Opal's garden fried with bacon and fresh dill. She was nervous again in front of the mirror pulling up her skirt, pulling down the short top.

So much had happened. She and Jamie knew more and more about geoengineering than they ever wanted to know, as a disgusted Lezah had claimed. She had missed him like crazy. It would be a new moon and she hoped to walk to the cave after dinner. She heard a car, looked like a new, sleek, green SUV was parked outside. Jackson opened the door, stood and stretched his arms over his head looking out to the sea. Lezah ran down the stairs and flew to the door then stood there frozen, her belly flip-flopping.

She waited and heard him say, "Stay back, you vicious animal" to Mesmer, which made her smile. She counted to ten after his second knock before she opened the door. A quick mutual look, smiles, shy eyes. "Come in come in, Jackson." His name on her lips meant everything. "I've got dinner ready. Are you hungry?"

"Yes, yes I am." He followed her, his eyes on her small perfect body, the way she floated up the stairs, the measured cadence of the beaded curtains as she parted them.

The huge painting dominated the room. He stood before it, his backpack in his hand. Blue water, a round moon and a mermaid reaching up, her face turned partly away.

"Wow? Lezah, that is amazing, so large, so lifelike."

"Come sit." She pointed to the retro chairs at the little table.

"Thanks."

"It's not finished." She removed the lid on the crab pot and the sweet hot scent of the salty broth filled the kitchen and fogged the windows. She set an opened bottle of white wine on the table and two glasses.

"Pour, please." She dressed the salad, served it, dished up the potatoes and put a crab on each plate. She took two large dish towels, folded them into halves and he copied as she tucked hers into the collar of her shirt. Pouring melted butter into two glass bowls she felt nervous but said, "I've missed you, Jackson."

He stood, kicking the chair, then recovering. He came to her and they put their arms around each other. Slightly bent over, his face in her hair. "Yes," he said. "Oh yes, I missed you too." Over dinner he watched fascinated as she cracked a claw with her thumbs. Her eyes on him. She dipped the sweet meat into the bowl of warm butter, which dripped from her plump mouth and ran down her chin. Her eyes still on him, her smile, feral. They finished, and not wanting any small talk or catching up she said, "It's a new moon. I want to go to the cave. Are you up for it?"

"Sure, it's getting dark though, got a headlamp, flashlight?"

"I know it by heart, in the dark, but I have both. C'mon I'll race you!"

"Kidding me? You're serious! Wait, my shoes."

"I'm going barefoot," she said over her shoulder.

"Is that a challenge? I've got soft, white, Portland feet."

"Okay I'll wait while you put them on," she sighed dramatically.

"Oh no, challenge accepted. Bare feet it is." They

walked to the downward path, paused, Lezah yelled "1, 2, 3, 4 go!" They took off running. He played with her. Yelling "Ouch, ouch, my feet, can you carry me, strong ocean woman?"

She smiled to herself as they padded onto the beach. Glancing through the dark water she shined the headlamp towards the haulout. All nine seals were there, no doubt asleep.

"This way," she called to him. He swerved left and followed. She heard the rumble of the low tide boomers far out. The sky black ink except for the sliver of moon. He was there. In the same space. She heard his footsteps coming closer. "Here, here is the cave."

The entrance, a V-shaped opening a few stories high. They jumped the little moat and entered. Their headlamps lit up the damp walls. Through the tunnel to the open sea they saw the low tide slowly coming in. Lezah took the headlamp off and set it on the ground. Then Jackson followed and the cave was dimly lit. The pleasure of their loving on the damp sand echoed and reverberated inside the bell-like chamber.

Coming out, Lezah sensed something had changed as they walked through the ever-widening half circles of water as the returning tide approached. Looking out to the open sea there was the faintest edge of light at the horizon. Not yet light, but a soft blue glow.

"Look," she pointed. "See the faint blue?"

"Yes, what is it, a boat?"

"No, it's *Velella velella.* Velum is Greek for paper or sail, and Ella means small. They are tiny oval-shaped creatures. Little wind sailors who have this translucent sail that is bioluminescent. Their movement depends on the strong winds way out in the deepest ocean." They stood astonished as the tide came in swiftly, the waves studded with blue flickering lights as the water was now the sky and the sky an expanse of dark water. Still filled with shared ecstasy, they held each other. Lezah felt an awareness of their connection beyond their passion, a bond somehow both familiar and strange, both ancient and new. And when Jackson kissed her she knew he felt it too.

They cuddled the next morning. Lezah brought homemade cinnamon rolls and coffee on a tray to the bed stand. "So how is Owen?"

"Doing well. I found a good sitter, and he is starting school."

"And his mother, how is she doing?"

"Sad story. She relapsed and is staying with her mother. Waiting to get into another rehab. I don't know," he rubbed his temples.

"And your job?" Her heart sped up.

"I'm training. It will be pretty easy to fly between Portland and LA. The money is, more than, well, I'll be able to pay off the hospital bills and maybe get ahead."

"New car?"

"Company car. Not complaining. It's really comfortable."

His cell buzzed. It was a call from Ski saying that they needed him as soon as he could get there. "Oh damn it Lezah, I'm sorry. I was so looking forward to this few days, but I'm the new guy and I have to go. Can I take a quick shower?" She removed their coffee cups from the side table in the alcove. His wallet was there also, lying open, carelessly tossed there. She waited a moment then picked it up. His driver's license was behind the little plastic frame on one side, his parking pass from EcoAir Aviation was on the other. She heard the shower water stop, closed the wallet and set it back on the table. Coming out, he looked as though he was from another time with the towel draped around his waist. What a beautiful man he was. His calm energy made her feel calm, his innocence and playfulness brought her childlike joy. She felt like she knew for the first time what making love meant.

"Okay, I'm dressed. Well, what time we did have together was great. I'll try to come back soon and hey I have days off, do you ever come to Portland?"

"I am going there next week. Hmmm coincidence? A private show for some big money guy, all artists are going to be there. So, do you have a regular schedule?"

"Yes, when are you coming?"

"Um, the show is the ninth."

"I'm free the tenth."

"Oh good." They held each other in the cluttered yard, the cat circling his ankles and purring.

She waved him off, blew kisses, teared up with a rush of emotion. On the way in she flipped the open sign to closed.

Wild joy brought her to the little stereo. She put the waltz CD in, the one she and Roe always danced to. She was really little when he taught her to waltz while her tiny feet were on top of his big ones. She danced around the shop, the Blue Danube playing at full volume. She was so…she searched for words. Excited. Ecstatic. Elated. Jackson!

She twirled like a girl until dizzy. *Whoa,* out of breath she went upstairs to the apartment. Slowly, she removed the sheet covering the large canvas, threw it onto the loveseat. She stood before it as if it were an altar. She went for water, inspiration bubbling as she laid out the brushes, the dip pan and the towels. Peeling the waxed paper off the palette, she stood staring at the image. A pale blue sky, a buttery moon, half in half out of the turquoise sea. A burnished bit of land, the morning sun brightening the cliffs in the background.

The foreground held the mermaid half submersed, reaching up, her face in profile. For three days Lezah barely ate or slept. Hour upon hour she spent painting the little white dots that created the rising foam around the mermaid. The ocean, which filled most of the image, was blue gray green undertones then patterned over with layers of cobalt, veridian, Prussian blue and turquoise. There were red studded coral shells woven throughout the long hair that floated out behind her. Her tail veiled, partly hidden, rested beneath the clear water.

She painted without knowing what or where just wherever she was drawn, using the brush to sketch the elusive image she had wanted to define. So obvious, now, this mysterious, missing part had taken so long to reveal itself. Backing up she stood before it, adrenaline rising. Hours passed again and the sketched image came alive. The moon's feathered light illuminated its anatomy and the gestured passion and connection shone through. Yes, she sighed. One more thing. She dipped the brush into water and spiraled it through the Alizarin Crimson paint on the palette.

"Ah yoohoo? Anybody home? Jamie?"

"Hey Lezah, nice surprise." He came out of the kitchen drying his hands.

"Doing breakfast dishes at um yep noon. What's up?"

"Just on a run, where is Zach?"

"He flew to Philadelphia this am, his dad is sick. Want something to drink? I've got ..."

"Just water." He filled a glass, handed it to her.

"What are you up to, how is the perfect fabulous guy?"

"Oh, yeah he came and stayed the night. You know how I was so curious where he worked now. Well he left his wallet out and I saw his parking pass. It's EcoAir Aviation," she rushed on. "And Jamie, I looked it up and it's a legit company that does stuff like ag spraying, transporting for the military, flying dignitaries to other countries, or they do set runs between Portland and LA delivering all kinds of …"

"Did you say EcoAir Aviation? Hold on, come with me to my office. I just saw something on that info site GeoWatch about this company." He sat down at his computer. "Man, Lezah this group has so much credible information. Let's see, here it is." He read it out loud. "EcoAir is a global aviation service company based in McMinnville, Oregon. Operating in 168 countries, EcoAir is a CIA front company using retrofitted 727s and 747s with liquid discharge tanks and aerosol spray devices used for weather modification, drug trafficking, delivering arms to various countries. These programs are funded by a secret presidential budget."

Lezah stood up. "Oh no, oh Jamie what if?" She paced the small room, "What if he is involved, oh my God."

"Lezah wait don't jump to …"

"I can't help it. I knew. How could he be part of this?"

"Well, have you actually asked him?"

"No, but I'm seeing him day after tomorrow. I'm going to the gallery for this event, leaving in the morning."

"Good, go to the source, don't overthink it. He's probably just flying the short routes, delivering stuff. He probably doesn't even know the bad shit they are involved in. Don't overthink your pretty little head."

"Yeah, okay. Gotta go run this fear energy off." She turned and rushed out. Jamie shut the computer down. *Man, she really loves him. Hope her intuition is wrong.*

Lezah flew down the path to the beach, angry tears blurred her vision. *Typical. I finally love someone and they turn out to be a fraud, a hoax, a liar.* She finally slowed to a walk after five miles, sweat drenched, spent, every muscle burning. She bent over breathing hard. Between her sand-dusted shoes a tiny crab stuck his head up out of the sand, twitched then burrowed back down. No more head in the sand for me, she thought. They had planned to meet at his house after the gallery event. No, don't want to go there. I'll call him, suggest we meet somewhere else, make up some reason. Walking back through the dunes she was grateful to be working the dinner shift. Less time to think.

Eleven

On the first day of training Jackson had waited for Ski a little nervously. The secretary had told him to go ahead and sit in Ski's office. He looked around the sparsely furnished space, desk, two chairs, and one picture of a dog on the wall. He heard Ski coming down the hall, asking if he'd arrived.

"Ah there ya are Jackson, good, right on time. I like that. I'm having an issue with your maiden flight today. The pilot who was gonna train you called in sick. I can't find a replacement so I'm gonna take you up. You'll fly, a piece of cake, and I'll show ya the ropes. Easy as pie. C'mon, let's go do it."

The C-17 sat on the runway. Ski was out of breath walking across the tarmac. Looks good, thought Jackson.

"So this is mostly what you'll drive. These birds are signature intelligence Air Force reconnaissance planes that have been modified and retrofitted with tanks."

They walked up the ramp. Jackson ducked as did Ski as they entered. The plane was empty of seats; instead, rows of tanks filled the cabin. Ski pointed out the chemicals, different mixes.

The cockpit was standard. Ski showed him where the designated flight pattern would appear on the computer screen, and where the dispersal data would come up.

"Easy peasy. Just take off, fly for three-hour shifts while sprays are completed. Fly back. Piece of cake. Since we are a private arm of the military we take orders from them and them only. Commercial birds steer clear unless their crafts are fitted out with spray apparatus. Whaddya think? Shall we go up?"

Jackson nodded and took the pilot's seat.

"How's your kid?"

"Doing well, thanks."

"Got a girlfriend?"

"Maybe. Seeing someone."

"Well ya know that's the hardest bit about this job. Secrecy. Ya can't let her know anything. Understand?"

"Yes," said Jackson as the screen lit up.

The designated flight patterns appeared. Portland to Northern California, Northern California to Southern California, then back again to Portland. Jackson asked, "Can these aerosols change the weather?"

"Sure can, I did this in Vietnam, caused the monsoon season to last so supplies or vehicles couldn't get through. Gave us the advantage for sure. Okay now see the nozzles are starting up. Your copilot will be monitoring the tanks and dispersals. You just fly." They rose up into the air, then leveled out. It was smooth sailing, the sky a bright blue. Suddenly, Ski leaned forward and groaned. "Damn it," he muttered, taking a bottle of pills out of his shirt pocket. He emptied some into his hand, then undid the lock on the water bottle, and gulped them down in one swallow, wiping his mouth with the back of his hand.

"You alright?" Jackson asked.

"Yeah sure, get these headaches sometimes. Hey great job, easy peasy huh?"

During Jackson's first week he and his copilot, Pete, were cruising through a classic blue sky. Two other planes were to his right. They would fly in a formation and disperse one after another. Jackson's plane was first.

"You got it, Jackson? Now you're in place, straight ahead, just cruise, here come the sprays." The plumes were laid down as the other two planes flew alongside, then rose above Jackson. The trails would bond and meld and become what looked like fog or thick cloud cover.

Pete said, "Okay good job. We follow the flight patterns, the satellites control the chemicals and basically that's it." He started playing with his radio.

"Sometimes we can get other pilots, even get other countries."

"Hmm," said Jackson. "That's cool." Pete searched, found a clear channel. Two guys talking.

"Oh, hey. I've gotta go to the John." He got out of his chair and walked out of the pit. Jackson watched the plume on the screen, all looked normal.

He listened to the conversation. "Don't pull that loyalty crap on me!"

"Hey man, you committed to complete silence and secrecy."

"Pilots are chatting all the time, bro. Get off if you don't like it."

"Anybody else out there?"

"Yeah me, hey I'm on a run between London and Germany under cover of darkness so as to fool those awake chaps. Ha ha, I've got school loans to pay for."

"Hey I'm in a DC-3 over Louisiana, low level, mosquito spray. Nasty stuff. Have a good shift."

"Yo, I've been deployed in a Cessna 172 to spray Charlottesville, North Carolina. Been feeling bad, guilty you know, anybody else?" There was static then the voices faded out.

Pete came back. "No more Mexican food for me."

"Pete, I heard some conversation while you were gone. How long you been doing this job?"

"Twenty months."

"Are we doing something good? Is this really to protect our national security and save us from the ozone layer?"

"Oh man, don't start! I can't answer and you shouldn't ask, know what I mean? Didn't Ski warn you?"

"Sort of."

Pete looked away. "Don't ask."

Ski stood at the window of the medical office. He had to slouch to see the woman's face. He wrote on the check and slid it under the glass.

"Do you need a follow-up appointment?"

He laughed. "Um don't think so, doc says I'm terminal."

"Oh my gosh." The young receptionist blushed. "I'm so sorry, I didn't know."

"It's okay, honey. We all go, ya know?" Walking to the parking lot he wondered did things look different because he didn't have long. Toby was licking the window as he got in. "Get back, girl. I know, I know." He buckled, then undid the belt. "Why the hell not?" Shit, no wonder those headaches were so bad. It's a big tumor, the doc showed him the X-ray. He drove through the five o'clock traffic, in that hypnotic state where he could drive with all that was needed to focus, yet he was in a state of disassociation thinking about what he needed to do to get ready.

Doc had said he would have a giant stroke or embolism. Be quick. Said he could have morphine if he wanted. Okay, he sighed. Could be worse. He pulled into Bob's Bigboy, ordered four double cheese burgers add onions. Two for him, two for Toby.

Lezah listened to the message. "Hey, hi. Got your message, will see you at the park in half an hour. By the swings and big cedar, okay? Bye." She had come to the gallery this morning to meet with Hank Berella, who was explaining how special commissions worked, which was the perfect reason to have Jackson meet her at the park instead of his home. Hank congratulated her on impressing the wealthy couple who were interested in her work as they were well-known collectors. She then walked to the park and sat down on a bench under a group of big cedars. She was nervous watching him park. His step was light, a big smile on his face as he approached. She stood up.

"Hi."

"Hey, so good to see you."

"Yes."

"Get the business taken care of with, what's his name?"

"Hank, yes."

He reached for her. "I've missed you. It will be good to be together." He slowly let go, sensing something. "Are you alright? Something wrong?"

"Um, I'm not sure Jackson. We need to talk."

"Okay," he said cautiously. "What's up?"

"Well you've heard me talk about my friend Jamie?"

"Yes."

"Well we've been noticing these strange lines in the sky for oh maybe five months. He's a science guy you know, a marine biologist. Anyway we started," Jackson held his breath, "we started researching and have discovered some frightening information."

"Like what, Lezah," he asked calmly.

"Well, it's called geoengineering. Have you heard of it?"

"Yeah, it's a general term for the many ways any environment can be altered."

"I'm not going to play games. Jackson, who do you work for? What's the name of the company?"

"EcoAir Aviation."

"Is it commercial?"

"Yes, partly."

"What are they about? What services does EcoAir provide?"

"Well, there is a whole list. Let's see, they transport worldwide. Goods, people, they fight fires, work with the forest service, do rescues. They fly dignitaries to other countries."

"What do you do Jackson?"

"I'm a pilot, I fly between Portland and Los Angeles. I'm not—I can't lie to you Lezah. I also can't tell you what I do. It's part of a secret program. I cannot, will not, since I signed official papers and if I did tell you there could be dire consequences. But to make you feel better, it's helping humans."

She moved towards him, her eyes held him. "God, I was so wrong about you."

"Lezah, listen!"

"No, you listen. How do you know it's 'helping'? Are you sure? There is evidence that people are being used, told it's okay when it's lethal. What do you know about this?"

"I can't and won't talk about it," he was pleading. "Lezah I wouldn't do something that was harmful."

"Right! I thought you were different. But no, just another guy going for the big bucks with no conscience or care for consequences." She shook her head.

"Aw, come on Lezah! It's for my kid, so he can live, ya

know. I have to pay down the hospital bills or he won't be admitted. Is that a good enough reason for you?"

"Your kid has trouble breathing, right? And you are," she hesitated, "you are poisoning the air he breathes." This hit him deep in his gut.

He pleaded, "I told you it's helping humans."

"Bullshit! You are being lied to. I'm sorry," she picked up her purse. "I'm not going to be able to see you anymore. I won't be with someone who knowingly hurts people."

"Shocked," he stuttered. "Really after all, we've, we've, shared? Don't leave please, can't we figure this out? I would know if it's what you are saying."

"You are so, so, clueless." She moved a few steps away then turned. "How did you vet this program? Did you check it out, see if it was a legit operation?"

"Of course, but it's the military, I can say no more."

"Like spraying chemicals, you would never do that, right?" The 'T' at the end of the word 'right' pierced him like a tiny knife. "No need to talk it through. Too bad it's gotten this far. I should have known. Have a good life, Jackson."

"Lezah wait!" He started running but her determined steps towards her car stopped him.

She turned, "You're just like all the power-hungry men drunk with greed, out looking for that next thing to make money. For money is God in our world. The way it's made does not concern people like you, no care about what the money-making venture does to anything, or any living thing. No consciousness equals no wrongs. You are poisoning the very air your child breathes to make money to heal him. That's insane, and if you honestly don't know what you are involved with well, how fucking naive…you have no idea that what you are doing is a crime against humanity and that you are raping the planet. Did you know a woman is raped every three minutes, no? Bet you didn't. There is no difference really. Our world is being ruined by your actions and lack of consciousness. I can't be with you. I won't." She spun around, her bag on her shoulder and walked towards her car.

"Lezah!" He started to go after her but stopped. He watched her leave the parking area. Sitting on the bench he was shaking beneath the giant cedars above, the sound of the empty swings moving in the wind. He was there for a long time. *What just happened? What did she know? What information had he not been told?* He paced. *Never seen her like that before. Anger spiked off her like a physical thing. She spit out words that came at him like weapons from her mouth. Rapist—what? The Mother Earth analogy? Was he doing something terrible?"* He called Ski's secretary to set up a meeting. The thought of losing Lezah left a cold sweat. No way, find out then deal with it.

Lezah had to really focus driving through the bottlenecked Portland freeways at rush hour, so that by the time she cut over to the coast via Eugene, Oregon she could process what had just happened with Jackson. He was spraying. Perhaps told it was for the good of humanity—she doubted it, doubted all in that moment that she would ever trust again. How could he? The child yes, but he could have, she searched, he could have taken a job for less money, made payments or taken out a loan or? No excuses. He knows. He doesn't care. Another man thinking he can control nature, even while the earth is dying.

She cried the whole coastal drive home. How could he? She kept thinking, saying it over and over. How could he?

She drove straight to Opal's. Roe's car was not there. She opened the door, surprising Opal who was knitting in the cozy room. One look and Opal stood, went to her, her arms around Lezah, "What? Lezah what?" She waited while the girl calmed.

Lezah caught her breath, looked into Opal's eyes. "He's gone."

"Who, where?"

"Jackson, he's out of my life. His new job is being a pilot with a company that sprays chemicals, like those trails I showed you and Roe. It's over. I can't see or be with him again," her voice faded. Her face fallen, she walked to the galley kitchen.

Opal called, "Yes, let's have tea." And she rushed past

Lezah and set the kettle on and tea things out. "So why is he doing this job do you think? He doesn't seem like a criminal or suspicious, but who knows. Why?"

"It's Owen. He is hundreds of thousands of dollars in debt. The child needs to be hospitalized often. Money of course and Owen's mother is in recovery again. His salary is five hundred thousand a year. When I confronted him he tried to convince me it's for the benefit of humanity and the planet. Seems he really believes it is."

"What do you think you would do in the same situation? Sick child, need money for care, the father unavailable. You are convinced that you are doing something valuable, then you meet someone who questions it all, it threatens your plans and you must decide. Appease this person or take care of your ill child. What would you do?"

"Yes, alright. But it's hurting people in an inconceivable way."

"Yes there is that," said Opal. "But he's not conscious of the danger yet, right? Question is, would he do it if he knew it hurt people?"

Lezah started crying quietly as Opal laid the tea tray and moved towards the living room. "It's just so…Opal why did this happen to me? I can't be with him and live with myself."

"The question of why it's happening to you might be replaced with what is the lesson in this situation? But before that can be addressed you must ask yourself if you have enough information to make this decision at this time, or is it just assumptions?"

"A part of me thinks he wouldn't do it if he knew. But the other part says he's a desperate father and that might overrule."

"What are his other options?" asked Opal.

"Well, a loan maybe or a payment plan with the hospital, other job searches, debt counseling, I don't know." She rubbed her eyes. "I'm going home. I was up all night. I need to sleep." She kissed Opal on the cheek. "Thanks for listening." She put the tea cup down in the kitchen sink, turned. Opal put her hands on Lezah's shoulders.

"Lezah, that part of him that you love, don't turn it off yet. Keep it tucked somewhere safe until you know more. Stay open."

"I can't be with him, or anyone who is part of this crime against humanity, regardless of the circumstances. It cancels out all the good, Opal. I'll be in touch."

After Lezah closed the door, Opal walked over to the little altar and lit the candles.

Jackson called Lezah again, this the fifth time. Just her message. He'd come home from the park, a feeling of confused shock about what had happened. Drinking shots of scotch, watching soccer, he went over it. What she thought was happening, was it true? Probably. He had enough signs. His meeting with Ski was in a few days. One more week and he'd get a check. Mary Kay was back in rehab, her third time. He would have to find a daycare for Owen. Not easy as he'd been turned away by others due to his health issues. He better start looking now. He took another shot. Oh God, and Lezah. He could not lose her. But he could not quit the job either. Not now. He downed another shot, passed out on the worn sofa, the TV casting a flickering blue-green light over him.

In the dream he is running, holding Owen in his arms running for his life or the boy's he does not know. He is desperate, desperate to get the boy to safety, to shield him from extreme danger. He looks down, his feet are bare, slapping the wet sand clinging between his toes. Where is he? Looking out at a huge expanse of water. He is running to the water. No! He must dive in with the boy and swim him to safety. No! He cannot. He can't swim, ever since he almost drowned in the lake near his boyhood home. But now he must or Owen will die. He rushes to the shore, the sleeping child in his arms. Something shimmers beyond the blowback, rises up, a tail arching, closer. He is shaking all over, squints. It's coming closer, goes under then bursts up out of the froth. It's Lezah, her eyes hard, her arms reach out and grabs the boy who starts screaming, "Daddy, Daddy." She dives into the water, a last look at Jackson, her smile one of satisfaction before she disappears underwater. Waking, he mutters, "whoa, weird," stumbling towards the bathroom.

Opal wrapped the fried egg and onion sandwiches in tinfoil. After packing them in the canvas sack she added a can of warm beer and a cloth napkin. All the time they had been together she had her evening walk while Roe fished. There was something about watching the sun disappear into the sea that completed her day. Once on the beach, she walked to the east as the last light glowed upon the darkening water. She couldn't stop thinking about Lezah and Jackson. Roe waved as she approached him, standing in the surf, waves sloshing around his rubber boots. He smiled at her, took off his ball cap, and bowed.

"Evening Miss, out for a stroll?"

"Oh Roe," she handed him the bag…and walked on.

"Ya still got those legs." He didn't see her smile but knew she did. Skeins of long lavender and orange clouds spilled across the sky. "See ya in a while."

The surf seemed restless, sets of waves intersecting chaotically like her feelings about Lezah and this seemingly good man. Regardless of her fears about Jackson and her past, Opal knew Lezah must take the risk and embrace the unknown territory of a relationship. Opal knew if one did not learn from a failed relationship the lesson would repeat itself in different forms or with different individuals, whatever that may mean.

Roe unwrapped the sandwiches. The first bite of the

warm sandwich made him sigh as yolk dribbled down his chin. He popped the top on the beer. He enjoyed just one every evening. Chewing, sipping, staring at the ever-changing water, he watched Opal's progression down the long beach. He knew that she was worried about Lezah, this man she loved that they hardly knew, and what he would think of Lezah's past. He was in the bay that early foggy morning checking his crab pots. Something floated past him. He heard the jangling metal panels on the dock and thought he saw Lezah. He and Opal had never discussed Brodie's death in, he counted…twenty-four years. He'd gone along with the story, never let on. Why? To protect Lezah? He truly did not know all of what happened and some part of him did not want to know, he reckoned. Still doesn't.

Opal knew trust for Lezah was an issue, but she had given Jackson her whole heart. The sun had sunk unnoticed due to her worried thoughts. The gloaming gathered, a slim moon appeared. Roe was folding up his chair.

"Hey there, ya free tonight?"

"Oh Roe."

"'Cause if you are, I got some nice halibut. Gonna clean 'em, leave the guts for Lezah's seals, then be right up."

The next evening, Roe put the fishing rod in its holder. He sat down, didn't feel much like fishing. Felt weird, weak in his limbs, kinda clumsy. That pain in his chest hadn't let up since noon. He waited, admiring the big, perfect boomers rolling in. Okay, go home now, getting dark. Started to get up—shit, couldn't. Damn, hot pain, upper back, shooting pain, left arm. What's happening? His heart, yes. Oh no, really, now? He bent forward, tried to catch his breath, looked at his hands in his lap, water rising. Turning, he saw the little home on the cliff, thought of Opal, Lezah, all that he ever loved. This place, the ocean. Fear engulfed him. He could not live without them. And then, an embrace of the purest comfort and well-being. Stars filling the sky, colors never seen before. The fiery lights exploded all around him forming galaxies that spun and spiraled. Ecstatic music, a symphony with violins and woodwinds and crashing cymbals. Oh Opal, look—the stars, so many stars...

Opal woke in the dark, the book still open in her lap. There were a thousand lights swirling around her. Blinking, she moved to the edge of the chair. Not a dream, more than a vision, loud, ecstatic music encircled her. Wake up, she told herself! But she was awake; as above her fireworks, intricate shapes and colors exploded as the music crescendoed with cymbals and violins, she stood up. What? Was? That?

Roe!? She looked at the clock, 10:15. "Roe, you in there?" No, he wasn't in the bedroom. Outside, barefoot she ran the few steps up to his workshop, which was dark. Worrying now, back to the house, checked the bathroom. No. She had done her usual sunset walk, Roe telling her he was gonna fish another hour or so. 10:15, he wouldn't stay out that late? Hurriedly, she pocketed her phone, put on shoes and rushed out the front door. Quickly down the steps to the path, slipping in wet mud, fell twice straining to see the beach. Once down she called him "Roe! Roe? Honey?" She could see the faint outline of his tall chair near the shore. Closer, she yelled "Roe!" There he was, couldn't hear her, that was all...She could see the back of his head, worrying now. "Roeland." Panting, aching sides, she came up behind him. The water up around the seat, his legs floating in front of him. His face, oh Roe, oh no, honey no no no no.

Her arms around his cold body, she stroked his hair, his weathered cheek. In shock, in terror, in horror, in disbelief she took his hand and looked out to the ocean where his now closed eyes last rested. Waning crescent moon, soaked to her thighs she felt hypnotized by the powerful set of waves coming in, one after another; she moved back, the oncoming surf too close, then wind-rushed blowback unseated the chair as she watched helplessly as it began to float. Panic, then resolve. She could do nothing—the upcoming wave washed his body ashore, left him curled on his side like a sleeping infant. She ran to him and laid down beside him.

There was no funeral or public celebration of life, but Roe was loved by many so a fish-fry potluck dinner was held at the old armory. Afterwards Lezah and Opal had come to Opal's with a car full of flowers. Opal made tea and could not hold the weight of grief in her body any longer and laid down on their bed and fell asleep. Turning over, reaching for him, shocked awake at the emptiness there, his missing form like an amputee's phantom limb.

Lezah filled Roe's old canvas rucksack from Vietnam with the many bright bouquets and loose flowers that had been centerpieces at the armory dinner. Shouldering it, she hefted it into position. Through Opal's open door, Lezah saw her sleeping face and tiptoed out of the house, down the path to the beach. Halfway there, she saw Roe's chair near the shore. Opal had found Roe in the chair, big waves had taken him out then carried him back up at high tide. The chair had washed up as well and now lay on its side in the dry sand, a stranded thing. Lezah lifted it and walked it close to the water. Pushing the legs securely into the wet sand she wriggled out of the backpack, set it on her lap in the high chair. Untying the several knots she pulled the flowers out and tossed them into the water where Roe had last sat, her cries and echoed keening muffled by the surf's roar.

Calming, she watched the flowers carried away in the approach, retreat of the moon's pull. Oh how she wanted him now, how she loved him. He was her first holdfast, the trusted anchor that nurtured and protected her. Yellow roses swirled around the legs of the chair. She wanted so badly to float out with them to be buoyed up and carried away from this pain. "Roe, my Roe."

Opal walked the sunset beach passing by Roe's fishing chair, amazed that no one had stolen it. Along with the autumn rainy season she felt dull, gray, and heavy. Tonight the sun smeared orange and purple across a cloudless sky. As she walked along the shore at low tide, the little waves washing in then out, she spotted a good-sized chunk of agate ahead and stopped, bent, and scooped it into her hand. She studied the perfect specimen. Over the years she and Roe had collected agates in competition with one another. "Mine is larger, but mine, look how the light shines through." This one in her hand was gold and smooth on one side with a band of green and white where the silica had filled in the crevices in the volcanic rock. The other half of the oval was dull brown and roughly pocked. Half done, she thought, as she slid it into her pocket. But then she decided to throw it back into the waves, knowing for it to be fully formed the agate would need to be in with other stones inside the moving water, the constant friction smoothing out the grit of time.

Waiting for the next wave, she threw the agate down and watched as the wave came in gathering the stones and broken shells, tumbling them, rolling them, the music a brief crescendo. Was she half finished? Half smoothed, half wise? Life without Roe, what future friction would she have to endure to bear life without him?

Twelve

"Come in, Maddox." Ski held the door open. "To what do I owe this displeasure?"

"Knock it off, Ski. The folks upstairs sent me to personally brief you on some new protocols. No record, no media, no emails, on the QT undercover, good ole-fashioned communication. Okay?"

"What's going on?"

"They are ramping up the sprays worldwide, country by country. Weather warfare will be on the rise. Cool huh, we can just freeze-dry those Russian bastards," he chuckled. "You are gonna need more pilots, as the program expands."

"Oh great, I can barely keep the ones I have."

"No worries, they are authorizing huge raises as we speak. There is a new twist though. Something, that if it's leaked, could jeopardize geoengineering altogether. They are starting a Biological Spray program."

"A what?" Ski leaned in.

"A Biological Spray program. Eventually the health of the people will be greatly influenced by chemicals, nanoparticles, and biological sprays."

"You mean like germs? Like bioweapons?"

"Yup, first it will be flus and colds. Once they figure that out there are plans for epidemics, even pandemics. Great tool, huh?"

"Get out, Maddox." He stood up and opened the door.

"Cool it, Ski." The man took hold of the door knob and quietly closed the door. "There's more you need to hear. They are shutting down EcoAir, turning it into an aviation museum. The expansion is worldwide, all NATO countries are on board. If you don't go along with this, stay in charge of the pilots, you could be in big trouble, Ski. You know way too much for the boys upstairs to let you walk away now. So ya better think about getting on board. Your new offices will now be at Portland International. Most commercial airlines are being outfitted. You'll be on the military side. So come on, pal, ya didn't have issues before."

Ski's head was throbbing, "Get out, go now!" The small, thin man opened the door slowly, then turned, his tiny eyes on Ski.

"All this hush, hush. Tell your pilots their salaries are

doubled as of tomorrow. Don't divulge the new plan. Bye."

Sweat dripped from his brow onto the desktop. Palming his handkerchief he blotted his pounding head, mopped up the desk.

He thought about what Maddox told him. He'd gone along all these years telling himself there was no definitive or scientific proof that the sprays caused harm. But this... another sharp pain pierced his temple. I can't think about it now, but, fuck, never thought it would go this far. He took two more Vicodin and placed his crossed arms on the desk and lowered his head to rest on them.

It was a Saturday morning, no wind. Jamie had jogged the beach loop from his neighborhood to Lezah's shop.

"Hey there." He jingled the bells on the screen door. "Lezah? You up or down?" She came in through the back door.

"I'm here, just emptied the garbage. Did you see the sign?"

"No, is it up?"

"I did it yesterday. Come and look." He followed her out. "Nice day huh? Bluebird Saturday, clear sky, blue ocean, sunshine. So come out here as if you are looking for the shop. Stop, right there—see it?"

On one of the porch posts was a colorful round sign, ENVIRONMENTAL AND GEOENGINEERING INFORMATION HERE. QUESTIONS WELCOME.

"Looks great, visible but not intrusive, bright colors, yeah it's perfect. The flyers from GeoWatch are ordered. I was thinking, always dangerous I know, is there room for a small bulletin board so we can post info and pictures?"

"There's lots of room since my girls went to the gallery. Good idea. I had an idea, what about a show, here, showing all the cloud anomalies with their new names? It's public by way of the revised International Cloud Atlas that anyone can look up so let's showcase it here at the mermaid. Or maybe just photos of trails? Want coffee, I'm here all day." He nodded his head yes. "Let's go up." They heard a car door close and the bell on the gate outside sound.

"Customer. Don't leave, I'll deal with them, then we can chat."

"Hi Folks." The Scottish couple came through the gate. "Good morning. Beautiful day!"

"We saw your sign and came by to chat. Do you have time?" Lezah looked at Jamie who recognized them from the meeting in School's Bay. He nodded.

"Well come inside." Lezah opened the door and arranged four chairs around one of the redwood burl tables. "Sit please." There was a moment when no one spoke. Finally, Lezah said, "Thank you again for the invitation to the gallery. It's been a dream come true."

"I heard your art is selling well. We are here to talk about geoengineering. We live outside of Glasgow, Scotland. For years now the planes fly over our apartment constantly. Our city has established an Institute of Environmental Health that is being funded partially by my trust. How long have you been aware of it, Lezah?"

"The last year or so. What does your institute accomplish, what are its goals?"

The wife, Maeve, spoke. "We are educating as many people as possible about the sprays and weather warfare. We have invested in flyers, info packets, and templates to write legislators, and lately we fly experts in this area to various locations for speaking engagements in universities, libraries, and corporations. We have financially backed several brilliant documentaries and are buying time in movie theaters across the nation. Education is everything. The people must stop it. Government wants it to continue indefinitely. The people must speak out against the poisoning of the planet."

"Why are you here in Banderlay?"

"Well it was fortuitous synchronicity. We wanted a retreat while supporting my brother's gallery and current show. We had driven through and fell in love with Banderlay. We knew it was a ways from Portland, but decided to commute to the galas and fundraisers. We saw you at the School's Bay meeting and then discussed your opinion of the geoengineering presentation. Remember? And now we see a new sign passing by. Tell us about your center?"

Lezah smiled, "Oh well we are brand new. This is Jamie, my partner in crime. He's a marine biologist. We've been researching and gathering information and decided to make a space in my shop to share information and educate people."

"That's brilliant, how can we help?"

Lezah looked at Jamie. "Well, we're not sure. We are so new and I think if we keep it simple we're good for now."

"Unless," Jamie interrupted. "Unless you have research and data to share? I'm researching and would be interested to see what your experts are finding."

"Of course. We have, I believe, Europe's most updated information on our website." He turned to his wife. "Maeve, can you give him the institute's card?"

"Well, we've got to move on. We are flying to the gallery today for an important meeting." Lezah walked them to the door.

"Keep up your good work and let us know how it's progressing. Thank you, Ta-ta."

After the couple left, Jamie and Lezah looked at each other. "Well that just happened," said Lezah, smiling.

"Good connection. Looking forward to seeing their info. That is if Zach lets me."

"What?"

"He's got this attitude that I'm obsessed and falling down a rabbit hole of conspiracy theories. Boy, the CIA sure knew what they were doing when they coined that term after JFK's assassination. Just erases everything and anything doesn't it? We've really been off of late. How are you doing with…I mean without—awkward, sorry—Jackson?"

"Terrible, I miss him, and I still can't believe he is working for EcoAir. He's left, I swear twenty messages in the last month. I'm in deep grief over Roe," she teared up…"I don't know how to erase him from my life." She sniffed. Jamie came over to her.

"Come here girlfriend." He hugged her. There were no words and they both knew it.

"How is Opal?"

"She is surviving. I think. I've been staying with her. The nights are the most difficult. For both of us."

"Well I better get going. Zach has a honey do list a mile long for me this weekend. Hangin, love you. Bye."

After he left Lezah walked to the shop phone and listened to Jackson's last message. "Oh hey there Lezah, it's me, again. Please, can we talk. I miss you and love you …" She hit the delete button hard.

"In your dreams," she said out loud, sounding sure and grounded and even confident, but she was haunted by memories in random places and times; without prethought she would remember things so sensual and loving. No, no she would tell herself, he's gone. But he wasn't gone, he lived inside every cell of her being and she would do anything to forget him.

Mary Kay entered the designated room at the hospital clinic. Her first time attending this Narcotics Anonymous meeting. She found a chair in the circle, hung her purse over the back and sat down. Almost all the ten seats were taken. The group leader spoke.

"Welcome, and congratulations on attending your first NA meeting at Granite Pass's Mountain View Hospital. I'm Rene Brown and I will be your facilitator. Today you will introduce yourselves and tell a little about your recovery story."

I hate this, thought Mary Kay, rubbing her sweaty palms together.

"Hello, and your name is?"

"Miguel Campara."

"Well Miguel, please tell us about yourself."

Obviously nervous, he stuttered at first. "Um hi, I'm Miguel and I, I am a drug addict. My story is short. I got hooked on heroin when I was in high school …"

Mary Kay was next. *How can you tell a lifetime in five minutes? I hate this so much and I hate myself…*

"So, Mom said 'Miguel, you are going to die just like your cousin Willy.' So here I am, I'm on methadone and that's about it."

Rene asked him, "How do you feel, how long has it been?"

"I feel honestly like coyote shit. I'm sick all the time. I don't want to die, but I don't know if I want to live bad enough to stop."

"Thanks for your honesty, Miguel." Rene looked at her list. "Mary Kay, oh there you are. Welcome, can you share a bit about yourself."

"I'm Mary Kay and I am an addict. This is my third relapse. I have a little boy, Owen, he is six. He has a disease called cystic fibrosis. It affects his lungs. They build up with phlegm and mucus and he can't breathe. His father and I are not together. He's been in my care mostly since he was born. It all started with all the nights I've spent up with him and his asthma attacks. Carting him to the ER, wondering if he was gonna die before I got there. I became used to never sleeping a full night. Don't get me wrong, his father is very good and supportive, but he lives in Portland. So …" she hung her head for a moment, looked up. "I started dating this guy and he gave me oxycontin to sleep. It was a miracle, but I had never drunk or done drugs before and once I realized I was addicted it was too late. My son's father was very understanding the first time I went to rehab and he took Owen to Portland. I overdosed again when I got out. Not sure why, maybe all the past trauma I dealt with as a child. I was lucky, able to enter another program, but but I," tears slid down her face, "I went out again, almost didn't want to live this time. His dad must have told him I was struggling again and this little precious boy sent me a video—my God, kids today," she wiped her eyes with her fists. "This message from him is why I am here today."

Rene interrupted, "Would you be willing to share the message with us?"

"Um, sure." She adjusted the volume. "Hi mommy, it's me, Owen. Daddy said I could Facetime you while he's in the shower. So, I miss you so much mommy. Dad said you have to take a test before you can come see me. Mommy, I know you can do it. Look at me I, take tests all the time, and it hurts and it's not fun but I do it because you and Dad always told me I was brave. You can be brave too, I know it. Remember how you always tell me I'm a hero? You are my hero, Mom, and you will now pass your test because from now on, every night I'm gonna round up all my dinosaurs and we are going to sing to you every night, 'GO Mary Kay, my pretty, nice mom, go Mary Kay be brave it will only hurt awhile,' and then you can hug me and I can see your smile. Go Mary Kay." She turned it off. "This sweet boy. I have to heal this, and I will for me first, but for him. His life has been so hard…I'm so sorry." Rene passed the Kleenex box to her.

"Mary Kay that was brave and we are all moved by your story," people nodded, dabbed at their eyes. "We believe you can and will get clean. Our next person to speak is …"

Please God, let it be, she thought, tucking the Kleenex into her pocket.

Lezah was driving back from another meeting at the gallery. She stayed afterwards signing a contract for a private commission. Hank had hovered after the couple left making conversation with Lezah who was about to leave, about the unusually warm weather, her plans for the weekend? He had stepped out, going for coffee and asked her to stay at the gallery until he returned. She was standing in the lobby, her purse, briefcase and coat piled on a chair next to her looking at the park across the street when suddenly a child that looked like Owen ran to the swing set. A man and woman followed him. Moving closer to the large glass doors it was Jackson carrying Owen's folded wheelchair. The woman was young and pretty. A feeling of dread washed over her. Already, he had moved on already? Hank came back, asking "isn't that your uh friend in the park?"

"Yes," she replied as casually as possible.

"Are you together with, I mean with him?"

"No, just a friend."

"Would you want to have dinner with me tonight?"

"Oh, um sorry but maybe another time."

A smile scrolled across his handsome face. "Well, okay I'll keep asking then."

Lezah shouldered the bag, grabbed the coat and purse, lowered her head and walked out.

Jackson was pushing the child on the swings. "My turn," called the woman. "Let your auntie Sarah push you while Dad goes to the restroom." Jackson turned around and walked towards the complex.

Lezah hurried to the car. Driving away she was shaking, angry with herself for still caring. The drive home was a blur as emotions tore her, negative judgments about her choices, the hurt she felt seeing him with the woman, which took up much time driving as she went over what she saw and heard in the brief moment as she was leaving. The woman said, "auntie Sarah," and Lezah did remember that was Jackson's sister's name, and she was blond like Jackson. These compulsive thoughts tracked her all the way home. Sunset, a fiery globe above a calm, teal sea. Once home she stripped, changed, and was soon running the path downhill. She cut across another trail, then two sets of rickety wooden stairs landed her on the littered shore.

Breathing in the moist air she walked among the trees that had sailed the sea, that came from ships and streams creating a boneyard at the base of the cliffs. Storm sent, these firs and redwoods came from the local mills or had been windblown down rain-swollen creeks and rivers. Roe had told her how when floating in huge rafts or even small slicks of driftwood, waterborne wood attracts plankton and small fish, which draws larger predatory fish like sharks and tuna. Shade, plenty of food, a place to lay eggs, and protection from waves provided new life from dead trees.

Moving among the helter-skelter of giant forms, the elaborate patterns of stacked logs turned every which way forming fantastic shelters, towers or sculptures an artist could humanize for hours. Wandering, wondering where a telephone-pole-sized trunk with unfamiliar patterned bark and palm fronds spiking its top, came from. Maybe Asia, as it stood on a shore its stiff sword-like leaves blowing, murmuring, sighing in a hot wind? How long did it take to travel thousands of miles across the sea? Was it adrift alone? Or with others? Is that what I am? Adrift? Sitting down on a smooth round log with sun warm on her face she remembered how she came here as a child and crawled through the low maze of tangled spaces, stopping to curl into the smallest ball her body could make, feeling protected and invisible, her baby cheek resting on the damp, grainy sand. She looked around spotting a large, thick root system that could be entered to provide shelter. Bending down, crawling inside, the curved roots cupping the sand, she gathered and removed a few small stones then lay down. Sun through slatted wood, the hypnotic rhythm of waves lulled her.

As she dreams of whales, sleep swims through the clear calm water. Her finned tail gently undulates, arcing lazily. Propelling her body downward, silver bubbles rise from her mouth. She hears their songs but cannot see them. Slanted sunlight cuts through the roof of the water above. Her strong arms pull in wide circles and as she searches the bottom, she sees bouquets of seaweeds anchored by their holdfasts. The cries again. A swiftly synchronized school of fish passes nearby, their choreography a flash of white, yellow, and black. She kicks out silently, turns her streamlined body downward, falling through the water's thick silence. Again, calls from below, sounding closer. Passing a constellation of sea stars crimson against the rocks, she dives deeper.

The whales, feeding below, rise. The mother and calf swim upward. Lezah feels the water cleaving around her, spinning her round and round. Their huge bodies rushing past her like islands encrusted with barnacles.

Helpless, their forceful rise pulls her upward too. The thrill of speed, eyes closed, allowing what is—up and up and up. Her head above water she sees the vertical towers of their bodies breach and seem to dance on the surface as they twist and dive again. She is sucked into their wake, rushes downward. The mother's big boat of a body slows as she floats towards the bottom again. The calf, curious, swims near Lezah. She can see its round dark eye. It nuzzles her with its nose. She reaches out, the skin soft and rubbery. The calf swims away, comes back, twists, spiraling fast around her body. She woke in the gloaming, the roots above her in shadow. Stiff, cold, she crawled out, sitting for a moment the stars just blinking on.

Thirteen

Lezah and Opal had finished lunch, chatting about the town's fall happenings. Lezah had been in Portland for a week for gallery fundraisers and show openings.

Opal's eyes brightened as she told Lezah about the meeting for the fall festival. "The mass disorganization that only a group of humans could create. Miscommunication to levels of absurdity."

Lezah noticed the sky darkening outside the window.

"And I said alright I will help with the Fiber Arts booth, but only four-hour shifts for this old lady ..."

Lezah said, "Yeah, eight hours is a killer at any age." She looked out of the open window and saw a set of black serrated, toothy clouds fly overhead.

"So Marion Johnstone volunteered and we are going to switch off. Can you donate something for the raffle?"

Lezah heard it before she knew what it was; what she heard was silence. "Hold on Opal, listen."

"Don't hear anything."

"Exactly." Lezah opened the front door. The clockwork of her life, the background sound that never ceased, the constant sound of waves was absent. "Opal listen—nothing, come look." The flattened water rushing out to sea leaving the waters around Seal Rock lower than low tide.

"Tsunami," said Opal quietly. "Right, Lezah?"

"Yes. The seals, I'm going. They have to move to high ground. They will be crushed by the weight of the water when it comes back."

"Don't go. They will make their own way."

"You know I have to. Go now...Opal, hurry up to the community center, I'll be fine."

She rushed out to the clothesline, grabbed the wetsuit and flippers, felt for her knife and fanny pack, leapt onto the path. How much time she wondered before the waves would come? It depended on the wind and its velocity.

She saw the seals on the closest haulout. She whistled and heads turned. A bull bellowed. Once on the other side, she threw the wetsuit down, held the shoulders and wiggled into it. Hurrying, she zipped it up, fastened the carabiner on the fanny pack around her waist and walked towards them. They came to her quickly, arcing, galumphing with all of their blubbered might. "Okay, it's alright, let me think. We must go up." She calculated at least three hundred feet. As a teenager in the summers she had led expeditions of rock climbers wanting to scale the seastacks. There used to be a path that circled the base of the nearest island. If they could make the distance to the island and then climb, there might be a chance. It was a short distance, doable as the seals could maneuver through the low water line and she could walk as they crossed to the other island. Both she and the seals paused to look at the exposed underwater plants and creatures where riotous colors had hypnotized tsunami watchers, she remembered reading, "so readily distracted they would approach the riches too long and end up drowning."

She whistled again. She led them to the island. Where was that path? She tried to remember. No way the slow-moving cumbersome beasts could climb a steep vertical.

The roaring wind surrounded them and the path was not in sight. Stopping a moment, searching the high rock walls and crevices, she glimpsed a line of green succulents traversing the middle section. She followed it downward with her eyes. There, it looked like a narrow path just ahead. They moved towards it, Lezah now concerned about the old one and the new mother hoping they could handle the rocky climb. Once at the base of the island they lined up behind Lezah.

So slow, so very slowly they maneuvered the first part

of the path. Galumphing, snakelike they followed one another in a slow but steady uphill drag, their heavy breathing audible. Lezah held onto clumps of sea grass and succulents reaching up, pulling herself upward. The wind picked up, the sea below them poised, still. Lezah knew they had to climb high to be above the wide waves rushing inland at hundreds of miles per hour. If liquid could be wound tight as a spring that's what the energy felt like, the water itself holding its own breath.

Lezah heard the warning sirens coming from Old Town and the community center. She glanced northeast at the jetty near the bay and watched pieces of broken boats, logs, and debris shoot out of the bay into the flattened ocean.

They were midway up, circling the island, when the wind came violently right at them. Lezah stopped, thinking they should wait before moving again. It was then that the young mother lost her balance and the new, late-born pup, fell to his death. The vocal creatures called and moaned, in their sad agitation. Lezah led them again to around the back of the island where she hoped to find a cave or shelter of some kind. The sun was dropping and her energy crashed, leaving her weak and shaky and scared. As night set in and the moon rose she saw the dark crevice ahead. It was a good-sized cave perched on the edge of what looked to be a solid enough refuge. With the howling wind pushing them up the last distance to the opening, Lezah went in first. A low ceiling, it was dark and maybe large enough to hold them all. One by one they crawled in, the three big bulls guarding the entrance. Torrential rain and blasts of wind so loud it sounded like gunshots inside the echoing cave.

The beasts were shaking. She scooted herself to the cave opening and watched as twelve-foot-high waves moving hundreds of miles per hour came slamming into the distant shore, the strength and power unbelievable. She shivered, the condensation dripping from the shallow ceiling chilling her skin where the ragged wetsuit was torn. Once settled, the mother cried even though the old one had moved closer to her. Soon all slept.

Lezah, exhausted, drifted between wild random thoughts and memories and questions about how they would survive. She had no water to drink. The seals got most of their fluids through food. They could wait a while but how long could she? Hunger ached inside her belly. She knew from fasting that the empty feeling would subside. Full dark framed her view of the cliffs and bluff. She assumed the power was out as only a few lights flickered from the Beach Loop homes. She floated between sleep and consciousness, flailing up out of a dream then falling back.

Where am I? Oh, the cave. Looking around, they were all there. Except the pup. Oh, the pup. The old one slept deeply, her whiskers twitching. Lezah knew the tsunami and its aftermath could last for days and there was no food available in the shallow cave. Traveling through time, all time being one time at the same time, she sees her mother in the ocean, her mother squatting, rocking back and forth in the low tide. She is naked and singing, looking out. Behind her stands the father. Her mother reaches down as waves surround her. Her head thrown back, she lifts the baby up into the air as the father comes close. They place her briefly in the water before she is breathing, the mother's hands holding her there, and then she lifts the child up onto her shoulder and they watch, their faces lit with love as she took her first breath. She had always doubted they loved or wanted her. Hmmm?

The young bulls bellowed the pod of seals awake and a barking chorus began, the banging wind played bass. Settling down, they adjusted their blubberous forms and slept. Lezah thinking, fear now her constant companion. Even if we stay in here until the tsunami is over, how will we all climb out and get down? The weight of the beasts, their inability to move quickly, and their general clumsiness would make it a dangerous descent. Hopefully the short wall built of sand, stones, and bird shit would protect them from the drop-off with its illusion of enclosure. It was all about the weather too, it must be clear, no storms. Her leg ached where she'd cut it climbing up. Slightly crusted over with a thin green scab, it began to throb. She couldn't think about tomorrow anymore. She curled up next to Pinni, her arm around her thick neck and slept and dreamt, and remembered the day Pinni was born. No one cared that Lezah swam in the water between the island and the beach's shore. Two seals were playing tag in the water when Pinni's mother swam over and birthed her pup right in front of five-year-old Lezah. When the pup was six weeks old it left the mother to learn to be on its own. The female seal had bonded with Lezah and followed her whether it was in the water or on the rocks.

The old one's breathing became labored, almost like a pant. Lezah felt the animal's life force waning, slowing. Holding her tighter she remembered how Brodie would stand on shore calling her to come in for lunch and nap time. She would stay in the water making him wait, knowing he would beat her for it, but also that it would postpone the horrible nap ritual.

Pinni nuzzled her. She woke remembering, actually seeing the group of them in the water when she was little, diving and playing and how it all stopped as Brodie stood on the shore calling her in. Pinni would come and circle swim around her, even jumping in front of Lezah as she slowly swam back to shore. How did the seal know? Perhaps it was the sound of Lezah's crying as he carried her along the beach. Over Brodie's massive shoulder Lezah watched as Pinni swam just beyond the waves her head up, watching, waiting, until they turned up through the dunes.

On the second day, she woke at dawn to hard rain, her dry throat aching from coughing all night. She unhooked one of the flippers from the fanny pack strap. Scooting on her belly to the cave entrance, moving as close as possible to the edge of the opening she held out the flipper and watched it fill with rainwater. She drank it slowly, relishing the coolness, the sweet flow of it.

The seals were stirring, waking up, groaning in the half light. "Hey," she called to them. "Good morning, Beasts." As light grew outside she could see that the houses on the bluffs were safe. No normal waves though the treacherous tides criss-crossed and boiled, then spread out, carrying fast-moving debris—the masts of broken sailboats, sleds, cars, and logs from the local mill. They would have to stay another day and night inside the cave. The seals could wait to eat, but could she? Never had hunger caused her pain like what she was experiencing. Probably due to what she could no longer deny. She grieved what she had not been able to do knowing it would haunt her the rest of her life.

The pod was lethargic most of the day napping, rolling around, draped over each other, snoring. She was dizzy, feeling weak by midday and nauseous, her mind fogged.

By early evening raindrops plunging, wind slamming, the ocean below. Very weak now, she hoped the vocalizing seals would stop their bawling soon. She nodded, unable to stay awake, falling into dream after dream, Jackson laughing with her on the beach, running from Brodie, her little girl legs shaking. Roe and a huge octopus swimming near her in the water. A mermaid, not one of her own, holding something in her arms.

She woke in deep dark, the cave a blur, the only sound the breathing of the seals. So hungry, her belly cramping, the weakness in her creating a crippling fear about having the strength to lead them out. No helicopter would ever find them. Yawning, overwhelmed by the mental exhaustion, she was lured once again into the safe oblivion of sleep.

Waking, overwhelmed mentally, physically failing, the cut on her leg infected. A noise in the back of the cave made her listen, the mother seal crying softly, the old one moaning. She turned in a circle and moved to the back on her hands and knees. The mother seal was on her back rolling around. Lezah noticed her swollen teats, most likely blocked by mastitis. She moved to the seal's side, face to face, the pain in her eyes held Lezah's as she reached over the seal's belly and grasped the leaking teat. Gently, she began to massage it to relieve the pressure for the animal. When the milk started to flow Lezah's mouth began to water. Again she unhooked the strap holding one of the flippers. Maneuvering the toe end of it into the right position she milked the fat rich fluid into the foot of the flipper until it was full. At first the emptiness in her belly cramped but then welcomed the warm milk. After finishing it she curled between the young and old seals, and exhausted from her fearful thoughts she dozed again.

Dawn, a clear day, the water had retreated leaving the beach exposed at the base of the cliffs, littered with pieces from houses that sat low behind the dunes. Some underwater, only their identical seagull chimneys visible.

IT WAS NOW. She raised up on her knees barely able

to withstand the pain in her leg. "Come on, come on everybody." She reached out, gently slapping the ones near her. "Let's move, now!" She crawled towards the back of the cave; the mother seal was coming towards her, then passed her. Lezah glimpsed Pinni curled in the very back corner, her eyes closed; her breathing labored, she moved her head. "Hey girl, oh Pinni, old girl." She opened her eyes, looked right into Lezah's, then she sighed and closed them and left her body there in the damp cave. Lezah put her hand on Pinni's head for a long moment. Opal had been her earth mother. Pinni had been her water mother.

Crawling back to the opening, the seals were waiting, agitated and vocalizing, restless. Good, she thought, we will need that spirit. Sun sparked the entrance, bouncing off the reflected water, blinding them. Lezah went out first, weakly standing on the cave's lip that jutted out above a cluster of boulders below. A short jump, her leg throbbing, she looked above at the lineup waiting to move across to the boulders and down. Two males in the lead then the females and young, then two males in back. She sat down, using her hands to straddle the boulders that led down to the narrow path. Slowly, so very slowly was their descent. Hours later the nine seals and Lezah were coming close to the island's base where they could swim back to Seal Rock Lagoon. Racing daylight, her body weak, dehydrated, she doubted she could swim the length of white-capped water to the lagoon. Once down, they moved to a pool of rainwater and drank deeply, Lezah cupping her hands, gulping with them. With whiskers dripping they paused as Lezah turned and spit up bile onto the sand. She would not make it, not enough strength, her body feeling weak all over. The lead bull barked as he swam out. This moment the only one, to go before the tide rose. The others followed splashing, turning on their backs diving, resurfacing.

If she stayed, the high tide would trap her there. Better to drown than be crushed against the rocks. The two males moved out, the females and pups stayed in the middle as the younger males headed up the rear. Lezah knelt and unhooked the flippers, put them on and dove in. The pod would stay close to one another swimming out slowly, their heads up, watching. At first Lezah felt light, buoyed up by the water, the cut on her leg numbed by the cold. So weak, the seals moved further away. She tried to stay with them. Panicking, she called out "Hey." The mothers stopped and turned towards her. She couldn't move, felt herself sinking, her head thrown back as she passed out. The female seals torpedoed through the water circling her, closing in with their bodies, holding her up. They floated out to the open sea between the two islands and stayed together in a floating bobbing knot.

Jackson heard news of the tsunami on his car radio as he drove home. It had peaked in Banderlay around six pm. He called Lezah, no answer. He had wished many times that he had Opal's number but knew that would overstep a boundary. *I'm going.* He parked in his driveway, left the car running. A few minutes later he came out with a change of clothes in his backpack and rain gear in case. Energized with adrenaline, he set out on the four-hour drive with a feeling of dread and faint hope she would see him.

He had driven straight through only stopping once for gas. The weather was wild most of the way. Thunder, lightning, and harsh winds. He pulled into the front of Lezah's shop. Pitch black. He took out his headlamp and went to the door. The doorbells had fallen on to the welcome mat. He put them back on the door knob. Knocked, called her name once more, sighed, checked the knob again. Open, hmm. He walked inside, the headlamp lighting up the way. "Lezah?" He thought, I need to check in case. Upstairs, "Lezah?" nothing. Back downstairs he closed the turquoise door. Driving to Opal's he hoped she would talk to him. God knows what Lezah told her about their breakup. He parked, looked below at the black water. He knocked softly as a light went on inside.

"Hello, who is it?"

"It's Jackson."

"Oh Jackson, hello."

"Are you alright? Where is Lezah, I was just there and …"

"Come in please. Lezah swam away with the seals."

"What?"

"She led them to safety. I couldn't stop her, as usual. I'm so worried. But as soon as the sun is up the helicopters will be out looking again. Meanwhile I'm glad for your company. I decided to stay here, wait it out, safe enough up here on the bluff." She moved to the stove and lit the burner. "Please sit down. I'll make us some tea and toast."

"I was so sorry to hear about your husband."

"Thanks, I miss him so...His absence is so, so large."

"I remember that. My dad died when I was sixteen. It was like this sudden void, especially the physical absence. How is Lezah?"

"She's not handling it well. Roe's been the only man she loved, trusted. Lezah has trust issues." She rose from the table, went to the window, silent for an uncomfortable moment. Jackson, waiting, then unable to stop the question he asked, "what happened to her, Opal?" He watched her body recoil, the look of uncertainty on her face, while she put cups on a tray.

Opal thought, *should I tell him? Does he deserve to know? Of course, he loves her, seems so deeply concerned. If she did how would it affect her relationship with Lezah now or in the future?* In the end it was the way Jackson's eyes held hers, waiting. Once she started, the story tumbled out uncontrollably, her unrecognized need to tell it stronger than the consequences. He listened intently, never asking a question. She left no detail out. At times he wiped his eyes or shook his head in disbelief. It was the recent confession from Lezah about Brodie that she held back for a moment, but only a moment because it came flooding out too with all of the tamped down emotion about what Lezah had endured. It was too much and she lost control, her fear screaming that Lezah was lost or dead. Jackson stood too and took her into his arms where for a very long time Opal cried and keened. Coming back around, she moved away from Jackson in search of her handkerchief.

"Here it is."

"Thank you. I needed that more than I knew." He had sat back down, his head in his hands. "How are you, Jackson? Do you understand her better now?"

He nodded. Why? But why? "Did that child have to go through that, Opal? And to carry it all this time? You didn't know?"

"I suspected there was more. But I couldn't prove it until she told me. This new information about...Brodie all of this coming up at the time when Lezah had just met you. Another layer of her healing coming forward at an inconvenient time, eh? Or maybe not, maybe you needed to know to decide if you truly want to be with her?"

"Oh I do more than anything, but I don't think she wants me, especially now. She won't talk to me or see me."

"Yes, her convictions are one of her best and worst qualities. She's in love with you."

"She is? Are you sure, because ..."

"I'm sure. But she won't be with you as long as you have that job."

"I quit. She was right, it was not what I thought or was told."

"She's carrying your child."

"What did you say? Um—my child? She said she was on birth control?"

"Something about missing a pill in the redwoods. She was never going to have a child. I went to the clinic with her but she couldn't do it." She poured their tea as Jackson paced.

He held his hands out. "Opal, how can I gain her trust? Let her know I want her and the child. What if she is lost out there or, or worse and I didn't have the chance to tell her?"

"We can only pray. You look so tired. Why don't you go rest in the loft. It's all made up and comfy. Let me show you. First though, I'll cook some eggs on the wood stove. Gotta keep up our strength." He slept fitfully most of the day. In the evening he carried wood into the house and helped Opal fix the workshop door that had come off its hinges. "You will find his tools inside. I can't, I can't go in there, Jackson."

"I understand, I can do this."

On the third morning Opal's cell phone rang. "Okay Curly, thanks. The Sheriff, the heli saw something between the islands not sure but it's moving towards their haulout. Let's go look." She picked up the binoculars and went outside. She could see the haulout from the stairs, saw nothing, passed them to Jackson. "Look by those three big rocks. That's where they usually …"

"I see something on the shore—a seal, I don't know, it's not moving. Oh a few seals in the water, diving and surfacing."

"Let me look, that's them, Lezah's seals—I recognize them. C'mon let's go down. I'll grab my shoes."

On the way down the path Jackson silently prayed, *please God, whoever and whatever you are, please let her live.* He held onto Opal's arm near the bottom. They hurried across the beach. Opal's cell rang again. "Yes, Curly we are going to the haulout now. Not sure what we saw but Lezah's seals are there. Okay, will do."

Jackson took off his shoes, glanced at the water, look at the other shore. For a split second fear gripped his gut, then disappeared as he swam out into the lagoon, veering towards the place where he'd seen something from the house. Adrenaline high, sweat in his eyes, he stumbled to shore looking all around. The seals were in the water watching him. Climbing around the giant boulders, "please, please," he pleaded. "Lezah!" He called "Lezah!" and then right in front of him he saw her lying on the sand, her feet in the water, her arms over her head, so still. *Oh God,* he ran, bent down, picked her up. She was unconscious.

When Opal saw him swimming back with Lezah she had hoped, but when he came ashore carrying her limp body Opal started screaming "No no no!" Jackson laid her down and started breathing, pushing, breathing.

The wild clutter on the beach blocked the helicopter from landing near them. After setting down on the bluff above, the medics were able to walk downhill with the stretcher. One started an IV, the other checked her pulse. "Faint but there," he called as he moved her to the stretcher.

"I have to go with her," Opal yelled.

"Okay mam, but you'll have to keep up with us up the hill, we will be taking off right away."

"What hospital?" Jackson asked as they turned and started walking toward the path.

"School's Bay."

"C'mon Opal, I'll drive you there now." He took her trembling hand and led her.

At the top they watched the helicopter lift off. "Will she live, Jackson?"

"I don't know. They found a pulse. Do you need anything from your house?"

"Yes, I should pack a bag and bring Lezah clothes too.

Just a robe and pajamas for now."

Jackson said, "I'll go get them. I'll lock the door when I leave and bring you the key. Be right back."

"Yes, look in the armoire. I'll be ready," Opal called.

As he drove the few blocks to the shop he saw houses with shutters ripped off, collapsed porches, a greenhouse upended. He left the car running, the door open, and sprinted to the porch. Once inside, looking around, all seemed in order. Moving upstairs, through the beaded curtain, he went to the armoire, found both a robe and pajamas, and put them into a backpack by the door. A gust of wind blew open the window in the alcove. Latching it, he turned, noticing the paint-stained sheet on the floor. The enormous painting overwhelmed the small space. Moving back a bit he stared at it, a strange sound came from his throat. Below the pale yellow moon and rising turquoise sea were he and Lezah holding one another, clinging passionately, desperately as if parting, her face tucked under his chin, his red hat resting on her long wet hair. Transfixed, frozen, then hurrying, backpack in hand he couldn't control the tears. Downstairs he took the keys from the register drawer, went out, locked the door. Once in the car he gathered himself, sitting for a moment, calming down for Opal and what lay ahead.

It took a whole hour just to get out onto the Pacific highway. Traffic both leaving and coming in caused bottlenecks in the small town. Jackson went to turn on the radio to cushion silence between he and Opal, but then remembered that he didn't have the EcoAir company car, but the radioless Honda. The hospital parking lot was almost full. They spent an hour in the waiting room. Opal finally was told that Lezah was in surgery. They said she would be in recovery soon, that she would be awake in a few hours.

In the hospital cafeteria people were coming in for the dinner shift. Jackson had forgotten what institutional food smelled like and took a pre-made sandwich out of the case. Opal, too upset to eat, had tea and picked at a pastry. Back at the ER desk they called Opal's name. She went to the glass window. Jackson overheard the nurse.

"Are you Lezah Boudrow's power of attorney?"

"Um I'm not sure. I'm her legal guardian. Why?"

"Well, the doctor wants a fetal ultrasound right away and Ms. Boudrow cannot give permission in this moment. Jackson stood up, walked to the window. Oh, are you the father because …"

"Yes, I believe I am. Can I give permission?"

"If you have a paternity test, easy quick cheek swab?"

"Okay." He followed her to the lab. When he returned he found Opal speaking with a doctor in the waiting room.

"Well that is all good news. Thank you so much." He nodded and walked away.

"Jackson, that's Lezah's doctor. He said she will be fine. They stitched up her injured leg and started her on antibiotics. Oh and the baby is good. Three and a half months term, and it is yours."

Jackson swallowed, nodded. "When can we see her?"

"They said she is awake now. I'll go first?"

"Yes okay. I'll wait here."

It was alarming for Opal to see all the wires and ways Lezah was hooked up to the machines. The nurse checking her pulse said everything looked normal. "Just don't stay too long, she needs rest." Opal moved to the bed, Lezah so pale, her hair tucked up in a floral cap.

"Honey?" Lezah opened her eyes as Opal took her hand.

"Hi. Opal," she said weakly. "What happened? My leg? The seals? The—?"

"Well not sure. After you left the house you were gone three nights during the tsunami."

Lezah sat up a little, groaning. "I found a cave, we stayed there. Once we came down I was too weak and sick. All I remember. Where did you, did they find me?"

"Seal Rock Lagoon."

"How? There's no way."

The nurse came back, "Well good. You are sitting up a little. Here is the ultrasound pic," she smiled. "Thought you might want to see it. Oh and I gave the father his copy. He is waiting to come in. I'll be back later."

After she left Lezah looked at Opal, "what father?"

"Lezah, Jackson came on the first night. He stayed with me while we waited. We had time to talk and ..."

"What did you tell him? Oh no, you didn't? He knows? About the...pregnancy? Opal how could you?" She started crying.

"Here she is." Jackson stood in the doorway as the nurse left.

"Lezah," he held the ultrasound picture in both hands, "I, I just want to say ..."

"Get out," she said. Her voice low and angry. "Stay away from me. I never, ever want to see you again." She covered her eyes with her hands, "Opal, make him leave. Now!"

Opal shook her head, looked at Jackson as he stepped back into the hallway and followed him. "I'm so sorry Jackson. She's not in her right mind. I'll keep you posted. I've got your number now." The last he heard was Lezah crying, saying I don't want him near me, I don't want him or it...Lezah turned her face away. Opal came back in, stood by her bed.

"Honey, you need to rest now. I've rented a motel for tonight right around the corner." She handed the nurse a card. "Here's their number, room 396. You need to sleep and heal, don't worry. We can go home tomorrow if your leg looks good." She bent and kissed the top of Lezah's head.

"Okay, we will call you if she needs you. Have a good night."

Fourteen

Ski yawned, his body feeling like jelly. He swallowed more pills.

"Oh yeah it could be worse." He looked around the office; all was in order. The letter to Jackson would go out in the last mail pickup. The letter to his niece as well. She in turn would get ahold of Jackson about Toby. All neat, tidy. He kicked off his shoes and reclined in the chair.

"Okay, oh so sleepy." He stumbled to the door, unlocked it, heard people leaving for the day, chatting in the hallway. He'd told his secretary to take tomorrow off. No use her finding him or his niece if he'd croaked at home. Probably the guy? What's the word? His eyes closed, head thrown back, he nodded out, came to. Oh yeah the janitor, that's who would find him. Good, that's clean. Reaching across the desk for the framed picture of Toby he slid it towards him, held it to his chest and took his last breath.

Jackson decided to drive home after the scene at the hospital. He was exhausted and so sad. Her last words repeated in his head. "I don't want him or it." That pretty much was the end of any hope he had harbored. What she had been through, the fact that she lived, it was insane, unbelievable. All he could do was check in with Opal in the next few days...The painting? It was THEM. When had she finished it? There was so much she didn't know. He looked at the manila envelope lying on the seat in the half light. The ultrasound image of their child. *Oh my God.* He swerved slightly, correcting right away.

All so unreal, thought Jackson. Owen would be going to school soon, the sitter would drop him off. He could barely keep his eyes open. Learning about the baby changed it all. If she didn't want to raise it he thought he would maybe, he was at least looking at that possibility. He would not want strangers raising his child. Suddenly sunrise in Portland, blush of light on the mountain peaks. He was so tired, longing for his bed as he finally pulled into the driveway. A light went on inside, he was hoping Owen would be asleep so he could get a few hours. But no such luck, the little guy cracked the door open, then came out and waved to him.

"Hi daddy, good morning."

"Good morning son." Shouldering the pack, he walked up the driveway. "How are you? School today?"

"Yes."

He ruffled his hair.

"Yes, I'm sharing my dinos. Glad you are safe from the stewnami."

Betty, the sitter came to the door as he entered. "Hi Mr. Craig."

"Hey Owen, give Dad a hug, and come get dressed. It's donut day!"

"Yay!" Owen put his arms around Jackson's knees."

"Okay, see you later when you get home." He showered and passed out.

Owen waved to the bus driver, went inside and set the lunch box by the door. "Daddy?" He looked in Jackson's room and saw that he was still asleep. Okay, he would get a snack and watch a show and not wake him up yet. I will not use the toaster or the stove. Hmm. He looked in the cupboard, graham crackers, okay. He took juice out of the fridge, poured some carefully into a mug. He set the bottle down on the table, noticing the big yellow envelope. Chewing the graham cracker, he turned the envelope over. Reading since he was four, he read *ultrasound image Boudrow-Craig.* He knew ultrasound 'cause he'd had so many of them over the years. Boudrow, that was Lezah's name, and Craig, that was his and his dad's name.

He squeezed the metal tab, it pushed up easily and the flap opened. He looked towards the hallway, carefully slid the picture out. It was weird, not a real picture. Dark and white shadows showed a lump with a head turned sideways. A small hand near a mouth. What is it? He looked at the writing on the bottom, Female 13 weeks, School's Bay Hospital. Oh no, was Lezah or Daddy sick? He put it back in the envelope, pushed the gold wings down on the flap. He took a sip of juice. Jackson stumbled out into the hallway.

Yawning and rubbing his eyes. "Hey Owen, you're home, I slept in. Be right back." He came out in shirt and flannel pants. "Already got your snack?" He reached for the coffee pot.

"Dad, what is this?"

Shit. Jackson started the coffee. *I'm not even awake and I for sure don't know what the fuck is going on with my life and now pre-coffee I'm supposed to explain it to a six-year-old.* "Um, it's an X-ray type of thing."

"It's weird, I looked at it. Is it a monster? Part human, part alien, part frog?"

"No it's not a monster. It's an unborn baby."

"Oh…is it alive?"

"Yes it is," he said, as he spilled the cream. *Quick, quick, should I tell him, no. Everything is too uncertain?*

"So Dad, you know what I read on this big yellow envelope, your name and Lezah's and School Bay Hospital, are you and Lezah sick?"

"No, Owen we are fine. Really healthy."

At the bottom he pointed to the small print. "I didn't know this word," he spelled it out, "F E M A L E. What does that mean?"

Jackson stirred the coffee with an unsteady hand. "It means, Owen, that the baby in the picture is a...girl."

"Oh...I see. Whose baby is it?"

"Did you have lunch? Are you hungry? 'Cause I'm starving."

"Yes Dad, it's Tuesday, I had lunch at school and I'm eating these grahm crackers now."

"Uh-huh, how was school? Did the kids love your dinos?"

"No, I didn't share them. They wouldn't come out of my backpack. They were too shy."

Jackson sat down across from the boy. "What should we do this afternoon? Maybe your dinos want to go to the lake?"

"We can decide later, not right now, Dad. Please tell me why is you and Lezah's name on this?"

Inner panic. *What should he say?* No matter how it all played out the child would know eventually, he'd never lied to him. "Owen, before Lezah and I stopped dating, remember we talked about that? She and I made a baby. It's in her belly now. That's a picture of it." He massaged the back of his neck, sighed, turned his head from side to side. Everything hurt head to toe from…

"So is that thing my sister, Dad?"

Here we go, "It's your half sister because you have different mothers."

"Oh, okay. When will it be borned?"

"In the spring, I think. There are many things to be worked out between me and Lezah about this baby."

"Okay, Dad." He put his hand on the envelope. Shook his head. "I told you aliens were real."

He smiled. "It won't look like that when it's born."

"Good! I'm a go get all my dinosaurs ready for the lake." He put his cup in the sink and ran out.

How could I possibly parent another child? There is no way. He heard Owen from another room say, "Tyrone, you have to wear a sweater, it might be cold. Dad, the T-rex won't wear his sweater!"

"Put it in the backpack in case." His phone went off. Mary Kay, *can't, can't talk to her now it will be an hour. Oh my God, what else? Don't ask,* he thought. "C'mon Owen, let's go." On the way out he checked the mailbox. Unfamiliar handwriting slanted to the left addressed him as Mr. Craig. "What? Hold on Owen." He opened the letter. Skimmed it, saw Ski's signature. "Wait, what? Hey,

Owen—can you watch a show for ten minutes?"

"Sure, Dad."

Settling into the chair, he read:

Dear Jackson,

Hi ya, Ski here. Well here goes, I'm kinda loopy from the pain meds. I've got an advanced cancerous brain tumor. Those damn headaches, ya know? So my doc says I've got a few weeks maybe a month. Should be quick and painless he said, but what the hell does he know?

Now I'm gonna tell you about the changes to EcoAir, which are not good news. They are ramping up the geo-engineering programs around the world. A big move to control the weather part of it, but they are adding biologicals to the sprays. You know flus, viruses, and worse.

Did you know I was in Nam and flew planes over the Ho Chi Minh Trail? We sprayed and made it rain for years. The gooks couldn't receive their supplies and equipment or get out. Weather Warfare, it works! I did some other things over there that I'm not proud of. Agent Orange. I just blocked it all out when I came home. I worked as an engineer for thirty years and when I got the job offer from EcoAir I couldn't resist the money. Mary Mother of God, was over the top. At first I believed that the spraying was okay, protecting folks from the sizzling heat coming through the ozone layer...You know the story. But when I started to pay attention, I noticed things and it got weird real quick. The global warming thing was becoming popular. But get this, I knew that geoengineering was heating up the atmosphere. WTF. At first I was told the chems used were harmless, uh yeah right. Barium, strontium, even aluminum. And then they started mixing in nanoparticles. This shit can't be good for whatever it lands on. Come to find out it's never been tested on flora, fauna, or us. We are all breathing it every day. I was gonna hang in another year and if ole man death weren't stalking me I would quit now. No more hurting people, I'm exposing all I can, sending out info packets to government agencies around the world. That should do it. By the way, I fired you this week, faked the paperwork, used your unavailability because of the kid's illness as a reason. You know nothing, right? Don't worry, there are other jobs.

I've left the duplex to my niece Stacy and money so she can finish nursing school and for after. She is getting my newer truck. You're probably wondering why I'm telling you all this. Well, it's about my dog Toby. Best dog in the world. Only four years old. I'm usually home a lot, but when I wasn't my niece took care of Toby. I can't see my niece having her full-time when I'm gone. I don't know what to do. I know this is a long shot, but would you and your boy want her? I will pay for all her expenses for her lifetime and pay monthly for her care. Ya know Jackson, when I got to know you and saw how much you love your kid it moved me. Not something that happens that often, but it reminded me, your boy is lucky too. Maybe you guys would want Toby? I mean that would be the best for her, but wouldn't it cheer up your little guy too? She's hypoallergenic. By the way, she loves to ride in the car. And she loves Bob's Big Cheeseburgers, and kids. Think about it, please. If it works for you, Stacy will get in touch with you after I'm gone.

Been nice knowing you,

Ski.

Wow! Jackson read it again. Okay, so I quit last week, but he fired me too? Holy shit, biologicals? Sure Owen would love a dog, especially a hypoallergenic one."

Another call. "Hey Mark"

"Jackson, did you hear, Ski died in his office last night? He did something. Shit is gonna fly."

"Thanks, no, I hadn't heard. I'm outta there. I quit last week. Good luck. Bye."

"Dad it's been 10 minutes and 21 and a half seconds."

His cell rang. "Hello, yes it is." Wow things were happening fast. "Yes yes Ski told me about you and the dog. Yes I just heard, I'm sorry for your loss. Whuh, I see, well, um, finals, huh. Okay, where do you live? Okay, yes I know that part of town. Your address—gotta pen, yes, 413 Oak Ct. Okay, I could come now I guess, about forty minutes—will that work? See you then." What the hell, he looked over at Owen.

"Son, the man I worked for has died."

"Why?"

"Cancer and he had a dog and there is no one to take care of the dog who is a girl named Toby. Maybe, not for sure, but do you want to go pick her up and see if we can help find her a home?"

"Okay, Dad, she can stay in my room until she finds a home, okay?"

Jackson shook his head, *what the? was happening?*

Jackson had never seen an animal-boy connection like the one Toby and Owen shared immediately. No sooner had they entered the duplex than boy and dog were all over each other. Stacy had all of the dog's toys (so many) and dishes and bed and leashes packed up, also a bag of dry food and gourmet meat cans. She was beautiful, a red-golden doodle covered in curls.

"Well, I will miss her," the young woman said.

"You can come visit her," piped Owen. She handed Jackson an envelope. Once in the car, the boy in back strapped in his booster seat with the dog between him and the window, both had big smiles. Life, thought Jackson... Wow oh, he almost missed the turn off to Bob's Bigboy. He made a U-turn. "Hungry?"

"Starved," said Owen. The dog became animated as they pulled in the drive-through line. Owen rolled the window down when it was their turn. The girl behind the window said, "Hi Toby Girl."

Surprised, Jackson said, "do you know her?"

"Sure, she's a regular customer. I know what she wants, a double cheeseburger, right girl?" Toby's tongue hung happily out one side of her mouth. "What can I get for you all?"

"Three cheeseburgers and two OJs."

"Sure thing."

After a few minutes she handed him the food. They parked and ate.

"Dad, look there's a bounce house, can we go after we eat, park over there and jump?"

"C'mere." He wiped ketchup off the boy's mouth. "Okay, for a few minutes." The dog followed him and dove right into the squishy colored balls after Owen. There was no one else around so Jackson let it be. He reached into his shirt pocket and removed the folded envelope.

Dear Jackson,

Well, if you got this from my niece then I'm passed on. Thank you, for taking Toby. This should be enough money to cover her for her life and a little extra for you. Do me a favor. Do something good with the money.

Ski

Jackson took the folded check out of the envelope and opened it. *No, no way, is this real?* To Jackson Craig, one million dollars & no/100. It seemed official, from a local big bank. He looked over at the bounce house, the kid and dog jumping for joy. If someone had told him even last year where he would be today he wouldn't believe it. Holy shit.

"Dad, Dada." Owen rushed towards him. "We have to go to the bathroom! Toby too."

"Owen, a dog is not allowed to go with you. Here Toby," he held out his hand to the dog. "Over there Owen, that green building." The boy turned and ran and the dog whimpered.

"It's okay girl, I have a feeling you two will be spending plenty of time with each other."

Opal cut carrots to add to the pot of chicken soup. Believing that food was literally medicine she had also baked bread and made a big salad. Lezah had slept straight through that first day out of the hospital, only waking to shower and eat some oatmeal. This morning, Opal hoped they would be able to talk about Jackson. She sensed that Lezah felt betrayed by her breach of confidence and maybe well she should, but Opal wanted her to know why.

Lezah woke at mid-morning, limping to the bathroom. Opal heard her throwing up. Came and knocked on the door. "You okay?"

"Yes." She came out, sat on the couch. Opal propped up her bandaged leg with a pillow.

"How's your pain?"

"Not bad. At least in my body. What happened with Jackson? Why would you tell him about the dock and Brodie?"

"I'm glad you asked. I actually spent two days with him. He arrived in the night of the first day of the tsunami. Had gone to your shop to check on you, then came here. I was grateful for the company, being I was alone and all. We talked for the next two days. He helped me bring in wood, fixed the door. We waited together to hear any news about your safety. He is so in love with you. He asked me at one point, 'Opal, what happened to Lezah?' He was so sincere, concerned and it all just came out and I needed to see his reaction. He has things, important news to tell you. And Lezah, for what it's worth, he is such a kind, wonderful man. He has a right to know about the baby and to have a say in what you decide now. That's it. If I hadn't shared it <u>all</u> I would never know who he really is."

"I can't be with him, Opal. Look out of the window even now, right after a tsunami they are spraying again. I can't …"

"You need to meet with him and hear what he has to say. It may change your mind. Regardless, he deserves to speak with you one last time."

Lezah gagged and hobbled to the bathroom. Leaning over the toilet all she could think was "No, no, I can't." The painting, had he seen it? Had she left it covered?

After washing her hands and returning to sit on the couch she told Opal, "I feel betrayed. I'll be honest."

"I know, but let me explain. Under any other circumstances I would have never interfered. My grandmother taught rule number one, you must have been asked or have permission before giving assistance. I had neither from you, and I must admit there was on a personal level a terrible need to share it with someone else that loved you, and," she paused, "Jackson asked me, Lezah."

"Oh, I see, so you feel that he is a good person?"

Opal didn't hesitate. "Yes, yes I do. Another reason I chose to tell him the truth. You know how so many couples today are unhappy in their relationships. And we know as women about the male-dominated world. There is a war between men and women, you see, and until that war subsides there will be no world peace. A power struggle between the old and the new is typical of change. And then I see you and Jackson knowing how you both feel about one another, your journey so far, and I believe you and he could rise above that pattern and be a loving couple. And family." Lezah stiffened, looked away. "Only five months until you have the child. Don't you think and feel that he has a right to participate? Running away, keeping the child from him? That's not going to work for anyone."

Lezah shook her head, "Opal, I can't be with him. He is knowingly hurting people. I won't be with someone like that, ever."

"Please trust me Lezah, things have changed in his life. I'm not at liberty…you need to see him, in person and figure this out."

"You are so sure and strong in your opinion. You've never been like this before."

"Yes, I know. Please take that into consideration."

Lezah was relieved to return to work, anything to keep her distracted. She was still in denial about the pregnancy. She told the nurse at the clinic the she was considering adoption, as she registered as a single mother. Opal hadn't brought up anything about Jackson in weeks. Every time Lezah tried to imagine contacting him she became anxious and depressed. To compartmentalize and stash the reality way way back in her mind worked, until the late shift on Sunday. She was drying glasses behind the bar when reaching up to place one on a high shelf, she felt a fishtail swish of movement in her belly. "Oh!" Was that the…then it happened again. Three hard pokes in a row. She set down the towel, walked through the empty room to the open back door. She stood looking out on the bay, a full moon reflecting on the water. A low rush of wind rippling the water caused the chains on the dock to clang and creak. She was that little girl again, screaming in pain, bent over on the toilet as she passed the fetus, Opal crooning "alright, alright it's over now honey." Not over, she thought. Never. How could she go through with it and survive—how?

Carey came out and lit his end of the night cigarette, blew four smoke rings into the air. "How ya doing, Lezah?"

"Doing okay, Carey."

He yawned.

"Hey go home, I'll lock up. Just have to finish the glasses."

"Okay, I will. See ya tomorrow." He threw his apron into the hamper and went out the back door.

After putting the wine glasses away she heard Jamie's voice in the kitchen.

"Hey, anybody home? Lezah?" He came to the bar. "Back door wide open, saw your car."

"Hi, oh good, yes I'm locking up. Want a beer?"

"Sure. Your leg all better?"

"Almost, still tender after a long shift. How was your night?"

"Good, motel's almost booked. Been better tips!"

"Jamie, I have things I need to tell you, I guess now is as good a time as any."

"Sure."

She brought him a beer. They stood outside, the moon sparking the windblown bay.

"Okay, after a lot of therapy, some you have known about, back in my twenties I felt I had dealt with the abuse issue. I walled off, blacked it out, dealt with, cured, finished. Well, not so fast because when I met Jackson memories surfaced from my childhood.

"I was pregnant at age twelve, you didn't know that did you? Opal helped me have a herbal abortion. A month later Brodie right over there on the dock," she pointed. "He put his hands under my shirt and picked me up and I screamed and he slipped and fell and hit his head, blood all over, then he stopped moving. I panicked and squatted down and rolled him into the bay. I've only told Opal. I needed to tell you, because..." She looked down and shook her head, "because ..."

He set the beer on the ground, turned, and faced her eye to eye.

"Lezah, I suspected there was more to the story for ten or more years now."

"What? How?" she asked.

"Roe. We sat on the beach one summer, and your name came up. I asked him how you were. You were in Portland doing art school and a lot of therapy. He started talking, you know how that was, and he just told me that he was in the bay that morning checking traps. He'd said fog was thick as snot. He heard a scream, thought he saw you running away. Then Brodie's body floated up right next to the boat. Lezah, he said that Brodie was chalk white, that he must have bled out on the dock."

Lezah stunned, took in a breath. "Oh Jamie, that means...he died before I pushed him?"

He moved in closer, put his arm around her. "Yes."

Shaking, tears streaming, "Oh Jamie, that means so much. There is more to tell." She bent down, picked up a rock and threw it into the water. "I'm pregnant."

"You are? How, I mean I know but you have been so careful ..."

"Yes, but I missed a pill while we were in the redwoods. Anyway, I'm almost four months already. I tried, went to the clinic, but couldn't go through with it."

"Oh girl, how did Jackson react?"

"I've barely talked with him since the breakup. I'm gearing up for adoption and then I might just move, go to Portland, disappear. I don't know."

"Whoa, that doesn't sound like the Lezah I know. You've never run away from anything. No way you two couldn't get back together?"

"No, never. I can't be with him."

"Okay, but you would be a great mother."

"No I wouldn't. How and why would I bring a child

into this world? A world where humans ravish the earth, rape and gouge its surface, mine it to extract the black oil that's killing us. We shoot beams deep into the earth causing earthquakes. We are polluting the sky. No Jamie, why would I expose an innocent being to this life? Air, water, food, our minds all poisoned."

"I know, I know, maybe he would want to raise the child?"

"Oh God." She bent forward, her hands over her eyes. "I can't, can't do this anymore."

"C'mere. C'mere, Lezah." He put his arms around her.

"I hear you, why would you want to bring a baby here. Well, maybe to help the world? By joining a family that works to make it better? And it's already almost here, girl, and it's yours ..." Lezah silent for a moment.

"C'mon." She closed and locked the back door, took her coat and purse from the office, locked the front. Jamie waved. "Gonna be alright," he called as she crossed the deserted street.

She put her hand in the air, blew him a kiss before she got into the Buick. On the big curve on Beach Loop where Seal Rock sat below the cliffs, in the middle of the Seastack Islands, she pulled over. Getting out, she walked to the edge. Looking below at the beach, watching the silken pewter waves, the wind strong on her back, she felt it again, circular spinning, then three swift soft kicks.

Fifteen

Morning broke with a low tide and a cold, thick fog, but Lezah knew by midday it would burn off. She ate a bowl of oatmeal, then packed an apple, cheese, and crackers for her lunch. She was in need of escape and truly excited—gathering and drying seaweed was one of her favorite things. She pulled on a pair of blue jeans cut off at the ankles, a tank top, and her ancient black sweatshirt. After putting on wool socks she laced her hiking boots carefully, remembering the time when tripping over a loose shoelace had caused her to stumble and fall partway down the steep incline to the cove below. After brushing out her long curly hair and wrestling it into a ponytail she sprayed the top and sides with water so loose tendrils wouldn't block her view down the cliff face. She put the food and a water bottle into a backpack, then went downstairs to the shop. She filled Mesmer's bowl with cat chow, giving him a quick, "Good morning, you old guy," as she briskly stroked his big, black body from head to tail.

Outside, the sun glowed faintly through the thinning fog as she went to the old shed to get a five-gallon bucket. The heavy door wheezed open. Leaning into the dark, dank space, a spiderweb brushed her cheek, setting off a shiver and a tightening in her chest. *No,* she told herself, taking in deep breaths as she grabbed the bucket and slammed the door. Still breathing the tightness away, she turned and focused on the new pink clouds, the long stretch of low tide. Then with eyes closed she inhaled the cool, freshened scent of the sea, after loading the backpack and bucket into the trunk of the Buick.

She drove along Beach Loop Drive. There were no other cars this early, only a few people out walking their dogs. She noticed some new houses being built along the cliff. She was always amazed at people's taste in architecture and style as they built their "dream beach houses." Such a variety, the only common denominator: they were almost always huge, lavish, and mansion-like. These owners who came for a few weeks in summer or on holidays were not really part of the small community. The little coastal town had prospered until the 2008 financial crash. Now, five years later, with the tourist trade dwindling, many homes were for sale and almost half of the quaint shops in Old Town had closed.

The sun burned brighter as she turned onto Highway 101. While she drove the ten or so miles to the hidden cove, she remembered the first time Opal had shown her the seaweeds. She must have been only six or seven. They had walked from Opal's house to the beach at low tide.

The seaweeds were so pretty! Bright colors and varied shapes. Opal collected and dried certain ones to snack on or to use in soups or stews. Lezah's child self had called them sea flowers instead of seaweeds from then on. Once, home on a break from art school in Portland, Lezah found dried ones on the beach after a high tide and began collaging them onto her paintings.

Soon the big, twisted cypress loomed, signaling her turn onto an unmarked road. The blooming Scotch gorse on both sides was an intense hot yellow. The plant, one of the most invasive, was the scourge of Banderlay. Fortunes were spent in attempts to eradicate it. It had greatly contributed to the fires that had burned the town to the ground twice, in 1914 and 1936. Lezah secretly loved it because its long, sharp thorns kept people out but protected birds, feral cats, kittens, and small brown rabbits. Crows rose up and scattered while she parked her car near the overlook. She gathered the few supplies and checked to make sure her shoelaces were tight and her knife was in her pocket. Bucket in hand, she stood at the narrow trailhead. Below she could see tide pools, their centers shimmering under the newly emerged sun. Further out, waves at the lowest tide formed long, silver lines pooling around the exposed bases of the regal seastacks.

At one point where the path turned she was able to stop for a moment to peer into the exotic center of a native white iris clinging to the cliff face. She skittered on loose stones, heard them falling and hitting the narrow beach far below. She remembered coming here with Opal when she was a teen. They had just gotten to this same point when Lezah somehow slipped and slid, feet first, the rest of the way to the bottom. Opal, usually calm, had let out a yelp, then she too lost her balance and tumbled down the last stretch, landing right on top of Lezah who was examining her bleeding elbows and knees. Both safe, they had laughed and laughed, tears streaming down their faces.

Today at the halfway point Lezah focused on the path, calculating each step, aware of any and all obstructions such as rocks, roots above ground, unexpected gullies, or pitfalls of mud or bird shit. The bottom seemed to come quickly, causing her to jump flat-footed onto the dampened beach. Walking towards the nearest tide pool she felt the now full-blown sun on her back. She sat down on a scooped-out seat in a cluster of boulders and pulled the sweatshirt and tank over her head with one tug. Warmth soaked into her chilled belly and breasts. Sighing, she savored the heat on her bare skin; the feeling of it melted deep into her bones. Surprised by hunger pangs, she opened the backpack and methodically removed the apple, cheese, and crackers. First a bite of apple, then a piece of cheese, then a cracker. While she ate, she eyed a squadron of pelicans, gliding and soaring, falling in and out of formation.

The surface of the tide pool glinted. She knelt in the wet sand, popped the lid off the bucket. There were a number of seaweeds floating on the surface. She submerged the lip of the bucket, gently tipped it, and held it steady. Several seaweeds floated into the container. First a piece of feather boa kelp, its green, fringed tendrils swaying in the water. Near it, red needle and thread, its long, beaded strands splayed on the surface. She checked to make sure it was not attached to a holdfast. Then with her fingers she pulled it through the water and captured it. Moving to the next pool she found her favorite, sea lettuce, the pale green translucence almost ethereal, the edges ruffled like a petticoat. Nearby, *Delesseria,* its delicate pinkish-purple leaflets rising from a midrib. Thinking she had enough, she picked some purple Irish moss off the rocks, knowing how much Opal loved to eat it. She stared out at the approaching waves that came in slyly, slowly, then slopped onto the shore. Wind fiddled, encircled the beach. The sun was suddenly shrouded by a cold, wet fog. Shivering, she pulled on her tank and sweatshirt. For safety she pounded the lid back onto the bucket with her small fists.

The trip back up the cliff was now compromised by thick fog. She put on her backpack and started walking to where she thought the path began. It took a few minutes of disorientation before she located it. Intent on balancing the heavy sloshing bucket and squinting through the fog swirling around her, she slowly, one step at a time, finally arrived at the overlook.

Once back home and sequestered in her warm apartment, tea in hand, Lezah sat down with the bucket and the plant press. Handmade by Roe, the press was one foot square, consisting of twenty layers of heavy cardboard secured by leather straps. Taking thick watercolor paper and dipping it into the bucket of seawater, she retrieved a piece of seaweed. She let the water slide off, leaving the seaweed centered on the paper. She then laid the paper in the press, placing another layer of paper on top to help absorb the moisture, followed by a piece of cardboard. Patiently she repeated the sequence until there was a stack of seaweeds in the press. Then she positioned the wooden lid of the press on top and pulled the leather straps around the press from bottom to the top, where the buckles would meet and could be pulled and cinched down tightly. Every day for six weeks she would undo the press, switch out the wet sheets of paper with dry sheets, then restack the seaweeds and cinch down the press again. This process was essential for the seaweeds to dry thoroughly.

Well worth it! she thought to herself. She loved the way the sea flowers floated realistically in the underwater world of her mermaid paintings. Washing her hands at the sink she heard the doorbells in the shop and walked downstairs. Jackson was standing in the middle of the room, Mesmer twirling and purring around his ankles.

"Hello Lezah, please can we talk. I have to tell you some things, please?"

She walked to the front door and flipped the open sign and locked the door. "Yes, come upstairs." *Here it is,* she thought as she opened the turquoise door. Mesmer followed her. Jackson's feet heavy on the stairs as she parted the curtain, held it open as he came in. They faced each other, their eyes anxious and fearful, both frozen in place. The intensity unbearable.

"I don't know where to start?"

"I'll make tea" said Lezah, breaking the spell. "Are you hungry?"

"No, no thanks." He sat down at the kitchen table, looked out to the blue white-capped water, his hands trembling in his lap. He said, "I have something important to tell you, before we, uh talk." Neither spoke as Lezah poured the hot water into the teapot, set the cups on a tray and brought it to the table.

"Alright, Jackson," her voice soft as she poured the oolong and sat down across from him. "Alright."

"First I, I need you to understand how desperate I was to get Owen the care he needed. I did not know about geoengineering when I took the job. It didn't take long though, for me to figure it all out. You were right, it's terrible, an unbelievable crime against humanity…I quit before my first paycheck and my boss fired me too, long story. I'm not who you think I am."

Lezah fixated on his words, the fetus spinning round and round.

"Can you forgive me for making a mistake, for falling for their BS? I've learned so much, it's about to get worse. It has to stop…and Lezah. I'm so grateful for what we've shared and …"

"You don't know me, Jackson." With her heart in her throat she asked, "Didn't Opal tell you about my uncle?"

His body slumped. Head down, he took in a few audible breaths, looked at her. "Yes, yes she did. She said that she had to tell me the whole story, to learn certain important things and...Oh my God Lezah I can't imagine," his voice sad and low, "what you had to endure. You were just a child...an innocent little girl who feared for her life. How can I judge you for that? I love and respect you even more now that I know."

Silence, the tea steaming, the distant tumble and rush of the breaking waves below. Jackson twisted in the chair, leaned forward. "So," his fingers softly drumming the table. "So Owen found out about the...um baby. He saw the ultrasound image and asked me what it was. I told him it was a baby you and I made before we stopped being together. He asked if it was his sister and said it looked like an alien." He smiled. "That kid. I told him you and I had to decide about the baby. 'Decide what? Just make up and give me my sister.' He sighed. "So here I am, Lezah. Remember me before geoengineering? How I loved you and you loved me? Do you remember us? I want you and this child, but I'm aware of your position and it's your choice, it's your life, but honestly I can't stand the idea of some stranger raising our daughter. So I'm here to say if you don't want to raise the child, I will."

When he said "our daughter," something insider her dissolved, a hardness dislodged as his words washed over her. He watched her rise, calling "This, this," as she approached the easel and grasped the sheet, letting it fall to the floor. "This is us, Jackson."

Staring at it for a moment he looked back at her. He stood up. "When I came to check on you during the tsunami I saw your painting, it's what gave me the guts to come here today." He took her in his arms, and as they embraced, the child within smiled.

Jackson in the shower holding Owen, the steam filling the room.

"Lezah call the ambulance, this is a bad one." The sound of Owen's wheezing other worldly, the intervals between terrifying. The small rural hospital ER had been alerted and the oxygen en route had helped. Still, Lezah in the waiting room couldn't settle herself down. Recently after Jackson and Owen had moved to Banderlay and they were still remodeling the shop, Owen had an asthma attack. Jackson thought maybe because even though they had been aware and careful there was dust and other irritants in the air. Owen recovered quickly with the help of his inhaler that time. This incident had led to a conversation about the care and management of a child with cystic fibrosis. Lezah read about the disease, and in distress questioned Jackson about Owen's predicted lifespan.

"These kids don't have a normal life or a normal lifespan. They are known to die mostly as young adults."

"Oh no, really?"

"It's a genetic disease; both parents have to have the gene, so our baby should be fine if you don't have the defect."

Sitting there, seeing Owen on the stretcher as nurses and doctors ran to the room, the sounds he was making. The voice, "Positive for red zone." Owen trying to talk between gasps. "Dad, Dad I can't." Jackson's quiet voice answering.

What if? What if this baby has it? Fear rose up, heating her face and neck. *Don't, don't what if.* Jackson came out.

"He's stabilized." Sitting down next to her, he rubbed his temples and yawned. "They want to keep him overnight. Good idea, that episode was beyond me, I'm used to his asthma, but that was more complicated. I need to call Mary Kay. How are you? Scary, huh?" He walked down the hallway for a few minutes, returned.

"One good thing, Mary Kay is doing well in her current rehab. I hope she can recover. We need to do this parenting thing together. I'm going to go with him to his room, say goodnight. Wanna come?"

"No, I'll wait here. Hug him for me."

"Will do, be back soon."

She had read that they would check the baby after birth for the CF gene. Poor Owen, his little life so affected by his health. Would she be able to handle one of these episodes on her own? Perhaps, if she didn't also have an infant to care for as well. That feeling in her chest, the rapid heart rate rising. *Breathe, she told herself. Shit. Breathe.*

"He said to hug you back. He's sleepy. You okay? You look—what's up?"

"Just tired. I have to admit that was...intense."

He sat down, put his arm around her. "I know it must have been frightening, I'm used to it I guess. You know what the good thing is? Because I paid off enough bills he was admitted here. My insurance covered it. I still can't believe Ski did that. So grateful."

"Me too and I love the way we changed The Mermaid into our home and the plans for the new gallery/shop."

"Let's go home," he said.

"Alright." In that moment she felt capable again, even a little brave. *Remember, you are not alone and Opal is there...*

Opal up at dawn, the moon sinking, expanding light at the window. Today was the day! She looked around the kitchen, coffee made, fresh cinnamon rolls cooling on the counter, sandwiches for Espe and her daughter Amarilla and her boy in the fridge.

"Roe." She went to the altar. Picked up the salt shaker

she kept some of Roe's ashes in and shook the gray grains into her hand. "Honey." She sprinkled them into the vase of hydrangea. "Our girl, we always shared everything about her with each other and now...She's going to have a baby in the next few hours! I'm to be a grandmother to a little girl—my heart could burst—the only thing, you're not here." Picking up a piece of blue sea glass she held it up to the window, banishing fear. Moving the Mary and child statue to the center of the altar, she prayed. Lezah's desire to birth the child near the ocean or if in stormy weather inside the warm comfortable tent Opal understood, and her need to be near the lagoon of course. And with the midwives up the hill at the A-frame it all felt safe and respectful of the new mother's wishes and boundaries...and the hospital was only ten minutes away. She lit a white candle. Next she set the Quan Yin statue on the altar and lit a red candle then looked at the Asian mother's face, her hands holding the world. "Peace please, in all things," she whispered, "let the past be past."

Next she placed the Celtic crone statue in front of the others. She spoke to the veiled woman holding a raven. "Mother of life, death, and rebirth teach me how to hold my new callings, that of crone, widow, and grandmother."

Lezah's message this morning let her know that she was in the early stages and that they were having breakfast with Owen and would check in when it was time to go to the beach. Lezah had shared her fear of the birth bringing up the past. She told Opal of the vision she had in the cave, of her mother birthing her in the ocean and how for the first time she knew that her parents loved and wanted her, at least in the beginning...Opal put the vase of flowers in the middle of the table for the meal afterwards. They had kept her name a secret. She couldn't wait to hold her...

By noon Lezah's surges were stronger. She had to stop and breathe in between. After Owen was settled at Opal's, happily playing with Espe's grandson and Toby, she and Jackson walked to the beach. He held her hand as they approached the tent that was enclosed by the driftwood structure that he and Owen had built. She bent down and crawled inside. It was so warm and pretty with Opal's quilts covering the mattress, a bouquet of white iris on the little table where water and an apple rested. A suitcase was packed with supplies that might be needed during labor.

"Look inside, Jackson, it's so cozy here."

He bent down, looked inside. "Oh it is."

She stood up and Lezah came out.

"Hopefully I will have her near the water." Jackson nodded, feeling a rush of nervousness.

"It will be alright, please don't worry, birth is natural—hold on." She closed her eyes, her face concentrated as she blew air through her lips. "I think I'm about four or five centimeters now. It will be more intense from now on. Hey don't look so scared. You're supposed to help me be brave, remember?" She reached up and kissed him.

"Well you know, Owen's birth was a nightmare. We didn't know if he would live or not."

"Well let it go, look at him now. I need to walk, come with?" She smiled but inside she felt a twinge of fear, questioning if this plan had been the right way to go. Suddenly she heard Roe's voice, "Ah c'mon, kiddo, you were made to do this, right?" She bent and picked up a mussel shell, let the sun spark its prismatic inside then threw it.

"Feel?" She took his hand and placed it on her rock-hard belly.

"Oh my God!"

"Yeah, that's the force that surrounds the baby as the contractions push it further downward." They were closer to the lagoon. The seals not hauled out anywhere that they could see.

"I need to keep moving." That morning before getting up she had talked to the baby girl, asking for her to come quickly, safely, easily. Her belly tightened again. For the next few hours they walked for miles in the rare bright day, an omen, hopefully, for what the night would bring. At sundown Lezah finally crawled inside the tent with Jackson holding her as her surges were one after another.

"Woah, I think it's time to call Opal."

"Okay." Jackson sat up. "Opal? Hi. It's going well, pretty intense, Lezah said to ask you to come now! Okay. Thanks."

"She's on her way. Look at the sky, Leez." Lavender and pink lit the edges of the falling sun.

Opal brought sandwiches and a thermos of tea. The tide was turning at sundown, pulling further and further out, exposing tide pools and red sea stars clinging to the rock faces. "I need to walk again." For the next hour they all walked, stopping every few minutes so Lezah could breathe and pant quietly. If it was an especially strong one she would let go of Opal's hand and face Jackson, her arms around his neck, swaying with rising discomfort, a soft song coming from her lips, then they would walk along the beach again mostly silent. Lezah felt a distinct change as the baby's head moved downward, stopping her in her tracks. "Um let's turn around, okay." Slowly, slowly they returned to the tent. Lezah went inside, grateful to lie down. She could see the lagoon and Seal Rock through the opening and the seals, their eyes moonlit. "Can't stay still." She rose up on her knees swaying back and forth side to side. "Help me up, Jackson." She took a few steps then stopped as her water spilled onto the sand. "Opal, is it clear?" Opal came over and held her headlamp above the sand.

"Yes, it's clear." Jackson sighed.

"I'm having more pressure. Can you put the blankets by the shore?" She bent over, panting. Once situated on the beach Lezah had little control as her body began to push the child out. Pain receded in between these new long contractions. Sometimes on her knees or suddenly squatting or standing, her body changing positions to accommodate the birth. Opal, her grandmother's rosary moving through her hands, Jackson sitting, waiting.

"Opal, bring the other blanket, Jackson take off my jacket."

"Oh oh oh." She was squatting and pushing. "Can you see the head?"

Jackson, looked "Yes!"

"I need you, Opal, to steady me." Opal came to her back and knelt so Lezah could lean on her.

"She is coming, you guys oh oh oh. Jackson, catch her!" The baby slipped into his big hands, her eyes already open. "Opal, help me up, Jackson," she put her arms out and held the child against her chest as the child took her first breath. After taking a few steps she squatted as the placenta released. She walked to a tide pool, after checking for creatures, she slipped down into it, the baby still attached by her cord and sank beneath the water, coming up quickly, the baby quiet, looking all around. "We need to cut the cord, help me please." They helped her climb out then while her arms were wrapped around the child, they walked slowly to the tent. Jackson helped Lezah get settled, the child already nursing. "Jackson, the scissors are in the suitcase." He came back. She showed him where and how to cut the cord.

Opal came in. "That was—oh my stars, Lezah you were amazing!"

Lezah smiled. "We were a good team. Ouch! This little girl is strong. What do you look like?" She gently unlatched her from her breast and held her out. She had never cried and seemed just so alert and aware.

"Hello, sweet girl," Lezah crooned, "Happy Birthday. Time for your daddy to hold you." She put her into Jackson's arms; he could not stop staring at her tiny face.

"Hey there ..." Glancing up he asked, "Is it me? Or parental pride? But isn't she just so so, beautiful."

Afterwards the little A-frame buzzed with excited energy welcoming the baby girl. No one was surprised that her birth was near the lagoon in a brimful tide pool, or that Lezah, an hour afterwards, walked up the hill. Espe and Amarilla announcing that they knew all was going well on the beach, because the blessed mother told them. All gathered round the doll-like newborn wrapped in a lavender angora blanket made by Opal, admiring her pink skin and wide blue eyes. Owen, standing near her, looked up to Lezah and Jackson. "What's her secret name?"

Lezah smiled. "Her name is Velella."

"Vanilla?" asked Owen.

"It rhymes with vanilla only with els. Velella. Her whole name is Velella Blue Opal Boudrow Craig. Velella is the name of a little creature that has a blue light seen at night, called wind sailors."

Owen stroked the umber down on the infant's head and said "Hello Velella Vanilla, you still kinda look alien but Dad, Lezah, can I hold her?"

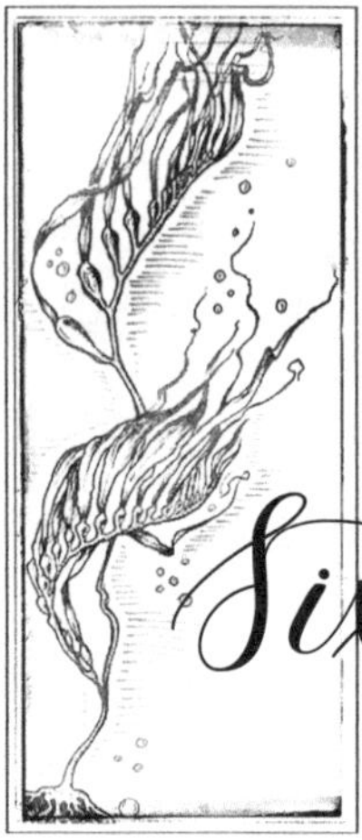

Sixteen

One Year Later

Lezah stood inside the new modular building that housed the environmental center and The Mermaid Shop and gallery. It looked so great, she thought, the big room painted all white, a whole wall presenting the history of Banderlay, including maps and photos of the seastacks. The gallery area displayed photographs of twenty-five chemical trails in different formations. On a table near the display were pamphlets and CDs discussing weather geoengineering. The opening was a few days away; she was almost ready. This evening she had explained to Jackson that she needed time to herself for the next few hours. He said of course, he would do dinner and tuck the kids in. "What's up?"

"I'm doing some, letting go… can I explain later? Don't worry I'll be getting rid of some of the trash out back. Thank you, see you in a few hours." It had drizzled all day so Lezah changed into some rain pants and a waterproof jacket. She carried a small suitcase as she walked to the back of the property. Stopping, she looked at the shed from a distance. Brodie would lock her in there, sometimes for days. She had asked Opal for advice about how to do a letting go prayer ritual. Opal said her grandmother taught her that the best way to banish, do away with or let go was often done with the element of fire.

The building had been stripped of the roof and walls leaving the four corner posts, floor, and a large pile of burnables in the middle of the floor. Walking closer she picked up the small can of gas and set the suitcase down. Twisting off the lid she poured the gas all over the bare bones of the shed. Moving a distance away from the building she opened the suitcase and took out scraps of watercolor paper on which she had written things to let go of. SHAME.

She walked back to the building and used the lighter to ignite the piece of paper, surprised by the loud sound as the remodel burnables blazed up into flames, shooting sparks into the sky. SHAME.

Her hand-wringing embarrassment about being dirty, wearing rags to school. The pity she saw in people's eyes. The disgrace of belonging to the town drunk. The ridicule of the school children, their condemnation of her clothes, her hair, the empty lunchbox. "Shame, I release you NOW!" One of the corner posts cracked, split in two and fell to the ground. Reaching for another piece of paper from the suitcase she drew FEAR.

Fear—she had come a long way from this monster, but living for twelve years in a state of impending danger, distress emotions high causing her to feel a constant sense of doom didn't disappear when she moved in with Opal and Roe. The nonspecific anxiety she carried along with her deep insecurity made her have to prove herself in all ways, be it grades, sports, work ethics, art. With each thought she tore off another piece of paper from the whole and fed it to the fire.

The last piece had the word Innocence written on it. The loss of innocence being perhaps the worst theft. Living life with a cynical eye, a distrust of all, even herself. The fire roared now, devouring the wood scraps, timber, and trash. Turning away from the intense heat she thought about the changes in her life. How there were people who loved her. Yes, it was time to forgive herself for being a frightened child who feared for her life.

The fire died down, sparks floated in the cold damp air. There was one more act to complete. Lezah bent and picked up the mermaid doll from her childhood, the one Opal had made her. It was torn and tattered, the metallic green yarn on the tail shredded. But the curly brown hair fell over the yellow top and the doll's smile was still visible. She held it to her chest and thanked it for all the comfort it had brought her. She whispered "Goodbye," and then threw her into smoldering coals.

Jackson rocked his baby girl. Even after a year he still found himself staring at her face. Her skin was Lezah's, darker than his, a honey quality compared to his fairer complexion. Her eyes, the lightest, bluest blue like his but she had Lezah's dark lashes and eyebrows. Her hair was a fluff of blond down. Her smile lit the night. She was so different from Owen as a baby, who was sick and fragile. This little being was healthy and energetic, thankfully. Her tests revealed that she did not have the cystic fibrosis gene. He looked over at Owen, sound asleep, cuddling T-rex, and felt an overwhelming rush of love…He slowly stood up, cradling Velella, kissed her forehead then laid her down in the crib.

There it is, oh yes there it is, Opal said to herself as she rummaged through the ancient suitcase. She lifted a piece of lace and held it up, fingering the intricate knots and tiny textured flowers. This had been a piece from her English grandmother's collar. She put it in the basket at her feet, remembering the old women with an accent who came to live with her family when Opal was a girl. They called her Gran. Mostly invisible, she either stayed in her camper, which she called her caravan, or she was in the garden she planted behind their humble house. Opal loved her and vice versa; their teacher-student relationship eased the reality of their poor and uninteresting life.

Yet people came from all around for herbal remedies

and Gran's prayer rituals. Opal was her assistant at the altar, placing a flower representing fertility in a vase at the right moment or lighting the candles in front of the goddess statues and laying a Celtic cross on the altar cloth. The tiny piece of lace would fit nicely somewhere and the energy of her gift in the garden "passed to the child's hands." Suddenly Opal teared up, as she never really thought she would be passing down generational knowing to a granddaughter. She would tell Velella and Lezah about her grandmother someday. In the meantime she needed to decide where to stitch the lace on the body of the doll. She had sewn the mermaid doll out of a piece of Lezah's discarded canvas. This material represented Lezah's overall strong protection of the baby throughout her life. After Opal "dressed" the doll the bright colors would represent art and expression.

Roe's fishing hat sat on the arm of the chair. The baseball-style cap's letters had never been readable. A khaki green cap with no symbol insignia or brand. Holding it, Opal was flooded with memories. Roe young and handsome on the wharf flirting with her while she worked. Roe with Lezah on his shoulders, the child wearing his hat sideways. Roe in his chair on the beach smiling at her as she handed him his evening sandwich and warm beer. She couldn't resist holding the inside headband close to her face searching for a trace of his spicy scent. She found a tattered piece of the green cloth and added it to the basket. Wishing the child the sweetness and patience of her grandfather.

She had stitched the face early on, big blue eyes, rosy cheeks, a long length of curly hair. She glanced at the clock, after one am! Better get rest, tomorrow is a huge day. She pinned the piece of lace so it became a lacy top. The tail she covered in a shimmery blue left from a prom dress she'd sewn for Lezah in high school. Yawning, she held it up. Baby V would like it, she thought, it reminded her of the one she'd made for Lezah so long ago.

Lezah, already so far away, watched the baby toddle through the dunes climbing the grassy hummocks, falling, getting up again, sand on her bottom as she ran for the beach. Lezah could not keep up with her. She called "Stop, No, No Stop," but she knew the child could not hear her...She was breathing heavily when she awoke, the last image of the dream the baby sitting close to the shoreline, waiting. Turning over in the big bed she heard whispering, then a small hand touched hers.

"Morning, Lezah?" Owen held Velella. Toby in tow, the room was filled with sunlight.

"Come here, come in." She turned back the comforter and patted the empty space. "Where's Papa?"

"He's on a run, he said when he gets back he will make special pancakes because it is a special day, right Vanilla?"

"And what special day is that?" asked Lezah smiling

as they scrambled up onto the bed, one on each side. The baby clapped.

"Happy birthday to you," Owen sang.

"Ice keem, ice keem." Jackson heard their laughter as he showered quickly.

"What's going on in here? I heard laughing, did I hear laughing?" The children screeched and pretended terror, hiding their faces in the pillows.

"Big daddy is gonna get you, no laughing."

"No, no, save us, Lezah."

"Of course, you are saved." She waved an imaginary wand.

"Get in with us, your hair is drippy," said Owen.

Velella plopped herself into Jackson's lap once he settled. "Is today your birthday?"

"Yes."

"What is a birthday?"

"Ice keem," she screamed.

He smiled, "distilled down to the most important element. What else, mama Lezah? Are we having a few friends for dinner?"

"It's up to fifty-eight I think."

"Are you ready? Can I help?"

"It's fairly covered. Zach and Jamie are bringing massive amounts of salads. Opal has been baking for days. Espe and Amarilla are bringing chile rellenos and Zach is barbecuing the fish and steaks. Did I tell you last night?"

"Night night?" said Velella.

"I forgot, I was so tired. The Portland Prestige news channel is covering the opening. Maraya Perez, head of GeoWatch, is being interviewed."

"Wow, that's so cool. The photography show looks great."

"Hungy Hungy" the baby whispered, her blue eyes wide.

"Me too!"

"Okay it's unanimous, pancakes coming right up, first a wrestle!"

"Yay, yay." Tickling, giggling. Trilled melodies of baby laughter filled the room.

"Okay Mom, I've got the vest and my meds, clothes, and books and toys all packed for my weekend at Dad's. I'm excited about the Grand Opening, why do they call it grand?"

Mary Kay smiled, "maybe it's to make people think it will be a 'great event.'"

"It will be. Dad and Lezah and me and Vanilla worked so hard to get it ready last time."

"I'll bet you did, I'm excited to see your new house and shop."

"Mom, isn't it so cool that we live closer now? Because you are in School's Bay and only twenty miles away. Only twenty miles. I like the week with you, the new school is good, and then I go to Dad and Lezah's on weekends. Perfect huh. I'll put my stuff in the car. Okay?"

"Sounds good." She looked in the mirror: a little make-up, her hair washed and curled, not bad. She was nervous, a little bit, but had gotten to know Lezah and found her to be warm and friendly and a good *other mother*, as Owen called her. She and Jackson had been so kind helping her find an apartment that was workable for her and Owen. Owen was thrilled with the location near both a large park and the beach. She'd found a job through her rehab program with the county mental health office as a receptionist. It had been hell the last year but she did it, recovered, and felt good about her life and being Owen's mother.

"Mom! You coming?"

"Yes, be right there."

Jamie pushed his chair back from the computer, stretched his arms over his head. So much he thought they were discovering, so much needed information. Geoengineering websites were being produced and people were talking more about the white skies, but mostly in 2014 people around the world were, he shook his head, mostly looking down at their phones. He actually liked doing the research, knowing what other people thought and theorized. The groups that first came to School's Bay had the best most current AND scientific info, he thought. Truth be told he might not have made it through the almost long-distance breakup with Zach if he hadn't been so engaged, really obsessed with studying all the data and information he could find.

The Scottish Enviro Center had been a great source and he felt lucky that he was now privy to their worldwide research. They were in full support of the center Jackson and Lezah were opening. The sprays were constant now, the norm, blue skies in the early morning, sprays, then white sky the rest of the day. They even sprayed at night. Jamie had seen the plastic particles in the air with a flashlight. Blood tests were showing high levels of aluminum, barium, and strontium. The big lie about "contrails" was alive and well. The buzz in the small movement was that legislative changes were a waste of time as the government and Military Industrial Complex created and supported the whole program. Educating the public was the only way to stop it. The powers that be were saying they were not spraying but would be trying it in the near future. How fucking stupid did they think people were?

"Jamie? Jamie?"

"In the office. Hey Zach."

"Hey there, I need your opinion. I'm finishing up the lil armchair for Lezah's baby girl. Could you take a look, tell me what you think about the trim for it?"

"Sure, are you having fun?"

"I am, I'm excited. It's a template for a whole line of teeny upholstered baby armchairs. Grans and gramps will go crazy, whaddya think? Come see?"

They walked to the garage studio. "Here she is." The small rocking chair was upholstered in a mermaid print in soft pastel colors.

"This, I thought at first because it made it pop. But the lighter trim keeps it soft and watery. What do you think?"

"I agree, the lighter one. You're right, you are going to sell those like crazy. You need a boy version."

"Umm, I'm nervous to see Lezah. You know before I left for my parents, I wasn't onboard with the chemtrail stuff. I said some things and I doubted both of you. Now you know how when I got to Philly and saw the extent of the chem shit show there I became a believer, but I never told Lezah or apologized."

"Zach, Lezah I bet took nothing you said personally. She will be so happy to see you."

"I want to tell her how it happened while I was at my parents'. How over the S. Philly skies there was no denying it, thick, constant sprays every day. We have way less here on the coast. Anyway, got your food all ready to go?"

"Sure do. Potato salad, mac salad, slaw, just have to pack it up. Wait until you meet Velella, oh my."

What had been the shop became their home and a new modular building had been set up next door becoming The Mermaid Shop, Gallery and Ocean Center. The sign said 'Grand Opening Today, Barbecue 3 pm.'

Morning came, with dense cold fog that hung about and lingered until mid-morning. The sun appeared around ten am, the doors opened at eleven. Lezah was prepping vegetables in the shop's small kitchen when she heard "Hey Hello? Anybody there?" Jamie and Zachary wandered in looking around, taking it all in, carrying their dishes, big smiles on their faces.

"Lezah, oh my God this is fabulous!"

"I know, I'm so excited, so happy you like it, Zach. Here, put your dishes here. Missed you, give me a hug."

"I like the layout," Jamie said, "I like the way the shop items and gallery are combined. Art on the walls and lovely things showcased on the floor." He walked over to the gallery wall. "These are amazing, are they Maraya's?"

"Yes James, a picture is worth a thousand words, isn't it. The Portland Gallery wants it next."

He turned. "Art and activism, hear that Zach?"

Zach sighed, "that is cool. Um, Lezah I want to apologize for being rude and questioning you and Jamie about the sprays. When I got to Philly it was so obvious. Every day, every single day morning through night...I was just so sure our government wouldn't ..."

"Zach, it's okay," she interrupted. "It's hard to believe, but Jamie and I have a saying, 'It's not about belief it's about observation.' How was your trip, your dad?"

"Good, he's better, recovering from the heart attack. Where is the munchkin?"

"That's right, you haven't met my daughter, have you? Opal is bringing her over any minute." Her cell chimed. "Hello, yes this is Lezah. Oh! Uh. That would be great. What time? Great, we will be ready for you. Guys, that was the *Schools' Bay News.* They're coming this afternoon to interview us. Jamie, you will be speaking, you know how I get nervous and all."

"No problem. I'll do it but you have to stand next to me, team effort as it is, okay?"

"Deal. Zach would you put the tablecloths on the tables? Hmm, could you two move the tables here?" she pointed, "end to end. It's a buffet. Maybe a group of chairs over here for folks to sit and eat."

"Where is Jackson?"

"Conference call with Terrance and Maeve. They got

the funding to expand the education program in the US. Such good news, it's been a challenge having Jackson in Europe so much. He will be based here from now on. Oh I hear someone." Opal came into the room carrying Velella, who was babbling on and on.

"Velella!"

"Mama."

"How's she been? Come and meet Uncle Zachary." She took her from Opal and walked up to Zach.

"OMG you didn't warn me she was gorgeous. Hello Princess."

They all watched as the child checked him out. She leaned in, her eyes on him, then smiled and held her chubby arms out to him. Zach, caught off guard, melted.

"Oh yes, come here baby girl." She went to him quickly. Opal, observing, remembered the incident last month in the gallery when Velella was toddling around while her mother helped a customer. The woman's husband said "Hi" to the baby and she held her arms up. He laughed and scooped her up off the ground. Lezah turned in that moment and saw him lift her and she lost it, rushing to him, taking the baby back, yelling, "what do you think you are doing??" The customers both in shock stood frozen.

Opal stepped in. "Here Lezah, I'll take her, time for her nap. C'mon baby Vee."

After she walked out Lezah apologized and tried to explain, the baby was so friendly to strangers and and there had been an incident recently and and and…

"We understand," said the woman, "you can't be too safe these days. Well thanks. Nice place, have a good day."

After she calmed down she realized that no matter what she did to deny it, she would never be able to fully protect her daughter. Owen and Mary Kay arrived, Owen so sweet introducing everyone to his mommy. Suddenly people started arriving. Lezah greeted them, introducing herself and Zach and Jamie. She began answering questions, walking people through the art exhibit explaining what geoengineering was and what The Ocean Center was all about.

The crowd held steady throughout the afternoon and the buffet meal was a success. Jamie and Lezah were interviewed by Portland's *Prestige News*, the tag line, "What are those strange lines in the sky?" They asked Maraya Perez to discuss GeoWatch's commitment to educating the public with facts and true science. After the crowds all left the family celebrated Velella's first birthday. She performed the ritual with the messy eating of a cupcake and clapped when they sang to her. Toby was under the high chair scarfing fallen scraps and Owen tried to teach her to blow out the candle with all laughing as she blew loud raspberries.

Zach went out to the car and brought in the little chair, the child running to it and sitting down.

“That is so adorable,” Lezah said. “You should do a Children of the Sea line of nursery furniture.”

Zach beamed. “My thoughts exactly.”

“Look Vanilla, it rocks.” Owen pushed the back of the chair gently.

“And Gran has a present for you too.” Opal handed her the mermaid doll. Velella hugged it to her chest. Lezah took in a breath.

“Do you remember the one I made for you, Lezah?”

“Yes, yes I sure do.”

During the event Jackson had run interference, being the best gopher and handyman, even fixing the leaking toilet in the middle of it all. They said goodbye to Mary Kay, Opal, Zach, and Jamie, and walked next door to the house.

“Wrestle me, Dad?”

“Okay dogpile!” He dropped to his knees as Owen came over already giggling. The baby crawled on Jackson’s back and Toby somehow did too.

“Get off me you rats.” He faked trying to escape. “Tickle monster gets you now.” They screeched with laughter as he tickled them, Toby now howling.

“Tickle Toby, Dad.”

“Okay.” He reached out and tickled the dog’s belly. “Now Lezah,” yelled Owen.

"Oh no, no way I'm getting involved in this chaos," she said, getting up off the couch.

"It's getting dark, I'm gonna make some Mac and Cheese. Anyone interested?"

Owen said "Me me," Toby barked, baby Vee said "yum yum," and Jackson got up and put his arms around Lezah and held her.

"Kiss her, Dad, kiss her."

"Well that's easy."

After the household slept, Lezah lit the candle on the table and sat with a cup of mint tea thinking about the opening day when her cell chimed.

"Hello."

"Lezah it's me, Carey. I know it's late and I meant to come today but it was slammed at the café and then this um other situation came up and jeez Lezah, I know it's late but I need to talk to you."

"Yeah, okay Carey, I'm awake, come on up."

Carey parked in front. "Look," he said to the girl in the passenger seat. "A friend of mine lives here and she maybe can help you. Her name is Lezah. Wait here a minute, lock the doors. Be right back."

"Come in. What's up?"

"There's this girl April, twelve or thirteen years old, new in town, always with her drunk father at the arcade. Dad plays pool all day. I saw them when locking up one night, the father staggering to his truck, the girl crying as he reached out and grabbed her ponytail, yanked her towards him. Rumor has it he "rents" her out for sex favors. I saw her during school hours on the dock crabbing. She brought me a couple of crabs last week asking if she could trade them for food. I gave her a fish sandwich and fries, it was so sad the way she took the bag from me and ran to a bench and gobbled the food. Something's not okay. I found her crying, hiding behind my car. She reminds me of you Lezah, when you were little, ya know? Anyways, can she stay here tonight? I'll call the authorities tomorrow."

"Sure. Okay."

"Thanks, I'll go get her. Be right back." Bursting back in, "Lezah, God damn it she's not in the car." Lezah grabbed her headlamp.

"I can't make it down to the beach."

"Okay I'll go look for her. Go home, Carey."

Lezah walked to the overlook where she saw the girl standing at the edge of the cliff, in the half dark. Afraid to alarm her she clicked off the headlamp and walked closer. The girl didn't see her. Lezah said "April?" The girl turned, "It's alright, please back up."

"No, leave me alone." She was crying.

"I can't do that."

"Why not?"

"Because Carey at the café told me you are having some hard times. I think I can help."

"No you can't." She shivered. "No one can. Are you a cop?"

"No, listen, I just live across the road, you can't stay out here all night. Come to my house and get warm. I'm Lezah, it's safe."

Back at the house she noticed the dirty sweatshirt tied around her waist and the bloodstain that had soaked through. "A shower will warm you, I have some clothes you can borrow, um, did you get your period?"

Embarrassed, she said "yes, my first one and he wouldn't buy me any …" She broke down again.

"Okay, well I have some pads and we can talk about… things after your shower." While the girl was in the bathroom she called Carey and told him she was there with her.

He said "well that's good because her lowlife father was arrested when I got back to town for breaking stuff up at the arcade. Thanks. I'll be in touch tomorrow."

Jackson came into the room with sleep-hooded eyes blinking at the lit candle on the table. "Lezah? Leez? There is someone in the shower." She briefly explained, he said "okay" and wandered back down the hallway.

The girl came out wearing Lezah's sweats, looking around fearfully.

"Hey, come sit, here is tea and a sandwich." Lezah pointed to the chair. "Your name is April, right?"

"Yes ma'am."

"So what's going on in your life, April? Are you traveling with your father? Where are you from?"

Wolfing down the sandwich, chewing fast, she paused. "Last place was Astoria. We don't live anywhere, back of the truck or whatever."

"What's your dad's job?"

The girl laughed. "He doesn't work. Sure you aren't a cop, you ask questions like one. I can't say anymore."

"Why aren't you in school? How old are you, April?"

"I'm almost thirteen."

"If your dad doesn't work than how do you live, eat?"

"Sometimes we don't eat. That was good, thanks."

"Let's go in the living room. You'll sleep out here. I'll make you a nice cozy bed."

"Okay."

"April?"

"Yeah?"

"Are you okay? Your dad isn't, you know, hurting

you, being inappropriate?" Lezah spread a quilt out on the couch, fluffed a pillow and looked at the girl then saw tears starting to fall. She looked away. "You can tell me."

"No I can't. He will beat me and starve me."

"What do you mean starve you?"

The girl was hiccoughing holding back sobs. "He won't give me food unless I, I either have sex with him or the men who pay him to do it with me. I'd rather die than go back with him"—her body shook—"and I will, I will figure out how to do it because he will never let me go ..."

Lezah walked closer to the hysterical girl. "April, I can help you."

"No you can't, how do you know?"

"Because it happened to me."

The girl was quiet for a moment. "It happened to you?"

"Yes, and I know for a fact that you are going to be safe because your dad was arrested last night. After what you have told me, he will never hurt you again."

"Really, you're sure?"

"Yes, I'm sure, he is in jail."

She walked to the couch, sat down, then lay down. She pulled the quilt up to her chin. "I'm so tired."

"Yes, you must be. You can sleep now."

"Will you stay with me for a while?"

"Alright." She pulled a chair closer to the couch.

April moved the quilt and reached out for Lezah's hand. Lezah held the girl's small hand long after she was fast asleep.

Appreciation and Gratitude

Lani Cartwright, Publisher at www.wisewomenink.com, Holdfast book design.

Original cover art, The Mermaid by Howard Pyle 1911.

Mimi Bailey for drawings, Holdfast Seaweed and Seal Rock www.bluefoxartworks.com

Anne Champagne, Editor Extraordinaire annec@green-words.ca

For credible scientific information and resources, newsletters, testimonials and the Dimming Documentary, visit www.geoengineeringwatch.org

Melinda Field writes poems, plays, and prose. Her first novel *True* was followed by *The Nest of Our Being*, which can be read as a standalone novel or as a sequel to *True*.

Based on excerpts from *The Nest of Our Being* Melinda was awarded a writing residency at the Can Serrat International Art Residency in Barcelona, Spain. She served as literary dramaturg for Strawberry Theatre's award-winning play, Postcards From Hotel Cassiopeia, which was performed at the Hudson Guild Theatre in New York City.

Melinda has written, along with photographic artist, Lani Cartwright, three sets of wisdom cards that were created to inspire and empower women of all ages on a daily basis. *The Journey*, *Wonder of the Mother*, and *Wisdom of the Crone* can be viewed and purchased at www.wisewomenink.com.

Visit Melinda's website at www.melindafield.com